Jeremiah cracked open the connecting door and peeked into the room. Laura inhaled audibly and reached for the phone. "José is talking things over with his Maker right now."

Laura put her hands to her mouth, holding her breath before gasping, "You killed him?"

Jerry gave a disinterested shrug. "I give no quarter to those who oppose me. Join me or die; that is the choice I have to offer. Everyone ignores the word of God."

"What do you want from me? Why me?" Laura asked, distressed and near tears.

Jeremiah laughed and shrugged. "Because you have charisma, believability, and access to millions of people. . . .You can hold a place of honor in New America."

"New America? You're insane."

He wagged a cautionary finger at her. "History is replete with examples of people underestimating the underdog." Jerry looked at the ceiling, a frown on his face. He took Laura's hand and held it tightly as he forced her to follow him into the adjoining room. "We'll relax. Get to know each other better."

JEREMIAH:
TERRORIST PROPHET

Michael A. Smith

A TOM DOHERTY ASSOCIATES BOOK
NEW YORK

JEREMIAH: TERRORIST PROPHET

Copyright © 1998 by Michael A. Smith

A Forge Book
Published by Tom Doherty Associates, Inc.
175 Fifth Avenue
New York, NY 10010

Forge® is a registered trademark of Tom Doherty Associates, Inc.

ISBN: 0-812-56189-9
Library of Congress Card Catalog Number: 97-34383

First edition: January 1998
First mass market edition: April 1999

Printed in the United States of America

0 9 8 7 6 5 4 3 2 1

To those whose lives flowed into mine:
Roy and Marie, Harold and Myrtle,
John and Jean, Leland and Anna.

The prophet that hath a dream,
let him tell a dream; and he that hath my word,
let him speak my word faithfully.
What is the chaff to the wheat?
saith the Lord.

Jeremiah 23:28

1

The prosecuting attorney's heart sank as he watched the six-year-old look around the courtroom. The excessively thin boy with the unmanageable blond hair and sad blue eyes looked confused, then panicked. He couldn't identify his attacker.

"Is the man who hurt you in this courtroom?" the prosecutor prompted.

"I don't know," the boy said, in a tiny wavering voice.

"Look again, son. Carefully." Although hardened from a thousand criminal trials, the prosecutor wanted this one badly. A year ago, the man sitting at the defendant's table had abducted the boy from a neighborhood park while his mother sat nearby on a bench, absorbed in a magazine. He drove away with the boy, stopping twice in secluded areas to rape him brutally before releasing him near a junkyard where police later found the child, so terrified and physically harmed that for weeks he could neither speak nor walk.

The prosecutor understood the problem. The defendant, Raymond Doyle, had been transformed from a wild-eyed, unkempt drunk into an apparent paragon of virtue, complete with a new haircut, suit, tie, and tranquilizers to steady his shaking hands.

Knowing he'd be chastised by the judge, the prosecutor decided on a desperate gamble. "Isn't this the man?" he said, pointing at Doyle.

The defendant's attorney jumped to his feet. "Judge! The state's attorney is attempting to influence this witness's identification. The boy already stated that he doesn't see his attacker in this room."

When court adjourned for the day,

two sheriff's deputies escorted Doyle from the courtroom to a hallway. In a closet-sized dressing room the defendant changed from his J.C. Penney business attire into an orange jumpsuit with the word PRISONER etched across the back in black lettering.

Willy White, one of the deputies, put a chain around Doyle's waist, connecting it to handcuffs and leg irons.

"Looks like the state's case is falling apart," Doyle said.

"How's that?" Willy asked, squeezing the cuffs extra tight around Doyle's wrists.

"The kid couldn't identify me. Without him, they got no case. My lawyer says they're gonna cut me a deal."

Willy shook his head wearily. "We both know you did it, Doyle."

Doyle, a wiry, hairy man with discolored teeth, smiled. "I'm innocent until proven guilty."

As his partner opened the exit door at the end of the second floor hallway, Willy shoved Doyle in that direction, none too gently. "Don't you even feel sorry for the kid, Doyle? You got a conscience?"

Doyle flashed a sickening brownish-yellow smile. "Kids enjoy it just like everybody else, Willy. It hurts women the first time, too, and they bleed. But they come back for seconds, right? Same with the kids."

"You're scum, Doyle."

"Just seeing the kid up there on the stand gave me a boner. You know what they say, Willy: sex by eight or it's too late!"

Willy roughly pushed Doyle out the exit door onto a landing at the top of wrought-iron stairs that led down to the alley, where a sheriff's van waited to transfer the prisoner back to the county jail. Following standard procedure, Willy's partner had moved to the bottom of the stairs where he waited to block any escape attempt.

As Willy locked the door at the top of the stairs, he watched Doyle breathe deeply of the autumn air, as if anticipating his impending freedom. Then the pedophile suddenly fell over backward, his body sliding and bumping down the steps until his head hit a railing support, which bent his neck at an angle and stopped his downward slide.

Willy jumped down several steps, bent over and looked at Doyle, who now had an ugly, reddish-black hole in the middle of his forehead.

"Shit!" Willy said, looking around fearfully. He quickly stepped over Doyle's body, bounded down the remaining stairs, and shoved his partner ahead of him toward the van.

"What the fuck's goin' on?" the other deputy

asked, as Willy yanked open the sliding door so they could scramble inside and seek cover.

"Call for help!" Willy yelled at the driver. "Someone just shot the prisoner!"

"No shit!" Willy's partner said. "Is Doyle dead?"

Willy looked over at the unmoving defendant, smiled, and chuckled softly. "He sure as hell is."

Nearly a quarter of a mile away, the shooter continued to look through his telescopic sight. Finally satisfied with his handiwork, he began to disassemble the German-made Heckler & Koch sniper rifle, the latest version used by the German Bundeswehr and U.S. Special Forces. In his professional opinion, the HK was superior to the army's M21, which he'd used when training in the mountains of Bavaria. Also, the HK could be disassembled quickly and packed into a carrying case that wouldn't attract much attention on the street.

From the fifth-floor office suite near the Los Angeles Civic Center, the sniper had a clear line of sight to the side entrance of the courthouse. He'd made one previous visit to the suite of offices with a rental agent, telling her he was scouting possible locations for his new tax-preparation business. When he dropped by the realtor's office today, saying he wanted a final look-see to make certain his furniture would fit, the agent readily handed over the office key, too busy with another customer to accompany him.

This is the beginning, he thought, *after so many years of study and preparation.*

Taking a small can of blue spray paint from his jacket pocket, the sniper spray-painted on the wall in a steady, flowing hand the words: JEREMIAH ONE, TEN. Jeremiah was the Bible's greatest prophet, chosen by God to point out to people their evil ways, as well as the path of righteousness and salvation. Jeremiah the First was his namesake, his model for a modern-day campaign against evil.

Then he spray-painted nine numbers on the wall: THREE, ONE, TWO, ONE, FIVE, ONE, NINE, FOUR, TWO.

Jeremiah the Second consulted a frayed Bible. On many of the holy book's pages, he'd underlined pertinent passages. In the margins he'd written his thoughts and comments—sometimes elaborating on God's word by making corrections, or providing additional detail and interpretation.

Today's pertinent passage defined his mission: "See, I have set you this day over nations and over kingdoms, to pluck up and to break down, to destroy and to overthrow, to build and to plant."

The Bible blended the Jewish Torah and historical books of the Old Testament with the Gospels and the epistles of the New Testament to create a composite of history, law, philosophy, cosmology, theology, poetry, mysticism, prophecy, and revelation that was as meaningful to the technocrats of the twentieth century as it had been to shepherds and nomads two thousand years ago. Christian fundamentalists erroneously believed the entire Bible had been dictated by God and was not open to interpretation. Some of the words were His; others had been written by men.

Hence the Bible often contradicted itself, or men inadvertently or maliciously misinterpreted the Word. For example, was one's response to evil an eye for an eye, as suggested in Exodus, or the offer of the other cheek, a philosophy Saint Matthew ascribed to Jesus Christ? Was wealth a sign of God's grace or an impediment to entering Heaven? Were men only created equal in God's image, or did the Creator want them to be equal in all ways? Is government Caesar's creation, or an instrument to be used by God's representatives to ensure justice and equality? Did one await the Apocalypse or attempt to shape it?

In his early Bible study, Jeremiah resolved such conflicts first with the help of his mentor, and then God. Not all books of the Bible were revealed truth, but God, ever so infrequently, did speak directly through chosen Prophets: Joshua, Elijah, and Isaiah during Old Testament times, and now, at the end of the twentieth century, Jeremiah the Second.

How did one separate truth and error and divine a path, a mission? One did not. According to the Gospel of Saint Matthew, one was chosen: "The Son of Man will send his angels, and they will gather out of his kingdom all causes of sin and all evildoers, and throw them into the furnace of fire. . . ." Or put them into the *line* of fire, according to the Gospel of Second Jeremiah.

The *"evildoer"* Raymond Doyle had defiled one of those destined to be first in the Kingdom of God: "But whoso shall offend one of these *little ones* which believe in me, it were better for him that a millstone were hanged about his neck, and that he were drowned in the depth of the sea." Or drowned in his own blood that spilled out of a hole in his head and ran into his nose and mouth, as he lay on his back staring into the fiery sun of God's vengeance.

Saint Matthew and Jeremiah the Second.

He left the empty office, walked down the stairs, and exited into an alley. He strolled casually, the lightweight rifle case swinging jauntily at his side. As he rounded the corner onto the sidewalk, heading toward his nearby car, he bumped into a woman holding the hand of a small boy.

"Sorry."

"No problem," the woman said, suspiciously eyeing Jeremiah's bald head and Vandyke beard.

Jeremiah put down the rifle case and knelt on one knee in front of the boy. "What's your name?"

"Brad."

"How old are you, Bradley?"

The boy with the glistening brown hair framing a cherubic face proudly held up three fingers. He wore a miniature Dodgers jacket and running shoes that emitted light through the heels when he walked.

"He's almost four," his mother said.

"You're very lucky to have such a fine, healthy boy," Jeremiah said.

"Thank you," she said, visibly relaxing.

"In God's new land, children will have nothing to fear at all," Jeremiah predicted, confidently, as he smiled at the woman and continued on his way.

2

"You read through the TelePrompTer material yet?" the floor manager asked, anxiously.

"Yes, and I don't like the intro to the education piece," Laura Delaney replied. She repressed an urge to chuckle as she watched his face fall. Laura considered herself to be easygoing, not like some of the other bitch goddesses of national television. Numerous surveys and focus groups had judged her to be smooth, believable, and sympathetic. In part that resulted from training; although Laura thought it had as much to do with the personality and physical features she'd inherited from her mother. Nevertheless, Laura had cultivated a hard-nosed attitude about good scriptwriting.

"I don't know if we can do anything now," the floor manager whined. "It's only twenty-five minutes until airtime."

"Sure we can," Laura told him, calmly. "Get some of those high-paid writers over here and we'll make the changes."

Within a minute, two writers materialized at the back of the set and marched grimly toward her desk.

"What's the problem?" asked the head writer, a

big blonde with a bad complexion and an attitude to match, Laura thought.

"There's no punch in the intro to the education piece," Laura said. "It would put the audience to sleep instead of motivating them to stay tuned."

"It seems pretty snappy to me," the blonde replied, steely-eyed.

Laura handed over a piece of paper on which she'd rewritten the lead-in. "I think the Pope quotation nicely frames the issue. See what you can do."

As the writers hurried off, Laura consulted her watch, to see how long it would take before word reached the production booth high in the air above the set that "the talent" was causing problems. Inside the booth were the show's producer, director, switcher, graphics generator, audio operator, and other technicians.

Within three minutes, Mel Crawford, the show's producer, approached the anchor desk, which sat in front of the *American Chronicle* backdrop, fittingly a panel of photographs of America's spectacular scenery from Maine to California.

"How's it goin'?" Mel asked. As usual, the long-haired, thirty-year-old wunderkind wore jeans, a buttoned-down oxford, and a sport coat to offset the hippie image.

"Fine," Laura replied, chirpily. "You?"

"No problems. They're scrambling to make the changes you ordered. Should be up on the Tele-PrompTer in a few minutes."

"Good." Laura noted that Mel seemed relaxed and in good humor, even though the responsibility for anything that went wrong on the show ultimately found its way to his doorstep. He knew she wouldn't put his ass in a sling.

"Course, if the catchy new intro didn't make it to the screen, you'd improvise, anyway, right?"

Laura nodded slyly. "Exactly. Don't worry, Mel. You know I always hit my marks. Everything will go smoothly. Trust me. Now go back up into the booth and hold your breath for about an hour."

He laughed and patted her on the arm. "You're the best, Laura."

Tonight the twice-weekly newsmagazine show Laura hosted would examine public elementary and secondary education, calling into question whether these public institutions effectively accomplished their goals. She'd done some of the on-site reporting, at alternative schools in Orlando and San Diego, as well as the voice-over for the B-roll footage.

A related story concerning the nation's military academies would ask whether they were the best way to educate the nation's military leaders, or an anachronism and breeding ground for fascism, sexism, and racism. A UBC senior correspondent would carry that piece.

Over the course of the show, Laura would direct traffic, question a panel of experts, ask the studio audience for input, and maybe take some outside calls. Following promos for Thursday's show, she'd sign off and drive home to her farm in the foothills of the Blue Ridge Mountains.

The floor manager gave her a countdown, and Laura flashed her trademark quizzical smile as she said: "Good evening and welcome to *American Chronicle*. Tonight we're going to continue our series on public schools." She paraphrased the TelePrompter material. "I remember a poem by Alexander Pope that I memorized in high school: ' 'Tis education forms the common mind, just as the twig is bent, the tree's inclined.' If so, should we expect our public schools to shape our children's minds in ways that help solve many of our social problems, or should schools restrict their efforts to teaching academic and vocational skills?

"This week we visited different types of schools across the country, public and private, traditional and innovative, and asked these questions of students, teachers, administrators, and parents. Here are some of the answers."

Laura looked at the monitor just out of camera range and suddenly saw herself in San Diego, talking to a group of students.

As usual, Laura remained at her desk after the show, watching the audience file out of the studio, while she waited for any phone calls forthcoming from Mel or other executives at the United Broadcasting Corporation. It would be a rare show that passed without comment or complaint from someone, she thought.

But when she picked up the ringing phone, Laura didn't recognize the voice.

"Great show, Ms. Delaney. As usual. You really are America's sweetheart."

"Who is this?" She pressed the memo button on the phone, to record the conversation. Something in the disembodied voice frightened her—a singsong quality, as if the person were reading verse.

"I'm sorry. How rude of me, Laura. My name is

Jeremiah and I'm going to be your main news source for the remainder of the year. Perhaps well into the future.''

''About what?'' *Why am I letting this conversation go on?*

''Important developments leading to a final, apocalyptic conflict that will take place before the end of the second millennium. The Lord has said to me: 'Behold, I have put my words in thy mouth.' I say those words to you, Laura, and you relay them to the public. That's how it will work. Aren't you pleased I've selected you?''

''You've selected *me!*'' Laura laughed at his audacity, whoever he was.

''Laura, you have that aura of believability, the ability to explain the inexplicable. We're going to be perfect together. In all ways.''

Laura sighed. *Another one.* ''Listen, buddy, thanks for watching the show, but I have to go.''

''I understand, Laura, but let me give you my bona fides first. Will you write down this series of numbers?''

''Why?''

''Because you can then report these numbers to FBI headquarters and they will verify that I am a legitimate news source.''

''The FBI?'' Maybe she had a real wacko on the line. If so, she should get as much information from him as possible.

''Here're the numbers, Laura. Three, one, two, one, five, one, nine, four, two.''

She wrote them on a pad and looked at the sequence, which made no sense to her. ''So what's this, Jerry, your Social Security number?''

"Well, the numbers do relate to my work. Three days ago I spray-painted them on the wall of a vacant office suite in Los Angeles."

"I assume you also do subway trains and overpasses."

Jeremiah laughed, genuinely. "That's good, Laura. You're every bit as engaging over the phone as you are on TV."

"Give me your phone number and address, Jerry, and I'll send you an autographed picture."

"In time, Laura, all in good time. But for right now, you give those numbers to the FBI and they'll tell you all about my work in California. That's just the start. You won't want to miss the rest of the story, Laura, which will be progressively revealed in *The Book of Second Jeremiah*. Next time I'll give you an exclusive."

"I can hardly wait," Laura said, now more bored than concerned.

"I hope you recognize my voice the next time I call, Laura, but I'll use that series of numbers to identify myself. It'll be our little secret."

Mel stood in front of her desk. "Is there a problem?" he asked.

Laura took off the mike pinned to the lapel of her suit coat. She popped the cassette out of the phone and handed it to him. "Listen to this and tell me what you think in the morning. I'm tired. I'm going home."

3

Shortly after Raymond Doyle was gunned down in Los Angeles, a hypertext connection called *The Book of Second Jeremiah* was added to World Religions Study Group, a World Wide Web site established by faculty and students at Ludwig Maximilian University in Munich, Germany.

THE BOOK OF SECOND JEREMIAH

CHAPTER ONE

1 From Joshua to Elijah and Isaiah to Malachi, the LORD anointeth Prophets to speak God's Word in a sinful and wicked world. So it is with Jeremiah the Second, who came reluctantly to his mission as a youth, saying he was unworthy. But the LORD gave Jeremiah a teacher, and when the Prophet became a man he spake the Word of the LORD without fear.

2 The LORD sayeth to Jeremiah the Latter: Lo, at the end of the Second Millennium since my son, Jesus Christ, walked on earth, I have looked

upon Man and see that he knows not the Word of God. Man was shown the path to Paradise, yet he chose the way of Sin.

3 Listen well and repeat these words to the People, sayeth the LORD to Jeremiah the Second. The sheep are to be divided by the Shepherd, and those on the left who are Evil will know fire and destruction, while those on the right who abideth by the LORD's Word will be led to a New Nation, blessed beyond all others on earth to this day; yea, even unto the end of time.

4 Remember the Book of Revelations, for the Seventh Seal has been broken and the final battle between Good and Evil is commenced.

5 The LORD sayeth to his Prophet:

In the land most blessed, of which much was expected,

Evil is allowed, nay, encouraged by word and deed,

so that those who observe my Law weep and suffer

while those who judge according to Man's law

neither enforce the law nor dispense justice; hence

Chaos rules where once I had established order.

6 O generation of Man, ye cultivate in thy bosom the seeds of greed, lust, pride, envy, gluttony, sloth, and wrath; forsaking purity, goodness, obedience, self-sacrifice, and devotion. America is awash in a sea of vulgarity, promiscuity, and violence! Those who mock Me by abandoning My values can expect no mercy in the coming struggle, nor at the Judgment Day.

7 Hear ye the LORD's wrath about the marketplace! I gave Man leave to know the Earth and know the Universe, yet ye know only trading, not only for bread and clothing and that which sustaineth life, but to gaineth an advantage in Money; to cheat and lie and manipulate and divide brother against brother and establish on earth classes of Men, according to Wealth. Know ye for certain, this is an abomination to God!

8 Forget thee the writings of the Old Testament and the words of Christ about the stain of riches! Mark this well, sayeth the LORD: he who divides Men and rules over them from a position of Wealth is Evil, and it is He against whom the battle is waged.

9 And, sayeth the LORD, whilst I gave you laws to observe
 and teachings to guide your actions,
 these ye forsake, instead adopting a government

in which Prideful Men strut and posture,

arguing endlessly about that which is already decided

while lining their pockets with ill-gotten gains.

10 These words the LORD sayeth: the rules of proper human behavior are set forth in the Ten Commandments, the teachings of Jesus, and now the prophecy of Jeremiah the Second, which is the Word of God. Faith, acceptance, and obedience are Man's duty; believe or believe ye not!

11 Woe to those who claim falsely to speak for Me, sayeth the LORD, twisting My words for selfish desires and Evil ends. Those who readeth My Word to find justification for Evil, Chaos, and Hatred will know My Wrath!

12 The LORD instructed Jeremiah the Second to tell this to the people: My purpose for Man can be seen in history, but mistake ye not the lesson, for it is not about conquest and hoarding riches, neither lust or power, but the gaining of Knowledge; that much is clear to he who is wise and listens. The reward of obedience is to eventually know the mind of God. From that which ye sprang shall ye be reunited in the end.

13 Thus sayeth the LORD: I have this day given unto Jeremiah the Second power to root out Evil, to destroy it, to rebuild the Chosen Nation upon solid ground, and restore the Word.

4

Steve Wallace walked the four blocks
from FBI headquarters to the Federal Triangle metro
stop, where he took the escalator underground and
waited for the next train. Either the blue or orange
line train would do, since both ran from the District
of Columbia beneath the Potomac River to Rosslyn,
the Virginia stop nearest the United Broadcasting
Corporation. He had an appointment with *American
Chronicle* producer Mel Crawford, and hopefully
would also meet the famous and beautiful Laura Delaney.

Crawford had sent over the phone tape, and Steve
knew that Ms. Delaney's Tuesday night caller—the
so-called Jeremiah the Second—probably was the
vigilante who'd shot and killed an accused pedophile
in Los Angeles. Or at least knew enough details
about the murder to be an accessory.

At first glance it wasn't exactly a high-profile case
that ordinarily would command the attention of the
head of the FBI's counterterrorism unit. Steve
couldn't deny that the opportunity to meet Delaney
in person was a factor in his decision to personally
look into this case; that and the fact that an ambitious

sniper with a national agenda could easily qualify as a terrorist.

The rounded, modernistic UBC building constructed of steel and silver-tinted glass' appeared to be a giant bullet dropped from the sky and embedded in the earth. It seemed sorely out of place less than a half mile from two icons of tradition, Arlington National Cemetery and the World War II Iwo Jima Memorial.

Steve stepped out of the elevator on the sixteenth floor, pushed through the glass doors of the United Broadcasting Corporation, and stood in front of a receptionist's desk, behind which a mural of the world showed the various continents linked together by a UBC chain. Whether Orwellian by accident or design, Steve didn't know.

Crawford appeared after a few minutes. "Agent Wallace?"

Steve flipped open his two-part identification wallet, featuring his picture subtly blended into the Justice Department seal, an anticounterfeit measure that went unnoticed by most members of the general public.

"Let's go back to my office where we can talk," Crawford said, leading the way down a hallway flanked by offices for various executives representing marketing, advertising, accounting, news, and production.

Spacious and well appointed, Crawford's office had an imposing view of the capital monuments, especially the Tidal Basin and the Jefferson Memorial.

"So, you guys give any credence to this crank call?" Crawford said.

Steve, dressed as usual in Mr. Hoover's favorite

dark blue pin-striped suit, made note of Crawford's counterculture appearance: boots, jeans, a patterned sport shirt, and long hair reaching to his collar. A navy blue blazer was draped over the back of Crawford's chair.

Steve opened his notebook and thumbed to the pages where he'd recorded notes about the conversation between Laura Delaney and her caller, "Jerry," as well as his telephone chat yesterday afternoon with LAPD Detective Ernesto Ortiz.

"Late last week, a sniper shot a man in Los Angeles," Steve began. "He painted a series of numbers on the wall that are identical to the ones he read over the phone to Ms. Delaney." Steve didn't mention the other evidence: the reference to JEREMIAH ONE: TEN, or the crudely annotated Bible left in the office.

"Jesus!" Crawford said. "Who'd this guy shoot?"

"A man on trial, as he left a county courthouse."

"On trial for what?"

"The assault and rape of a child. He was a pedophile with an extensive record."

Crawford squirmed in his chair. "What's the connection here?"

"Don't you think Ms. Delaney should be a party to this discussion? This may concern her safety. Things get lost in translation."

Crawford nodded and contacted his secretary through the intercom, asking her to find Laura.

Laura was taller in person than Steve had estimated from her television persona, and even more

beautiful, with luxurious midlength blonde hair, shining blue eyes, and high cheekbones. She wore navy blue slacks and a frilly white blouse. Trying not to stare, Steve frowned and concentrated on his notes. But when Laura introduced herself and took his hand, he almost had to gasp for air.

Laura listened intently as Steve reprised his conversation with Crawford.

"So do you think this is a John Hinckley/Jody Foster type of thing?" she asked.

"It's possible. We don't know anything about his motivation right now. Clearly you're a well-known personality who comes into everyone's home twice a week. He could have developed a proprietary interest in you, or he may just want to use your celebrity for his own purposes."

Steve watched in fascination as Laura cocked her head to the side and considered his opinion, just as he'd seen her do on television while listening to a correspondent provide his or her analysis of a news event. Then, as now, she responded in a calm voice.

"But he emphasized that I would be his *messenger*," Laura said.

Steve nodded his agreement, trying not to stare at the lovely face and mesmerizing eyes. He understood Jeremiah's infatuation, if that's what it was.

"Well, there're a few things we can do," Steve said, speaking professionally. "I've got a psychologist and a voice analyst reviewing the tape recording you sent over. They'll try to pinpoint the caller's cultural and geographical background, and likely motivation. They'll construct a psychological profile. Also, we'll compare Jeremiah's message to other telephone threats received by public figures."

"You can do that?" Laura asked, with a journalist's interest.

"The right computer program will do it quickly and accurately."

"Fascinating."

Steve had to agree, but he coughed, looked downward, and struggled to maintain the continuity of his thoughts. "We should tap your phones here. There's a good chance he'll call again."

"I don't know about that," Crawford said. "You mean record every incoming call? Christ, Kingsley and McNulty would go into orbit. They're both paranoid to start with. Right, Laura?"

They laughed at their private joke. Steve watched Laura characteristically swipe the blonde hair from her eyes and flash that dazzling smile.

"Kingsley, as you may know, is president and CEO of UBC," Laura explained to Steve. "McNulty is president of the News Division."

"We can equip the most likely phone with a switch to activate the tap," Steve offered. "That way we're only intercepting and tracing a call when you activate the system. You would be in charge."

"Yeah, but who's to know if you FBI guys worm your way into our whole system?" Crawford replied, jokingly.

Laura leaned over and touched Steve's arm, her eyes twinkling. "As you can see, paranoia is contagious here at UBC."

Feeling a shiver run through his body, Steve replied, "We'll work with your security people. I'm certain they'll understand the technology and protect your interests."

Crawford nodded. "I can sell that. After all, we need to protect Laura."

"You'd better!" she said, playfully. "I got a wrongful-death-on-the-job clause in my contract that would bankrupt the network!"

Crawford guffawed. "Now, that will get Kingsley's attention!"

"I don't want you to be unduly concerned," Steve said. "This guy could be just your run-of-the-mill nut, looking for his fifteen minutes of fame on television. More likely he's taking a lead from the Unabomber. He's got some perverted philosophy he wants to communicate to the public, and his outrageous deeds are a means of getting a platform. You may never hear from him again. But if you do, we'll know it's him if he repeats his ID numbers."

"Maybe next time Jeremiah calls, we'll just cut him off!" Crawford said.

"Good for you," Steve relied. "Most people at the FBI didn't agree with the Justice Department's decision to pressure the *New York Times* and the *Washington Post* into publishing the Unabomber's diatribe."

"Don't let Mel fool you, Steve," Laura said. "He only opposed publication of the Unabomber because his rant was book length. If he could've reduced it to a fifteen-second sound bite, we'd have been competing for his business with every other television news show."

Crawford laughed boisterously. "Well, that's different, especially if Jeremiah becomes someone important, like the Unabomber!"

Steve chuckled. Crawford and Laura were obviously good friends and he liked them both.

"Do you think Jeremiah's for real?" Laura asked.

"Possibly. It's a new day in America. The time of the terrorist."

Crawford stood suddenly, as if he had someplace to go. "Okay, we'll take your advice and consult with our security guys, but I think the phone tap is a good idea. Anything else?"

"When Jeremiah called, how'd he get through to you directly, Laura?" Steve asked.

She shrugged. "I don't know. He called on a private number that bypasses the switchboard. I've given it out to only a few relatives—my parents in Texas, my sister and brother—and a few close friends."

"Then we must assume Jeremiah is a resourceful person," Steve said. "He may also know where you live and have your home phone number, also."

"That's unlisted," Laura said, although not confidently.

"Just the same, I'd suggest an identical tracing device for your home phone," Steve said. "Do you have a home security system?"

"Yeah," Laura replied. "One of those alarm systems monitored by a private company. I live out by Middleburg on a small farm. The property manager and his wife live in an apartment above the barn. Seth and Gladys Schuyler. He takes care of the horses and the grounds and she does light housekeeping. Cooking now and then."

"They're obviously not trained personnel," Steve said, looking at Mel. "I'd suggest a professional bodyguard for a while."

"I agree," Mel replied, without hesitation. "We'll take care of that."

"Do you think this is all necessary?" Laura asked.

"It's your call, Ms. Delaney, but I'm in the bad-guy business. You people are in the television business. I wouldn't advise you about camera angles. You might consider accepting my professional judgment."

"You're right, of course," Laura conceded.

"In fact, I'd be happy to come out to your place and check out the security."

"That sounds like a good idea, Laura," Mel said.

Steve watched with anticipation as Laura looked at him and finally said, "Okay. I'll call you and we'll set up an appointment."

"Good enough. One more thing and I'll be on my way." Steve opened his briefcase and took out copies of the LAPD's sketch of the possible sniper. He handed them to Mel and Laura.

"These are computer-assisted drawings," Steve explained, "providing several looks for the same guy."

"How'd you develop these?" Laura asked.

"The LAPD has a witness who may have seen the sniper on the street, right after the shooting. She bumped into a guy near the building where the shooting took place. He might have been carrying a rifle case. Her description may or may not be accurate."

"I understand," Laura said, intently looking at the drawings.

"Ring any bells? He's described by the witness as six two, a hundred and eighty pounds. Very fit physically. Head shaven, wearing a mustache and goatee, but of course, those could be part of a disguise."

"No," Laura said with conviction, while Mel shook his head.

"Needless to say, if you see anyone resembling this man, call me immediately." Steve stood, handing his business cards to Laura and Crawford. "But don't get paranoid about this episode. Believe me, you can transpose this guy's face onto everyone you meet on the street."

"I think I'm going to stay off the street for a while," Laura replied, flashing a warm smile.

Walking back to the metro stop, Steve decided he'd pursue this case, after all. Ten years experience had sharpened his intuition. He had a feeling Jeremiah was more than a sniper or publicity hound.

5

Jeremiah flew into Atlanta, rented a car at the airport, and set out in search of his prey. An article Jeremiah had copied from the Atlanta *Journal-Constitution* provided details about their habits and location. Jeremiah's disciples in Atlanta had provided him with their high school yearbook photos.

Jeremiah planned to conclude his business before the day's end, so he didn't have a suitcase with him, only a camera case. The only other tool he'd need was a .38-caliber handgun, with an attached silencer, which he knew would be under the front seat of the rental car.

With the aid of a metropolitan map, it didn't take him long to get to Dunwoody, in the Atlanta suburbs. The newspaper article mentioned the town, neighborhood, high school, and one of the martial arts establishments frequented by his targets. Jeremiah parked near The Southern Karate Institute. He'd been told the two teenagers "practiced" there every day.

Jeremiah walked to a McDonald's at the far end of the shopping center and ordered a cup of coffee. He went outside and sat at a picnic table, listening to the teenage chatter of two girls and a boy sitting nearby. The chubby boy with a full head of curly, black hair had a pleasant demeanor.

Jeremiah leaned over and said, "Excuse me. I'm a reporter from Cincinnati. Maybe you can help me out. Are any of you familiar with The Southern Karate Institute over there?"

"Sure," the boy said. Both of the pretty girls regarded him suspiciously—*as they should in this day and age,* he thought.

"Isn't that the place where those two kids—what's their names, Davidson and Yates—used to study?"

A worried look crossed the boy's face. "Still do."

"You know them?"

"Oh, yeah," he said, his voice indicating it hadn't been a pleasant experience.

Jeremiah handed the boy a business card, with a fake name, address, and telephone number, identifying him as a writer and television producer. "Maybe you could provide me with some background information, son. What's your name?"

"Robbie," he said, looking at the card hesitantly.

Jeremiah understood. Trust had been severely eroded in the modern world. "Let's just step inside, Robbie, so I can get a coffee refill." *Where there are other people and you'll feel safe.*

The kid followed Jeremiah inside the McDonald's and they sat in a booth where they could see the karate institute. At midafternoon they almost had the place to themselves.

"Here's a fifty," Jeremiah said, laying the bill on the table and pushing it toward the boy. "You can buy dinner for your friends."

"Really?"

"I always pay my sources for information."

Robbie nodded, indicating he understood that money and obligations passed hands simultaneously.

"Could you help me identify Glenn Davidson and Jason Yates?"

"Why?"

"I'm writing a story about them." Jeremiah made his gambit. "Telling readers in Cincinnati what scum they are."

The kid nodded his agreement. "You don't have to convince me."

"You have a run-in with them?"

"They were in my grade school," Robbie remembered. "They've kicked me around at one time or another and stole money from me like they did from everyone else."

Jeremiah jerked his head toward the other end of the shopping center. "Would they be down there now, at the karate place?"

The kid looked out the window. "Maybe. I see their car."

Out on bail for assault and battery and suspicion of rape, but going about life brazenly, Jeremiah thought.

"Which one?"

Robbie identified a Camaro and described the "boys." Yates had a small head and dark, oily hair. He had "hate" and "love" tattooed below the knuckles of his fingers. He described Davidson as a tall redhead with crew-cut hair, who often wore a varsity letter jacket he'd stolen from a real athlete.

Jeremiah thanked the kid and stood up.

"Better watch out for them," Robbie warned.

Jeremiah smiled and nodded his appreciation for the advice. "Off the record, Robbie, what do you think ought to be done about these two?"

Robbie didn't hesitate. "I wish somebody would kill them."

From the mouths of babes. Jeremiah waited in his car for about forty-five minutes, until the pair emerged from the karate institute. Robbie's physical descriptions fit them to a tee. They got into the red Camaro and drove off, and Jeremiah pulled out after them.

First they went to a 7-Eleven where they passed money to another unsavory, older youth, who bought them a twelve-pack of beer. Davidson, the driver, then led Jeremiah out of the suburbs into the countryside. Eventually the karate kids pulled into a heavily wooded county park, drove the Camaro onto a graveled space in a picnic area, and walked through an opening in the trees.

Jeremiah slowed the car on the asphalt road, watching as the pair of juvenile delinquents sauntered toward a secluded picnic table, far off the road and surrounded by tall pines. *Perfect*, he thought. *When your cause is righteous, God rewards it with fortuitous developments.* The newspaper article, Robbie's help, and now this isolated park. *Justice can be cost-effective*, the modern-day prophet thought, compared to the tens of thousands of dollars that the school/police/judicial systems had lavished on these two, to no avail. Now, for the cost of an airline ticket, a fifty-dollar consulting fee, and a hundred feet of good rope from Wal-Mart, justice was about to be done. Truly.

Jeremiah parked the rented car on the shoulder of the road, got out, opened the back door, and took out a camcorder carrying case holding an 8-mm Sony, fully charged, with a blank videotape inside. The tightly wound, plastic-wrapped rope lay atop the camera. Two elastic straps attached to the bottom of the case held in place a lightweight telescoping tripod. A pocket on one end of the case held two pair of handcuffs; the pocket on the other end, a roll of all-purpose duct tape. Tools of his trade.

Jeremiah reached under the seat for the .38-caliber Smith & Wesson, screwed on the silencer, shoved the gun under his pants belt near his spine, and walked to his appointment. He looked around the mostly deserted park. A middle-aged couple sat at a faraway picnic table, completely absorbed in their conversation. In the center of the park, two young men and a collie noisily played with a Frisbee.

He walked right up to them and set his camera case on one end of the table.

"What the fuck you doin'?" Davidson asked, a beer can poised inches from his lips.

Jeremiah smiled. "I'd ask you two assholes the same question, but the answer's obvious."

"Who're you calling an asshole?" Yates said, coughing, having just taken a hit off a marijuana cigarette.

"You a cop?" the redhead asked, suspiciously.

"Nope. I'm judge, jury, and executioner. You're both guilty and the penalty is death."

He watched as fear rippled across their faces and hoped to see that emotion again, so he could record it for the satisfaction of their many victims, and as a warning to those who would emulate them.

Davidson stood and Jeremiah backed away, respectful of the alleged martial arts skills. He pulled the gun from his belt, sneaking a glance over his shoulder. No witnesses.

"What the fuck!" Yates exclaimed.

Jeremiah nodded toward the tree line behind the table, where a sign outlined a 1.5-mile hiking trail. "Get going that way."

Davidson laughed, suddenly full of confidence. "You planning on robbing us, *asshole*?!"

"No, but you better walk this trail or Jason here will carry you after I kneecap you. The choice is up to you, Glenn."

"How do you know our names?" Davidson asked.

"I know everything about you two. Known you all my life, in fact."

"What the fuck you talkin' about?" Yates asked, stupidly.

Jeremiah fired the gun into the middle of the picnic table. The splat sound didn't carry much beyond their intimate circle, but the .38-caliber bullet blew clear through the three-quarter-inch board, making a statement.

"Now, walk ahead of me, single file."

They walked silently into the woods, and Jeremiah prepared mentally for them to make a break. When they ran in opposite directions, he immediately shot Yates in the thigh.

"Stop or I'll shoot!" Jeremiah yelled, setting down the camera case and running after Davidson. He'd give the redhead three more counts before dropping him, which would be unfortunate, since he'd have to shoot to kill. Then there'd be only one criminal to bring before the bar of justice.

Davidson slowed to a walk, however, and turned around, looking helpless and defeated. Seventy-five feet to the west of them, Yates bawled like a baby. Jeremiah motioned with the gun for Davidson to get back to the trail.

He walked to where Yates lay on the ground, rocking back and forth, grasping his thigh, crying, and wailing. Jeremiah kicked him hard in the cheek with the toe of his shoe. He kept the gun on Davidson, but glanced back toward the picnic area and the opening in the trees leading to the road. No one had heard the commotion.

"Get him up," Jeremiah said to Davidson. "You make any more noise, Yates, and I'll knock out more of your teeth. Don't be such a crybaby. It's only a flesh wound."

Davidson did as he was told, but said, in a whiny voice, "Listen, man, our folks got money, okay? You let us go and I can get you five, ten thousand."

"Really?" Jeremiah replied, sarcastically. "Get moving down the trail."

"Where we goin'?" Davidson asked, as Yates hopped along beside him, whimpering softly and spitting out slobber, blood, and bits of broken teeth.

"I'm looking for the right spot," Jeremiah explained.

Within ten minutes he found it, as the trail intersected an unpaved fire road used infrequently by forest rangers and utility trucks, since grass grew in the tire ruts. About fifty yards down the road, Jeremiah spotted an ideal tree: a big oak with a thick limb jutting out at a right angle.

He herded the two defendants toward the tree, where he set down the camera bag, signaling that they had arrived at their destination. He smiled and absorbed the deathly quiet of the surrounding forest. The late afternoon light created the perfect ambience; soft, nonglaring, but with an ominous quality.

"What do you want!" Davidson repeated.

"Justice. You two budding young criminals have been getting a free ride up to this point."

"Hey, man, we ain't no worse than most kids."

"Precisely the point, Glenn. There're millions of fuckups like you all over the country. You just have the bad luck of being made a national example."

A sudden comprehension gripped Davidson. "You a relative of one of those kids?"

"You mean a relative of the boy you viciously beat up? Or his girlfriend you raped?"

"Hey, man, we ain't had our trial yet. The girl was putting out to us willingly when her boyfriend attacked us. We just defended ourselves."

Jeremiah smiled sadly. "It's a good defense strategy. It might even work. Who suggested it? Your lawyer? From what I've learned about you two assholes, you've been stealing, lying, and beating up on people since grade school. The courts slap your hands and the schools pass you from one grade to the other. You probably got to thinking you were bulletproof, huh? You know better now."

Jeremiah squatted by the camcorder bag, took out the handcuffs, and threw them at Yates's feet. "Cuff Glenn's hands behind his back, Jason. Tight. Do it now and I won't shoot you in the other leg."

Jeremiah watched the sniveling bully limp to his task.

"Okay, Davidson. On your knees. Lean forward, put your head against the tree. You, Yates, back off."

Jeremiah checked the handcuffs on Davidson's wrists, squeezing them together tightly until the red-head winced with pain. Then he cuffed Yates, who in his pathetic emotional and physical state posed no threat.

Jeremiah took the rope out of the bag, unraveled it, and cut it in half, creating two fifty-foot sections. He quickly fashioned a noose on each end and threw the ropes over the tree limb, so they hung side by side. He slipped a noose over their heads and tied each rope to the base of a small-diameter tree, pulling tightly so they boys had to stand on their tiptoes.

Jeremiah placed the tripod about ten feet in front of his captive audience of two, attached and focused the camera, checked the light meter, pushed the record button, and stood slightly to the side, out of frame.

"Okay," Jeremiah said. "Confess."

6

The emerald-green dress flattered her figure and coloring, Laura thought, taking a final look at her image in the backstage mirror. She walked out onto the set of *American Chronicle* and smiled widely in response to the cheers and applause—and one wolf whistle—that greeted her appearance.

She toed her mark in front of the audience and accepted a hand-held mike from a staffer. "Hello, welcome to *American Chronicle*," she said to the audience, knowing she had about a minute to waste before airtime. "Hold up your hand if you're from out of town."

She kept her own hands together to hide her nervousness in advance of this landmark show. Millions undoubtedly would tune in to watch Jeremiah's execution of two young criminals. Network executives, media critics, and government officials, including those at the Justice Department, would ruthlessly critique the show to make certain it didn't exceed First Amendment parameters. Laura's eyes scanned the studio audience, hoping to see the handsome FBI agent, Steve Wallace.

Suddenly the floor manager pointed his index finger at her, and Laura spoke into the camera, "Good evening, and welcome to another edition of *American Chronicle*. I'm Laura Delaney and we are live this evening from UBC headquarters in Rosslyn, Virginia.

"Tonight we will devote the entire hour to discussing domestic terrorism. As you know, it is increasingly part of our social landscape and includes such tragic events as the bombing of the Word Trade Center in New York, the Murrah federal office building in Oklahoma City, and the eighteen-year reign of terror by the Unabomber.

"Another terrorist, calling himself Jeremiah the Second, apparently has taken up a vigilante campaign against criminals. We know for certain he killed two teenagers Tuesday afternoon near Atlanta, Georgia. He filmed this murderous deed and supplied UBC with the videotape. Let's go now to Curtis Griswold at our affiliate in Atlanta for the background to this case."

Laura retreated to the anchor desk as Griswold's image appeared on several studio monitors. Griswold explained to the audience that Glenn Davidson and Jason Yates had extensive juvenile records for a variety of crimes, including theft and assault. They had been arraigned recently on charges of malicious wounding and rape, and had been released on bail pending their trial.

"They were either lured to a county park or surprised there by Jeremiah," Griswold said. "He was somehow able to overwhelm the two teenagers, handcuff them, and lead them deep into the wood."

Laura introduced UBC national reporter Roy Webster, who earlier had taped a report from the site of the hangings.

"KATX, the local UBC affiliate, received a call about five o'clock P.M. from Jeremiah," Webster told the audience. "He identified himself as God's prophet and said he'd executed two criminals, and that their bodies would be found at this site. A KATX camera crew arrived about five-thirty P.M., discovered the bodies, and called the local police."

Mel had already decided they wouldn't dwell on the fact that the KATX crew shot videotape of the grisly scene, and got it back to the station in time for the six-o'clock local news. UBC national news ran with it an hour later.

"Wednesday morning a courier service delivered a package to our office here in Rosslyn," Laura said. "It was addressed to me and it contained a videotape of the execution, obviously filmed by Jeremiah.

"We've struggled over what to do with this tape," Laura continued. "We immediately provided a copy to the FBI and the Justice Department. Our decision as journalists is to show you, our audience, an edited version of this tape made by the killer, not for the purpose of titillation or to sensationalize this tragic event, but to understand the killer's motives and gain some insight into what possibly could be the beginning of a unique terrorist campaign. Clearly that's the killer's intention.

"I must warn you that this film is graphic and violent and certainly not appropriate for children. The voice you hear in the background, out of range of the camera, is that of the killer."

Suddenly Davidson and Yates appeared on the TV screen, standing on their tiptoes to avoid being strangled by the ropes around their necks. They confessed to savagely beating a boy they knew and raping his girlfriend.

"It was Glenn's idea," Yates mumbled over broken teeth and a swollen lip. "I didn't want to do it!"

"You lying sonofabitch," Davidson responded. "You were the one who said you knew where they always made out in the woods. You led the way."

"Yeah, but I was only gonna scare them."

Yates's physical and emotional condition was even more pathetic than Laura remembered from an early viewing of the videotape. She watched again as the wounded, distraught teenager made a direct appeal to his tormentor.

"Please, man. We were drunk and stoned! Just let us go and I'll plead guilty and go to prison. I promise!"

The camera switched to Laura, who said, "The killer ignored this appeal for mercy. Now you will hear excerpts of a speech by Jeremiah, specifically directed at you, the American public."

While the camera focused on the two teenagers awaiting their fate, Jeremiah spoke. "My colleagues at the United Broadcasting Corporation, including Laura Delaney, have already cataloged the past crimes of these two defendants for the audience. And they've just confessed to even more dastardly deeds. By now viewers of *American Chronicle* surely have concluded that these two apprentice criminals can be expected to continue to wreak havoc throughout their lives. They won't change and we can't rely on the judicial system to protect us from them."

Off-camera, Laura shook her head in disgust at Jeremiah's irreverent reference to their "journalistic collegiality.'' Only a demented individual could attempt humor during this grim exercise.

"Imagine that an army invades America," Jeremiah continued, still standing out of camera range. "It ravishes the countryside and cities alike, killing twenty-five thousand Americans each year and wounding ten times as many. Its soldiers rape tens of thousands of women. This army appropriates property and disrupts the economy so that losses are measured in billions of dollars.

"What would the nation do? I'll tell you. We'd demand that our armed forces do what they did to the Iraqi army during Desert Storm. Confront the Devil's Army, cut it off, corner it, and kill it!

"But we've failed to confront the army of criminals in our midst who do this amount of damage each and every year. We declare that juvenile criminals are not responsible for their actions, which they adopt as their motto. We allow judges to conduct a bail-bond lottery, guaranteeing that a large percentage of criminals are set free to commit new crimes. We may jail a small percentage of lawbreakers for a few months or years, allowing them to learn more criminal skills from their jailhouse mentors. We then grant them parole under the guise of leniency, although it really means we won't spend the money necessary to build enough jails to keep all these animals off the streets.

"It's almost as if we are powerless to act. We seem to operate under some misguided belief that democracy and justice require us to endure this occupation of our country by those who observe no laws.

"I say: no more! I am the Jeremiah of this generation, called forth by God at long last to identify the evil among us and to compel decent people to act.

"These two bags of human garbage don't deserve a second chance. The country's full of them, my fellow Americans. I urge you to seek them out, corner them, kill them. We'll all be better off for your efforts, which have God's blessing."

Along with the studio and television audiences, Laura watched the monitor as the executioner suddenly came into view. He wore a black suit, black gloves, and a black ski mask that revealed only his eyes. He walked behind the two teenagers with nooses around their necks.

"Please, please, man," Yates wailed. Jeremiah grabbed the rope, put one foot against the tree, and pulled hard, hoisting Yates a foot off the ground. Jeremiah tied off the rope as Yates kicked, gurgled, and strangled to death in front of the camera lens.

Jeremiah walked toward the other rope tied around an adjacent tree.

"Just a minute, man," Davidson said, maneuvering on his tiptoes so he could turn slightly and look at Jeremiah. Laura watched the redheaded teenager muster a last bit of courage and defiance. "I ain't gonna cry for you, motherfucker! You can kiss my ass!"

Jeremiah hanged him, instead.

"I'm certain you agree that this is very disturbing footage," Laura said, trying to soothe the audience's fears, which she could literally hear and see as many let out their breath or moaned. Some cried; a few got up and left. "Obviously we are dealing with a madman. He is attempting to use the news media—this network and this show especially—to publicize his violent act and his message of hate, and to incite imitators. These are issues we'll discuss at length, following this message from our sponsors.''

After the break, Laura introduced the talking heads: an African-American woman representing Harvard University's Center on Free Speech and the Media; a criminologist from the University of California at Berkeley; a retired assistant director of the FBI; and a British author of a book on terrorism.

"What do you think?" Laura asked them.

"I don't think you should have given him this forum," the Harvard academic said, bluntly. "Without it, he's just another vigilante."

"I disagree," the criminologist said. "You're forgetting about the Internet. He doesn't have to go through commercial television to gain an audience of millions."

"We can't shy away from discussing this subject openly, as distasteful and unfortunate as it is," the British author said.

"It's true Jeremiah gets wide publicity on a show like this," said Alexander Bennett, the former FBI assistant director. "But his appearance also could generate leads from the public leading to his arrest."

Not ordinarily a peripatetic host, Laura walked toward the audience to acknowledge one of the many waving hands.

"It worries me when vigilantes start hanging criminals in the South," a black man said. "Some white racists will see this as an excuse to hang young, black men."

"Jeremiah has made several thoughtful points," a grim-faced woman said. "We worry too much about criminal rights in this country, and not enough about the victims."

During the uproar that followed, Laura noticed that Ken, a UBC computer expert who monitored on-line chatter about the show, was waving at her. She walked over to where he sat and said, "Yes, Ken?"

"I got a guy on-line who says he's Jeremiah. He's asking for an audio hookup."

"What?"

"Apparently he's got a software program that will convert script to audio."

Laura didn't recognize the computer voice as that of the man who'd called her, but he soon convinced her.

"Laura, you should tell your audience about Raymond Doyle, also. It shows my range. As for your panel members and audience, I'm not insane, I'm not a racist, nor part of any group, although I am soliciting disciples who want to follow my example."

"What are your beliefs?"

"As stated in the Book of Revelation, the ultimate battle on earth is between Good and Evil. We need to begin that battle now by ridding ourselves of those who are evil, beginning with murderers, sadists, rapists, and child molesters. God will judge them in heaven, but it's our mission to dispatch them to that judgment."

"Has God spoken to you as a modern-day prophet and given you that mission?" Laura asked.

"God has spoken to me and revealed to me a new book of the Bible, *The Book of Second Jeremiah*, which the public can read on a new Web site, Jeremiah2.com. Well, Laura, we're running out of time, so I'll sign off until the next show.''

To her chagrin, Laura discovered that Jeremiah had consumed all but the last minute of their allotted hour. The floor manager frantically signaled for her to wrap it up.

7

Following the *American* Chronicle show, tens of thousands of people logged on to Jeremiah2.com, a Web site that proposed an impartial examination of the writings of the self-styled prophet Jeremiah the Second, as well as the study of revolutionary movements in history. The Web site had been recently updated to include graphics from the *American Chronicle* broadcast. Visitors could click their way to related sites, including one maintained by a German university where chapter one of *The Book of Second Jeremiah* had been first published.

The BOOK OF SECOND JEREMIAH

CHAPTER TWO

1 The LORD first appeared to Jeremiah on a ship at sea, as dawn broke in the east, quieting the frothing waves. The LORD sayeth to Jeremiah: Evil is everywhere but Man understands not its nature.

2 Evil takes many forms, but does not originate with Satan, but only in the breast of Man,

through the exercise of his Free Will. 'Tis not the fault of the family, nor society; nor is Evil in the genes of Mankind. Man is responsible for his Evil actions, no one else!

3 The greatest lie of the weak and the False Prophets, who pretendeth to know the Word, but who God knows not, say eternal salvation can be won by a deathbed confession. Nay! It is the reward of a lifetime of good deeds. Mercy and rehabilitation are the lies of Evil. Order, unfailing obedience, only these habits does God reward.

4 Life evolves according to the Plan of the Universe; competition, a fact of animal life, is the bane of civilized life, whereas Cooperation among Men is the highest good. He who useth skill or wile for advantage is an animal and should be treated as such.

5 Why do so few observe thy Commandments, LORD? asketh Jeremiah. Because they have freely chosen Evil, sayeth the LORD. Know ye the Evil Ones by their riches and power over others, their indulgence of every vice, their cult of individuality, and their refusal to be part of a community or observe limits to their actions.

6 This is the new Social Contract, sayeth the LORD, which blends the old with the new and replaces all man-made law:

7 Thou shalt not question the Word of God as written and told by my Prophet Jeremiah, now or in the future.

8 Thou shalt not kill.

9 Thou shalt not rape.

10 Thou shalt not steal.

11 Thou shalt not lust after money, for it is a false idol and greed is the greatest sin, as it leads to all other sins.

12 Thou shalt not establish classes of human beings, for any reason.

13 Thou shalt not degrade another human being, by word or deed.

14 Thou shalt not commit adultery.

15 Thou shalt not bring children into the world and neglect their needs, abuse them, or abandon them.

16 Thou shalt not lie or mislead, cheat or misrepresent, nor bear false witness.

17 Thou shalt not imbibe intoxicating alcohol or drugs, except those revealed to cure serious mental or physical afflictions, for these foreign substances are a direct cause of Evil.

18 Thou shalt not gamble nor wager, for gambling is part of the lust after riches.

19 Thou shalt not despoil in any way the earth that God has created.

20 All will strive to the highest fulfillment of their natural talents, but ask not to be given that which they do not deserve.

21 Those who do not work do not enjoy the benefits of community.

22 No man shall deny another man his rightful calling and work, although all within a civilized society must participate in necessary labor as de-

termined by the community of men and its leader, Jeremiah the Second.

23 Those gifted intellectually or physically are especially called to the service of their fellow man, not to take advantage of them. Humble is their demeanor and grace is their reward.

24 But few observe your laws, LORD, sayeth Jeremiah. What of these men?

25 Mark these words well, sayeth the LORD. There is no right of life for Evil Men; Good Men shall pluck Evil Men from society as weeds are plucked from a beautiful garden. The Social Contract knows no exception, nor qualification. No need exists for judges and juries, prisons and parole, rehabilitation and pardon. Obey or die!

26 Those who would journey to the chosen land, New America, yet to be revealed, will swear to this Social Contract. Death is the reward of those who break these rules. Those who would join this community, but not be part of it, shall be cast out. So sayeth the LORD to his Prophet, Jeremiah, in these the latter days of the Second Millennium.

8

Steve exited north from Interstate 66 at The Plains, nearly an hour away from FBI headquarters and only a half hour from the Appalachian Mountains, which rose before him in the west. The gentle, rolling countryside alternated between stands of hardwood forest and meadows, illuminated by a full moon set in a clear night sky.

Following Laura's telephone directions, Steve turned west off the state highway onto an asphalt road which led within two miles to Laura's estate. He stopped the car in front of an imposing iron gate. On a numeric keypad he punched in the access code she'd given him, and the gate opened, beckoning him inside.

The long, winding driveway brought him toward the top of a hill on which sat a huge, old farmhouse—three stories, with a wraparound porch, a ground-to-roofline turret on one corner, and bay windows on the upper stories. The wood exterior gleamed from a recent slathering of white paint. The interior undoubtedly was a labyrinth, making the house a security nightmare.

Laura stood on the porch, leaning nonchalantly

against a pillar. "Isn't this a glorious night!" she said, as he stepped out of the car.

Before he could answer, a muscular young man with dark, curly hair came out of the house.

"Steve, meet José Alfredo Inglesias, my bodyguard," Laura said. "José, this is Steve Wallace of the FBI."

"My wife, Maria, will be joining us Monday," José said. "We usually work as a team."

"Pleased to meet you," Steve replied, as he performed a bone-breaking handshake with the bodyguard. Steve already knew Inglesias's background, having looked him up on the computer: Navy Seal, Philadelphia cop, now a junior partner in a popular security/protective agency doing very well in the nation's capital.

"Let's talk later, Steve, when you have some time," José said. "Right now, I'll leave you two to your business and take a spin around the grounds."

"Come in," Laura said, opening the screen door. Steve couldn't help but glance at the motion of the tight, faded blue jeans she wore, along with a white turtleneck sweater.

Laura led him into a house from another era: large foyer, mammoth oak staircase, high ceilings, and wood-trimmed, wide-open doorways leading right and left. They went into the dining room and then down two steps into a living room dominated by a stone fireplace taking up most of one wall.

Steve grimaced as he looked at the double-wide French doors leading to the lawn north of the house. Someone wanting to gain entrance could simply ram a car through them. He planned to see if the home-protection agency would allow FBI communications experts to tap into the alarm system, so they'd also be aware of any unauthorized entrance into the house.

"You want to see upstairs?" she asked, leading the way.

After touring both upper floors, Steve concluded he'd talk with Inglesias about installing a new security door leading to the third level, dominated by a massive ballroom that hadn't been used in years, according to Laura.

Steve stopped to examine a photo in the hallway outside Laura's bedroom.

"Those are my parents, brother Bill, and sister Cathy," Laura said.

"Handsome family."

Laura put her hands on both hips. "I owe everything to them. Mom was beautiful and Daddy was smart." She touched his arm as if to impart a confidence. "Sounds like a country song, don't it?"

The southern drawl surprised Steve and he offered a guess. "Texas?"

"It took me years to lose that accent. Where were you raised, Steve?"

"Colorado. Golden. My dad was a state trooper. There was just my older brother and I. Our mother died when I was eleven. Where'd you grow up in Texas?"

"On a ranch outside Austin. Daddy was into cattle, wheat, oil, and politics, although not necessarily in that order. He was a Texas state senator for sixteen years, and Reagan appointed him ambassador to Panama in 1981."

"A political family."

"We were a family of unbridled energy and ambition," Laura admitted. "Everyone had a hobby—no, a passion, if you will. Brother Bill was a sharp-shooter with a rifle, Cathy a champion equestrienne. On the Olympic team in 1984."

"And you?"

She smiled, wistfully. "Beauty pageants. It was really my mother's passion, from her youth. We traveled all over Texas, entering every pageant available. Miss Austin, Miss West Texas, Miss Panhandle, Miss Quarter Horse Festival! You name it, we were there."

"It doesn't sound like you enjoyed it," Steve guessed.

"It was a mixed blessing," Laura admitted. "I followed in mom's footsteps and was named Miss Texas in 1978. Competed in the Miss America contest where I was fourth runner-up. Bet you didn't know that."

Actually, Steve did, having looked up Laura's biography in *Who's Who*.

"Course, I can't complain," Laura continued. "The Miss America contest got me my first TV job in Kansas City. I was the weather girl, but not for long." A note of triumph sounded in her voice. "Unfortunately, I've yet to live down the beauty queen image. Some people assume I got where I am because of my pretty face and glib tongue."

"I can't imagine anyone thinking that, not with your accomplishments at NBC, and now UBC. You've become a legend in the television news business."

"Well, thank you, Steve. You want to go back downstairs?"

Instead of showing him the door, as he'd feared,

Laura led the way back into the living room and sat on a sofa.

"Why do you think Jeremiah selected me to deliver his message?" she asked. "He could have chosen any number of people at the other networks."

Steve sat on a chair across from her. "I thought about that and came to a couple of conclusions. You're certainly one of the best-know newscasters in the television business."

"Actually, I'm a newsmagazine show host," Laura interjected. "People in the news department at UBC would be the first to make that distinction."

"Your background's unique, though," Steve persisted. "You were a news anchor in New York, and before that, a well-known foreign news correspondent."

She smiled brightly. "Thank you, sir. Yes, I am proud to say I'm more than one-dimensional."

Steve thought it well to remember that several handsome, powerful men who'd been interviewed by Laura had paid a price for becoming momentarily mesmerized by her charm. Then Laura unleashed the hard questions. *On the other hand, I doubt she has any interest in me.*

"The other attraction for Jeremiah probably is UBC itself and the audience it attracts," Steve said, continuing his analysis.

"Maybe. UBC has developed a reputation for broadcast muckraking. That's why some of our critics and competitors refer to the network as the Undercover Broadcast Corps."

Steve laughed. "There aren't too many institutions you haven't infiltrated. I keep waiting for the FBI to join the list."

"Believe me, it's been discussed. As you know, Arthur Kingsley, the founder and president of UBC, made his fortune in the newspaper tabloid business and he brought that attitude to UBC. Sometimes it's a cross all of us have to bear, but I have to admit it's been a successful format. Despite the occasional sensationalism and misfires, we do some of the best investigative work in the business."

"UBC's unique," Steve agreed. "Especially the rest of the programming. The emphasis on amateur sports. The idiosyncratic individual and group adventures."

"Like the four septuagenarians who tried to climb Mount Everest?"

"And all the time set aside for public access."

"God, if I hear one more discussion of extraterrestrial kidnappings, I'm going to throw up."

"The point is, it's a great audience for Jeremiah's message, as I understand it, anyway," Steve said.

"I suppose, although UBC got raked over the coals by the other media, following Thursday night's show. They think we're pandering, and indirectly encouraging terrorism." Laura shrugged. "They may be right."

"I don't know about that."

"Enough of the security and television business, Steve. Tell me something about yourself. How'd you become an FBI agent?"

Steve welcomed the turn of the conversation. He wanted Laura to know him as someone other than a federal cop. "Originally I wanted to go to law school but couldn't afford it, in part because I got married in college. My high school sweetheart. Anyway, I came from a law enforcement family and the FBI seemed a natural choice. Besides, I thought they might finance my law school education. After training at Quantico, they posted me to San Diego. Then two years later to Denver, the dream posting. Jennifer, my ex-wife, was ecstatic. We were near our parents, relatives, and friends. She was equally heartbroken when they transferred us here five years ago.''

"She never got over it?"

He shrugged, not really knowing himself, although he didn't mind talking about it. "Jennifer was unhappy at first, but seemed to settle down when she went back to college to complete her master's degree." He shook his head, still unable to fathom it all. "I don't know what happened, really. We started out as friends and became lovers and then strangers. One day she went home to Denver, with the kids." The memory raised a lump in his throat and he felt like a fool for revealing his feelings.

"I got married in eighty-eight to a guy who worked for the L.A. *Times*," Laura explained. "We were both stationed in Europe at the time. NBC sent me to Washington a year later and he went back to L.A. Then I went to New York. One or the other of us would fly to the opposite coast every weekend, or whenever possible. Small wonder it didn't work out. Marriage is hard enough without all those handicaps."

"Careers exact a high price, if you let them," Steve replied, happy she'd shared an intimacy. It seemed a good sign.

"When I fall off the mountain, which may be sooner rather than later, what with the Jeremiah thing, I plan to stay right here. My own private

Texas. I'm gonna raise horses, maybe prize cattle, too. Own twenty pairs of jeans and one good dress. And not have one television set in the house!''

Steve suppressed an urge to take Laura into his arms and explain the beauty of shared dreams.

Laura stood suddenly. ''Say, you probably want to see the rest of the property, don't you?''

''Sure.''

''Let's take a ride, then. It's a beautiful night, with the full moon.''

''You're talking about horses?''

''I got two beauties in the barn, including a dapple gray that's just right for you.''

They came out of the house and found José sitting on the edge of the porch. Steve immediately felt awkward. Did the bodyguard think this business call had turned into a date? Even Steve was confused.

''We're going for a ride, José,'' Laura said.

''Just to look around,'' Steve added, hastily. ''Is there any reason to be concerned?''

''No, everything looks fine,'' José replied.

''I've got my gun,'' Steve said, ''and a cell phone. I programmed in the number here, so I'll call if need be.'' He desperately wanted to change the subject. ''They took care of the phones here?''

''Yeah,'' José said. ''Yesterday.''

''I think we'll piggyback into the alarm company's telephone line. We should do something about that door leading to the third floor, and those French doors.''

''Good ideas,'' José said.

Laura walked toward the barn and Steve followed,

relieved to put an end to his clumsy conversation with the bodyguard.

The cavernous barn had stalls on the ground level. Lights shone through windows on the second level, and Steve assumed it was the apartment Laura had mentioned.

"The property manager and his wife live there," Laura explained. "He'll be down shortly to help us."

"How many horses do you have?"

"Four," Laura said, "including a foal born in the spring."

She turned on a light switch and the horses began to neigh, and Laura baby-talked them. A door opened at the top of the stairs and an elderly man walked down.

"Steve, this is Seth Schuyler. Seth, Steve Wallace of the FBI."

"Nice meeting you, Mr. Wallace."

"Seth, I'd like to saddle Bella, and the dapple gray for Steve."

Ten minutes later, Steve put his foot in the stirrup, grabbed the pommel, and pulled himself into the saddle, accompanied by the sounds of creaky leather. The big gray gelding followed Laura's chestnut mare out the barn door toward the north pasture.

They trotted along the east fence before turning west toward the mountains silhouetted against the moonlight. Laura steered them toward a small pond, with cattails growing in the shallow end. They dismounted and led the horses by their bridles.

"You were right, Laura. This is gorgeous."

She undid two straps at the back of her saddle and took down a blanket, which she spread on the grass.

"Let them go," she said of the horses. "They'll stay nearby."

They sat silently on the blanket, side by side, their arms resting on their knees, listening to the sounds of the night: cicadas, frogs, the slapping sound of water, the noise the light wind made as it blew through the cattails and long grass.

"Look at the stars," Steve said, lying on his back. Laura followed suit and their shoulders touched briefly. He could smell her perfume and hair spray; almost taste the lipstick. His imagination ran wild and he cautioned himself that this might not mean anything. He shouldn't do anything rash. *God, she's gorgeous,* he thought.

Nevertheless, he was about to kiss her when he heard her name spoken, "Laura." Clearly, but not loudly. At first he thought he'd let her name slip out. Then he noticed a puzzled look on Laura's face.

"Did you say my name?" she asked, the question tinged with fear.

Steve returned to reality with a jolt and sprang into a crouch, looking around the darkened pasture as he groped for the gun in his shoulder holster. He pumped a round into the chamber when he finally saw him: a dark-clad figure standing perhaps a hundred feet away on the dam of the small pond.

The stranger said Laura's name again, faintly, and Steve immediately moved toward the man, pointing the gun. "Who are you? Identify yourself or I'll shoot!"

The figure just as quickly disappeared, seeming to drop down the steep slope of the dam away from the pond.

Steve jumped as Laura grabbed his arm. "Was that a man or an animal?" she asked.

"I'm not sure." Although he was. "Let's get to the horses. Leave the blanket!"

Steve backed up, slowly moving the gun from left to right, prepared to shoot at the slightest motion. He turned only when he sensed the big gray horse behind him. He vaulted into the saddle and they galloped toward the house at full speed.

At the barn, Steve left Laura in the care of old man Schuyler, who cradled a shotgun in one arm. Steve and the bodyguard took a Jeep equipped with a spotlight and searched the pasture and nearby back roads. José drove, with a Heckler and Koch M-5 submachine gun slung over one shoulder.

But they found nothing and Steve decided to downplay the episode, in part because he wasn't certain what had happened. "It could have been someone fishing illegally on her land," he said. "I may have scared him as badly as he did us."

"Did he say anything?" José asked.

Steve hesitated. "Not really. Maybe Laura's name."

They returned to the farmhouse and Steve told José he'd be staying the night. "You keep a watch until, say, three A.M. and then I'll spell you." When he and Laura were lying on the blanket, he'd fantasized about spending the night, but this wasn't what he'd had in mind.

9

Jeremiah's vigilante activities and his televised appeal for viewers to "follow my example" inspired imitators, including one in Dallas. Mel Crawford sent Laura there to investigate a bombing. She hoped there really wasn't a connection, since their job was to report the news, not make it.

On Harwood Street, about a mile from the city's center, Laura stood on the sidewalk looking at the remains of a ranch-style house, now just a large pile of shattered wood atop a concrete foundation. A chain-link fence surrounding the property had yellow police tape woven between the links.

In this mainly African-American neighborhood, she'd found few people willing to speak to her on-camera, and Laura wasn't certain what kind of show UBC could make out of the event anyway. Would viewers be horrified that someone had taken Jeremiah at his word? Or would a follow-up show just inspire others to take the law into their own hands?

Finally one elderly woman provided some information.

"Whose home was this?" Laura asked.

"DeWitt Lewis. He ran the Harwood Street Crew, which was also called the 'Homebo' Shopping Club.' "

"Why?"

"Because if you wanted somethin', DeWitt would find it and sell it to you."

"Anything?"

"That's right."

"Is it true Lewis and his crew ran the local drug trade and had a hand in prostitution and the loan shark business, too?"

Laura watched the old woman scrunch up her face and raise one eyebrow before replying. "There was rumors 'bout that, but I don't know for sure, you understand?"

Laura understood a lot about parsing the English language. She saw several young black men standing on a nearby street corner, eyeing her and her camera crew. Laura had dressed down for this visit, wearing blue jeans, a maroon turtleneck, and leather jacket, so as not to attract too much attention. Still, she had a job to do.

Laura walked across the street and approached the five men she judged to be in their late teens or early twenties. Two wore the ubiquitous-inner-city uniform of low-riding baggy jeans, oversized shirts, and high-topped, unlaced basketball shoes, while the other three sported expensive designer clothes.

"Hi, I'm Laura Delaney from UBC. Any of you know what happened here?"

One pointed out the obvious, "The house got blown up."

"And DeWitt and his crew along with it," another said.

"I understand from the police there were several survivors. Do you know anyone who got out alive?"

"I know who you are," said one who wore his hair in dreadlocks. "You put on that show where Jeremiah hung those two white kids. The folks at DeWitt's party was talkin' about it that night.

"You were there?"

He nodded emphatically. "It was just like any other Friday night. People listenin' to music, gettin' down, havin' a few drinks." He'd intentionally unbuttoned a red silk shirt halfway down to showcase a necklace of seashells resting in his chest hair.

"What were they saying about the show?" Laura asked, her interest piqued.

"That it was about crime and racism, the only subjects that much matter in America."

"Go on." Laura signaled for her cameraman to begin filming.

"They was sayin' this Jeremiah guy started killin' white folks so's not to make it seem like a racist thing, which it damn well is!" the guy with the seashell necklace said.

Others in the group now willingly voiced their opinion, Laura noticed.

"When any white man starts talkin' 'bout killin' criminals, you know he's really talkin' 'bout killin' the black man!"

"That's right!"

"Jeremiah's just tryin' to throw people off with this prophet shit."

"White television people like you are promotin' this sick fucker."

Laura looked anxiously at the teenager who made the last remark, and he glared back.

Someone else spoke up. "Nobody's gonna 'liminate crime in America. It's like the flag, apple pie, and yo' momma, if you dig what I mean." Laura laughed, which broke the tension. All five men now seemed anxious to continue the interview.

"You 'liminate crime and you throw a helluva lotta people outta work, and I ain't just talkin' about the niggers standing on this street corner!"

"Tell it, brother!"

It was a dizzying dialogue, and Laura nearly lost her balance several times trying to switch the microphone from one speaker to the other.

"Hell, half the governments in South America would cave in if you cut off their drug money. The CIA and the DEA use the drug cartels to keep the socialists and commies outta power."

"Yessir!"

"American companies make the chemicals you need to produce these drugs. Airlines, trucks, and ships bring the *shit* into the country. It don't just appear all of a sudden. Who owns these companies?"

"There it is! There it is!"

"Givin' black folks drugs and then makin' 'em illegal is a good reason for whitey to have more police, so they's safe in their homes and black folks is penned up in the ghetto!"

"You really gonna put this on television?" one asked.

"Yeah, but we'll do some editing," Laura said.

"If this Jeremiah muthafucker starts killin' the white-collar crooks who is launderin' this drug money, half the brokerage houses and banks in the country would go down the tube! Then there'd be a goddamned depression."

Two of the teenagers broke off and walked away, laughing as they left.

"So how did you get out alive?" she asked the seashell-necklace guy.

He sobered up, as did his friends. "DeWitt told me to relieve the lookout at the end of the alley. I wasn't the only one who left 'bout that time, either."

"Who else?"

"Black dude who delivered the beer. I seen him walk in carrying two cardboard cases and put 'em in the kitchen. Opened one box and put several bottles of Bud on ice."

"Did you know him?"

"No. I figured he was from the liquor store."

"You think the dynamite was in those boxes?" Laura asked.

He shrugged. "Don't know how else it got in there."

"And a fuckin' brother, too!" another said, angrily. With that, the group melted away, leaving Laura and her two-man camera crew standing alone on the street corner.

Later she talked to a Dallas Police Department captain, who said evidence collected at the scene indicated industrial-grade dynamite caused the explosion. Given the damage, he estimated it to be about twenty pounds. It blew down most of the walls inside the house and opened an eight-foot-diameter hole in the floor down to the crawl space. Four-inch construction nails placed on the dynamite served as shrapnel.

"How many dead?" Laura asked.

"Nineteen, with six seriously injured." The captain smiled. "DeWitt Lewis and most of the Harwood Street Crew are no more, and that ain't nothing to grieve about."

"Word on the street is that this could be the work of a rival drug gang."

The captain showed Laura a rectangular piece of aluminum. "If you look closely, you'll see some numbers scratched on one side."

Six numbers: SIX, EIGHT, THREE, FOUR, NINE, FIVE. Her heart sank. After Jeremiah mentioned Raymond Doyle on *American Chronicle*, newspapers all over the country ran a story about the ID numbers the terrorist had spray-painted on the walls of the Los Angeles office suite.

"We got an anonymous call within an hour of the explosion," the captain said. "The caller told us we'd find this aluminum calling card inside the stove in DeWitt's house. One of the few things to survive intact. And he correctly identified the numbers."

"What else did he say?"

"Said he was a New Age garbageman, and that we'd hear from him again."

Laura planned to fly to Austin and drive to her parents' ranch for a short visit. As she and her crew hailed a cab outside police headquarters to take them to the airport, Laura heard a street vendor shouting out a description of his wares.

"Get your Jeremiah sportswear here!"

Along with her cameraman, Maury Gannon, Laura walked over for a closer look. Bumper stickers displayed on the vendor's cart read: JEREMIAH SPEAKS THE LORD'S WORD, and in small print at the bottom, *www.Jeremiah2.com*. A legend imprinted on hanging sweatshirts warned: *HEED THE PROPHET'S TEACHINGS OR GO TO HELL!*

"What are you doing?" she asked indignantly.

"Selling stuff, lady. What do you want?"

"This is outrageous! You can't do this."

"The hell I can't. I got a valid city license."

"But you're encouraging him. Making him out to be a hero. He's a killer!"

The vendor sighed. "Look, lady, last year my biggest-selling item was Nazi stuff. You know, fake Iron Crosses, helmets with the swastika on 'em, T-shirts with lightning strikes and the identification for some Panzer division. Jeremiah's hot now."

"Whadaya think, Laura?" Maury asked, trying on a *J2* hat.

"It looks ridiculous, Maury."

"In that case I'll take it. How much?"

"Ten bucks."

"I'll give you six."

"Sold."

As the vendor made change, Laura grabbed his arm. "Do you know that some Jeremiah copycat blew up a house right here in Dallas, killing nineteen people?"

"Yeah!" the vendor exclaimed, his eyes shining. "Right now I got some guys printing up T-shirts that say, 'Six, eight, three, four, nine, five. The combination that cures drug use.' What do you think?"

"It's sick. Sick, sick, sick."

The vendor frowned. "Look, you don't like the guy, I got something for you. It'll be just right." He cast an appraising eye at her. "You got the chest to display it on, that's for sure. Check it out." He held up a while T-shirt proclaiming that "Jeremiah Sucks."

Laura arched an eyebrow. "How much?"

"For you, sweet pea, five bucks."

"I'll take it."

10

Monday morning, Steve convened his investigative team—Leslie Ulrich and Jack Kincaid from his counterterrorism squad; Lyle Grayson, a Bureau computer expert; and Dr. Michael Ellsworth, a psychologist from the Quantico unit. They had just sat down to business in a conference room when Deputy Director Peter Thompson appeared unannounced and took a seat at the table, causing everyone to look about nervously.

Known for his coolness under fire, literally and figuratively, and for his sartorial splendor, Thompson wore tailor-made suits that perfectly fit his compact frame. Thompson's ambition—many thought he wanted to be attorney general—caused him not to suffer fools gladly, especially subordinates whose ineptitude reflected adversely upon his leadership.

Steve figured Jeremiah's public relations successes had compelled Thompson's presence today. The deputy director wanted the terrorist caught, and soon.

Steve rubbed his hands together as a sign that the group should begin serious discussions. "Okay, Leslie, have you been able to track Jeremiah's movements in Atlanta?"

The only female agent in Steve's squad was athletically gifted, loyal, and competent, but nevertheless the butt of many jokes by her colleagues in a male-dominated Bureau. Steve often teamed with Leslie in the field, although not begrudgingly.

"From tire imprints, our Atlanta agents were able to track down the rental car," Leslie said. "Unfortunately, it already had been vacuumed and cleaned up by the agency employees at the airport as they prepared to put it on the street again. No prints, no fibers, no nothing.

"But we got a copy of the credit card receipt Jeremiah used to rent the car. American Express card. Also, he presented a driver's license as a second ID. Used the same name and card to buy his airline ticket. Flew directly out of Chicago O'Hare to Atlanta."

"Why does this seem too good to be true?" Kincaid asked, sarcastically. Steve thought Kincaid embodied some characteristics of the extremist groups he studied and occasionally infiltrated, including the Mafia, Klan, skinhead and neo-Nazi groups, various state militias, survivalists, constitutionalists, anti-immigration committees, anti-United Nations groups, and certain fundamentalist Christian sects.

"The card and driver's license belong to a sporting goods salesman who lives in Elmhurst, a Chicago suburb," Leslie added, looking daggers at Jack, whom Steve knew to be one of her tormentors.

"Counterfeit ID?" Steve inquired.

"Definitely the driver's license," Leslie told him. "Agents from our Chicago field office interviewed this guy Saturday. Name's Ralph Patterson. He had his driver's license on him and he had an ironclad alibi concerning his whereabouts last Tuesday. He was at a company training session with about a hundred other salespeople."

Steve watched the electricity jump around the room, from person to person.

"Jeremiah knows this guy!" Kincaid said, appealing to others in the group for confirmation. "They're friends or business associates, or Jeremiah lives in the same neighborhood. He stole Patterson's Social Security number! That's how he faked the driver's license."

"Possibly," Leslie said, cautiously.

"We should show the sketch of Jeremiah to Patterson's friends and neighbors," Kincaid said, using one hand to routinely level his rigid crew-cut hair.

"What about the credit card?" Steve asked.

"The American Express card was newly reissued," Leslie answered, "and mailed from Philadelphia about a week before Jeremiah struck in Atlanta. Someone with all the right answers made an eight-hundred-number call to activate the card."

"It wasn't Patterson," Steve guessed.

"Nope. He says he never got it."

"Jeremiah stole it from Patterson's mailbox!" Kincaid exclaimed, trying another angle. "It's another indication he might live in that area."

"Maybe," Steve replied. "Let's check it out but not get our hopes up. It's more likely Jeremiah had someone steal the AmEx card at the manufacturing plant in Philadelphia, or at the post office there, or the post office in Chicago."

"Exactly," Ellsworth said, stroking his beard for inspiration. "Jeremiah's plan is unfolding nicely. Think of how smart and efficient this guy has been to date and then square that with dumping his neighborhood location into our lap.'' The stocky psychologist's salt-and-pepper beard matched the pattern of his herringbone sport coat. The Behavioral Science Unit where he worked compiled psychological profiles of serial killers.

"On a positive note, we have a lot of crime-scene evidence," Steve said. "Footprints. Rope and videotape we might be able to track to a specific retail store. The best is the fully intact bullet that passed through the leg of the Yates kid. Now all we need is the gun."

"We know from Thursday's show that Jeremiah has computer expertise," Grayson, the computer expert, said. His gangly, rumpled appearance contrasted directly with Thompson's impeccable tailoring. "If he stole Patterson's card, then he, or his accomplices, had enough information to hack into the American Express mainframe and find out Patterson's home address, phone number, Social Security number, and other identification. Patterson is really a random victim. It only looks like Jeremiah knows him."

Steve looked at his fellow agents and most nodded unenthusiastically, including Kincaid. Conceding that Jeremiah had outmaneuvered them again wasn't anywhere near as exciting as thinking they were closing in on him.

"Lyle, if Jeremiah or one of his lieutenants broke into American Express's mainframe, there'd be a trail, wouldn't there?" Steve asked.

"Maybe, depending on how good they are."

"Well, it's your job to find out, Lyle, so Leslie can follow up this lead," Steve said, irritably. "Anything on the various Internet postings? I've given all of you copies of the Bible verse Jeremiah is writing. It's obviously a blueprint or a recruitment device, or both.''

Grayson raised his eyebrows in an expression of minor frustration. "I contacted our legate in Munich, but haven't heard from him. The first chapter came from there."

Thompson stirred to life. "Really? Germany?"

Lazily chewing gum, Grayson elaborated, "A religious study group based at a university there."

"Any chance of identifying the person who posted the file?" Steve asked.

"I doubt it," Grayson replied. "A sophisticated user like Jeremiah, or his people, can simply steal access codes. They could have posted this file from Japan and made it look like it came from Germany."

"What about the new Web site Jeremiah mentioned on the *American Chronicle* show?"

"That's a different story," Grayson explained. "We traced the design of that Web site to two individuals who were hired by the New Covenant, an organization headquartered in Seattle."

"Let me explain," Thompson interrupted, causing all heads to turn toward him. "The New Covenant fronts as an import-export company doing business worldwide, but they are known to be involved in smuggling, drugs, brokering arms sales, and indirectly supporting terrorist organizations by raising money, hiding fugitives, and facilitating communications among various groups."

Steve watched the others digest this bombshell of information, with its widespread implications.

"One more thing," Thompson added. "Although

there's conjecture on this point, some evidence points to Germany as the country of origin for the New Covenant.''

''Jesus!'' Kincaid marveled.

''On the topic of sponsorship, Jack, what have you found out about Jeremiah?'' Steve asked.

''Nothing,'' Kincaid answered bluntly. ''No one's claiming this guy as a member.''

''I've turned up something intriguing,'' Ellsworth interjected, suddenly, ''more so now that I know about the New Covenant. They also sponsored a survivalists' expo in Seattle recently.''

''We talked about that,'' Kincaid recalled.

''When I was in the office last week gathering information for this session, I asked Jack if any of these fringe groups hold public meetings and he mentioned a 'survivalists' expo' in Seattle this spring,'' the psychologist said.

''Our local agents videotaped the exhibits and the crowd,'' Kincaid said, ''and collected some of the literature being sold there.''

Ellsworth looked at Thompson. ''It took me a full day to dig it out of the mountain of files in our storage areas, most of which, I might add, are not indexed.''

''We've made an appropriation request each of the last three fiscal years to put more of our hard-copy files on microfiche,'' Thompson explained patiently, ''but it's been turned down each year.''

The psychologist shook his head. ''Anyway, on a hunch I hauled some of this stuff back to Quantico and I've been reading it for several days. It's the run-of-the-mill right-wing propaganda, warning about an international cabal of Jewish bankers, the Club of

Rome, U.N. helicopters, and others plotting to overthrow the government. As evidence, they point to military markings on road signs, presumably to guide foreign troops to battle. But there was one interesting tract that immediately caught my attention because of its reference to criminals as being like an army of invaders.''

The psychologist paused, waiting for his students to catch up.

''Which Jeremiah used as a metaphor in Atlanta,'' Steve said, thinking out loud, ''right before he hanged the two boys.''

''Exactly,'' Ellsworth said. ''And there's almost the same phrase, word for word, in one of these expo tracts entitled *The Chosen Few*.''

Ellsworth passed a bound volume to Steve, who fingered the textured blue cover and gold-embossed title. No author's name was printed on the cover, although Steve saw that the copyright had been registered in the name of one John James.

''It could be a tongue-in-cheek nom de plume,'' Ellsworth suggested. ''The Hebrew meanings of John and James, respectively, are 'God's Gracious Gift' and 'the Supplanter.' ''

Kincaid muttered under his breath and Steve agreed, thinking the psychologist's conclusions seemed far-fetched.

''Turn to the page with the paper clip and read the highlighted passage,'' Ellsworth said.

Steve did as instructed and then hurriedly fished through an expandable file folder on the table in front of him until he located a transcript of the videotape Jeremiah had filmed for Laura and UBC.

''Damn!'' Steve exclaimed, reading. ''They're

identical.'' He passed the book and transcript to Thompson.

Kincaid stood, eyes blazing. ''Anyone wanna fast-forward through our video of the expo?''

As Kincaid hurried out of the room to fetch the videotape, Ellsworth took back the blue volume. ''This book is organized into four sections,'' he explained to the others. '' 'Good Versus Evil,' 'Greed in the Marketplace,' 'The Failure of Government,' and 'The Chosen Few.' ''

''Have you read the entire book?'' Thompson asked.

''Yes, it's less than two hundred pages.'' The psychologist looked over the top of his glasses at the deputy director. ''And the similarities between this book and Jeremiah's spoken statements and published verse are startling.''

''If Steve is right that this literature could be a blueprint, we might conclude that Jeremiah's next victims are likely to be in the business community or the government,'' Thompson said. ''Now if we could only figure out who and where.''

The task force members silently watched the videotape, as the camera operator walked about the exhibition floor at a major Seattle hotel, filming exhibits and participants. Exactly twelve minutes into the film, according to the VCR clock, the cameraman focused on a table with a banner suspended above it, reading: THE CHOSEN FEW.

''Hold that!'' Ellsworth shouted.

Kincaid put the VCR on freeze-frame as they all stared at the three people sitting at the table, behind a pile of books similar to the blue volume Steve held. A woman in her late twenties or early thirties, a black man about the same age, and . . .

"Well, I'll be damned," Steve said, softly.

The third man appeared to be in his thirties, sandy-haired, as was the masked killer of the Atlanta youths, FBI analysts had concluded, after enlarging Jeremiah's videotape and examining the hairs on his neck. Also, the third man closely resembled one of the sketch options developed for the L.A. sniper, who claimed to be Jeremiah the Second.

"Well, gentlemen and lady, I'd say your work is cut out for you," Thompson said, as he stood and adjusted his suit coat. "Steve, I'm sure you know what to do, and you'll have all resources necessary to accomplish the job. Any problems, call me. This case may be bigger than I originally thought. I probably will involve some other people in this eventually."

Like the CIA, Pentagon, and possibly the White House, Steve thought. As Thompson prepared to leave the room, Steve coughed. "Ah, sir, one last bit of information you'll be interested in."

"Yes?"

Steve squirmed, knowing he had to inoculate himself before rumors were spread by the bodyguard. "Friday night I was at Laura Delaney's farmhouse out near Middleburg. We tapped her phones, as you know, and redid her home security system. UBC has provided her with two bodyguards.

"While I was there, Ms. Delaney wanted to take a horseback ride, and I went with her." He saw a small cloud appear on Thompson's face. "There was a bright moon and it seemed harmless enough. Anyway, we encountered a man in the pasture near a small pond." *Jesus, whatever I was thinking at the time, it certainly wasn't about security.* "He may have said her name. Laura. I attempted to apprehend this guy, but he disappeared. I took Ms. Delaney back to the house, and the bodyguard and I made a thorough search of the farm, but we couldn't find anyone." Steve shrugged. "It may be nothing. I just thought you—all of you—should know."

"I wouldn't doubt it was Jeremiah," Ellsworth pondered. "He has chosen Ms. Delaney as his spokesman to the world. It's not surprising that he may have taken a proprietary interest in her."

Having outed his indiscretion and painted it in muted colors, Steve sought an additional advantage. "I think I should maintain close contact with Ms. Delaney and her bodyguards, in case he comes back."

Thompson hesitated before responding. "Okay, Steve. The last thing we need is for a media celebrity to get killed under our noses."

11

Thirty thousand feet above Indiana, Steve and Jack Kincaid plotted their strategy for Seattle.

"You talked to our guys in Seattle?" Steve asked.

"Yeah, talked with Fleming, the agent in charge," Kincaid said, directing a stream of sour breath in Steve's direction. "He and his guys will meet us at the airport. They got search warrants for the New Covenant offices and warehouse. A court issued an order for phone taps yesterday, so they should be in place already."

The New Covenant had sponsored "Survivalists' Expo '95," Steve knew, where a man sold a book that Jeremiah the Terrorist Prophet now quoted, and they'd help set up Jeremiah2.com.

"What about this guy Adam Doyle who manages the New Covenant office?" Steve asked, having already determined that Adam Doyle wasn't related to Raymond Doyle, the assasinated pedophile.

"He's a self-appointed colonel in the Oregon Militia," Kincaid said. "Once he was a major in the real army, but they passed him over for promotion a few years ago and he took a cash settlement and early out."

"Was he West Point?"

"No, I don't think so."

They landed at Seattle/Tacoma International at 9:00 A.M. local time. They each carried a garment bag so they wouldn't have to waste time in baggage claim.

Three men intercepted them.

"Steve Wallace? I'm Matthew Fleming, agent in charge of the local office." He pointed at the two men with him. "This is Travis and Boyd."

"Nice to meet you. This is Agent Jack Kincaid."

As they all shook hands, Steve remembered meeting Fleming once before, at Bureau headquarters. Now, as then, he went against the grain of tradition, today wearing a handsome gray windowpane suit instead of the more acceptable black, navy, or gray, with or without pinstripes.

"We talked about Doyle on the plane," Steve said. "I understand he's ex-army. Is he likely to take offense at the search warrant and cause trouble?"

Fleming smiled confidently. "I don't think so. We're well aware of him here and he's mainly an organizational type. Lots of bluster but no balls."

"I understand there are two offices?"

"The New Covenant has a downtown address in an office building, and then there's a warehouse near the docks. You want to raid both places simultaneously?"

"I think we should go downtown first. We're looking primarily for leads, documents, not contraband. We'd most likely find that kind of stuff in his office, don't you think?" It was good politics to allow Fleming a say in the decisions. "Besides, your people will be listening to any phone calls between the office and warehouse, and maybe that'll generate a lead or two.''

They drove the interstate to downtown Seattle through beautiful, hilly suburban areas and then over the Alaskan Way Viaduct, from which they saw warehouses on Harbor Island and along the landward side of East Waterway, a channel leading off Elliott Bay. Fleming pointed out the New Covenant warehouse, but Steve couldn't quite distinguish it from the other look-alike buildings.

They exited in the downtown area and parked near an imposing office building on Stewart Street. Off to the northwest, Steve saw the distinctive World's Fair Space Needle. Stepping from the car, he smelled the sea breeze and heard the sounds of a tugboat horn above the car traffic sounds. Checking his bulletproof vest, Steve wished he were just visiting Seattle.

En route Fleming had used a cell phone to confirm previous arrangements with the Seattle police department. A black-and-white unit waited for them, and Fleming told one of the cops to stay outside where he had a view of the alley and fire exits. He sent the other cop to occupy the lobby. The five FBI agents took the elevator to the fifth floor.

Responding to his receptionist's intercom call, Doyle soon appeared and Fleming handed him the judge's order. ''This is a search warrant granting us full access to your office and records, business and personal.''

Baby-faced and barrel-chested, Doyle looked alarmed. Steve saw a line of sweat form on the ex-army officer's upper lip.

"It's this kind of Gestapo activity that led to the formation of the Oregon Militia," Doyle said, finally, his voice squeaking uncontrollably. "You're trampling on the Constitution!"

"Quite to the contrary, we went to extraordinary lengths to preserve your constitutional rights," Fleming said. "Now, do you intend to comply peacefully with the provisions of this search warrant?"

When the militia colonel's shoulders sagged appreciably, Steve heaved a silent sigh of relief. Obviously they had the element of surprise. Doyle either lacked the willpower or firepower to resist.

Fleming directed his two agents and Kincaid to search the office, while he used a walkie-talkie to communicate with the uniformed officers and let them know the danger had passed. Steve followed Doyle into his office.

"Just exactly what are you looking for?" Doyle fumed, dropping into a black leather chair behind a large, walnut desk. Steve stood so he could see if Doyle tried to open a drawer and pull out a weapon.

"You organized an expo here this spring," Steve said.

"Damn right! Patriots have a constitutional right to assemble! We have the right of free speech."

"No one's questioning those rights," Steve assured him. "In fact, I presume nearly all of the expo participants were law-abiding citizens. We have an interest only in those who are wanted by the law."

"Who?" Doyle asked, his indignation ebbing as his curiosity increased.

Steve handed over a still-frame print of the exhibitor who resembled Jeremiah.

Doyle looked at it, his face registering surprise,

then suspicion. "Where'd you get this?"

"It's from a video our agents took at the expo."

Doyle bounded out of his chair. "That's illegal surveillance!"

"No, it isn't. There are several statutes reserving the FBI's right to conduct surveillance of organizations with members suspected of plotting against the government of the United States."

Doyle smirked, sat down, and said, sanctimoniously, "Somebody *ought* to be plotting against the federal government."

Weary of the verbal sparring, Steve nodded at the photo. "You know these three people? You rented the booths at the expo. I can't imagine you didn't meet them or that you don't have records on hand, including an application form and a check for payment of their fees."

Doyle glanced briefly at the photo, as if afraid to examine it closely. "Could've met 'em," he said, "but there were over a hundred exhibitors and nearly two thousand people who visited the expo. This photo is pretty grainy. It doesn't ring a bell. I can check my records, though."

According to the records, John James rented the booth and paid the two-hundred-dollar exhibit fee in cash. Martha Kennedy, one of three people issued badges for the booth, had signed the application form, which indicated that the exhibit material would consist entirely of a book written by Mr. James, titled *The Chosen Few*. The other badges were in the name of Elijah Potts, presumably the black man in the photo, and John James, aka Jeremiah. Aliases all, Steve assumed. He doubted the addresses on the exhibit application were worth checking out.

"You know anything about this book?" Steve asked, holding up his copy of *The Chosen Few*.

Doyle smiled smugly and shook his head.

Within two hours the agents had packed

all the material they wanted into six boxes, including copies of all the office computer files, and carried them down to the car in two trips.

"Okay, Mr. Doyle, we'll be on our way," Fleming announced.

"When do I get my stuff back?" Doyle asked indignantly.

"We'll copy what we need and return the originals before the end of the week," Fleming answered.

They took two cars back to the Harbor Island area and the New Covenant warehouse on Eleventh Avenue, Southwest. They parked a block away and Fleming conferred by telephone with his office, as well as other agents posted in the warehouse district.

"There was a telephone call about twenty minutes ago, telling someone named Monroe to get out," Fleming said. "But we got the area sealed off and my agents told me no one has left."

"Monroe?" Steve asked.

Fleming shrugged and shook his head.

Stepping out of the car onto a sidewalk, Steve worried that he and his fellow FBI agents were too conspicuous: men in dark suits, wearing dark glasses, walking purposefully in an area of frenzied activity. Huge stationary cranes loaded and unloaded crates from the ships while forklifts darted about helter-skelter, occasionally scattering cursing longshoremen, conspicuous because of the yellow hard hats they wore.

A weathered, two-story, gray wood building housed the New Covenant office. The building attached to a corrugated-tin warehouse whose wide roll-up doors faced the dock area.

Travis and Boyd took up positions on the docks. Steve, Kincaid, and Fleming climbed the stairs to the second-floor entrance.

Steve pushed open the door, which made a scraping noise before yielding. Three pairs of eyes focused on them, belonging to two women and a gray-haired man, all sitting at desks in an open area to the left of the door. Behind the desks, an expanse of windows provided a panoramic view of the port.

"How can I help you gentlemen?" the gray-haired man asked, standing and walking to a pitted and scarred wood counter that separated the entryway from the office area. Straight ahead, beyond an old-fashioned swinging gate, Steve could see into the warehouse. To the right of the gate a hallway led to bathrooms, according to a sign on the wall.

"FBI," Fleming declared, flashing his ID.

"What do you want?" the man asked, stiffly.

Steve handed over the photo and asked him: "You know any of these people? They around today?"

A toothpick appeared between the man's lips as he looked at the photo. "Never saw any of 'em before."

"Mind if we look around?" Steve asked.

"You got a warrant?"

Fleming held out the paper as Steve motioned for Kincaid to go through the swinging gate toward the warehouse entrance.

Steve followed Kincaid and looked down the hallway toward the rest rooms. "Wait here while I check
this out," he told Kincaid.

Suddenly a black man charged out of the men's
room, hitting Steve in the head with the barrel of a
gun. As he slumped to the floor, fighting pain and
nausea, Steve heard gunfire. One, two, three shots.
He cringed but didn't feel the bullets' impact.

Several seconds or several minutes later, Steve
stood and shook off the numbing effects of the blow.
He felt a sore spot and welt above his left eye, which
explained his blurred vision. He pulled out his 9-mm
and looked ahead at Kincaid lying on the floor. Steve
rolled Kincaid over, while checking on Fleming
sprawled near the front door. The man behind the
counter seemed frozen in place and one of the
women cried hysterically.

Kincaid had a bullet hole in the center of his forehead and an expression of astonishment on his face.

"Are you okay?" Steve yelled at Fleming, who
struggled to his feet while examing his chest.

"Yeah, but I took two in the vest!"

At that moment agent Travis burst through the
door, nearly knocking Fleming down again.

"I heard gunfire!" Travis yelled.

"Follow me!" Steve ordered, running into the
warehouse. On the landing at the top of the stairs, he
looked at the floor below and saw several longshoremen looking up at him.

"FBI!" Steve yelled, bounding down the stairs,
pointing the gun in front of him. He saw Boyd at the
entrance of the warehouse and heard Travis following behind.

"The black guy, where'd he go?" Steve yelled at

the nearest longshoreman, who said nothing but glanced apprehensively toward the back of the warehouse.

"Get out of here!" Steve shouted at the workers, as Travis ran by him to take up a position behind a crate.

"Help's on the way!" Fleming hollered from the top of the stairs. Steve looked up at the frazzled agent in charge, who held a gun in one hand and a walkie-talkie in the other. *He's a perfect target!* Steve thought.

Steve, Travis, and Boyd alternately covered each other as they worked the aisles in the warehouse, searching for the gunman within a labyrinth of crates and boxes. Steve tried to make sense of it all. Was this the Elijah Potts from the expo? Who was Monroe? Obviously the warning call to Potts, or whoever he was, had come too late. Why hadn't he surrendered? Why shoot it out with them?

Suddenly Travis fired his weapon, and return fire came from the back of the warehouse. Just as Steve thought they had him cornered, the man drove a forklift out into the open. Protected by an iron cage, he fired at Travis and Steve, causing them to scramble for cover.

The gunman leapt from the forklift and dashed for freedom, making it to the outside of the warehouse, where he exchanged gunfire with Boyd. Steve and Travis moved at an angle until they had the black man in a cross fire. The three agents poured a withering line of fire at him until he collapsed.

They approached him cautiously. One on the downed man's legs quivered involuntarily for several seconds. A gun lay on the pavement, several inches from his hand. Steve kicked the gun aside while Travis knelt and felt his neck for a pulse.

"He's dead."

Steve held the photo at arm's length for comparison. The dead man definitely was Elijah Potts from the survivalists' expo.

The police arrived and Steve made his way back up to the office, where two paramedics bent over Kincaid.

"Is he dead?" Steve asked, foolishly.

They stepped aside as Steve knelt beside Jack and looked at him as if they'd never known each other. He couldn't help but reach out and gently level off the neat, black crew-cut hair.

12

The federal prison at Leavenworth, Kansas, had a storied reputation as the oldest level-five penitentiary in the United States, housing the "worst of the worst," a distinction that attracted Jeremiah, who planned to make it a demonstration project.

He considered Leavenworth to be nothing more than a graduate school of crime for twelve hundred of the most incorrigible criminals in America, including murderers, armed robbers, arsonists, rapists, and kidnappers.

"You know what the prisoners here at Leavenworth do all day?" Jeremiah asked, as he and his two helpers drove a stolen van west across the Missouri River bridge.

"What, boss?" asked Winston.

"Same thing they did on the streets. Roam the grounds all day, hang out, talk trash, loaf, fight, deal drugs, run scams, and generally prey on each other and the guards."

His other helper, Paris, grinned. "Don't sound like much of a punishment to me."

"It's just a bump in the road for these guys," Jeremiah said. "Did you know someone convicted of murder in the United States only spends four years in prison on the average?''

''That ain't right, boss.''

''Nope, and we're going to do something about it today.''

Jeremiah and his colleagues drove past Fort Leavenworth, an Army post known for the excellence of its tactical school. They parked the Chevy van on the side of Route 73, just opposite the entrance to the prison, situated about two hundred yards north of the road, atop a small hill. Lettering on the side of the van read: LEAVENWORTH WATER DEPARTMENT.

Winston and Paris placed yellow caution codes in back and front of the van, and then began unloading their equipment.

Jeremiah dialed a number on his cell phone and asked for the prison warden. ''Warden Ballard. This is the Leavenworth water department. If you'll look out your window, you'll see we're repairing a leak in the water line. The water pressure inside will be low for about an hour. We'll let you know when we're finished.''

Jeremiah smiled as he looked up at the formidable prison. A redbrick wall enclosed the twenty-two-acre complex that included the cell block buildings, a hospital, printing plant, textile shop, and furniture factory. The wall rose thirty-five feet above ground and extended the same distance below ground, he knew, to prevent both vaulting and tunneling. In the history of Leavenworth, only one convict had escaped and never been recaptured, and that was in 1910.

Four seven-story-high cell buildings, as well as an administrative hall, extended like spokes from a cen-

tral rotunda capped with a grand silvery dome that
rose 150 feet above the Kansas prairie. Befittingly,
Jeremiah thought, the prison architecture resembled
the United States Capitol building.

The four cell blocks each contained five-story,
double-sided cages inside a limestone building,
which resulted in a greenhouse effect during the summer, especially on the upper levels. For that reason,
the criminal community referred to Leavenworth as
the "Hot House."

From the back of the van, Jeremiah took a three-
foot-long metal bar with a T-shaped handle and a U-
shaped hook on the other end. In a grassy area just
beyond the shoulder and ditch, he located a twelve-
inch-diameter cast-iron cover recessed an inch below
ground level, removed it, and set it on the straw-
colored grass. Etched on the cover were the words
LEAVENWORTH WATER DEPARTMENT. Using a key,
Jeremiah unlocked a box and opened the lid. He inserted the U-shaped portion of the bar into the top
part of a valve and turned the handle until he'd shut
off the flow of water in the four-inch pipe below
ground.

Using shovels, it took Paris and Winston about
twenty-five minutes to dig below the frost line and
expose a three-foot section of water pipe. They used
an electric circular saw plugged into a gasoline-
powered electrical generator to cut out a two-foot
section of pipe. Their effort caused a brief waterspout
and they used coffee cans to bail out the water.

Jeremiah's helpers cut threads into each end of the
exposed pipe, inserted a T-shaped piece of replace-
ment pipe, and attached female couplings to the
newly carved threads. The vertical portion of the T-

shaped piece protruded about six inches above ground, the last few inches already threaded.

While they shoveled dirt back in the hole, Jeremiah carried from the van a rectangular metal box, two feet by three feet, and six inches thick, with several black dials on its side. The box had a four-inch-diameter hole in its center, which fit perfectly over the vertical pipe. Jeremiah removed the two halves of the top of the box to reveal an internal maze of copper lines, joints, and valves. He screwed onto the ground pipe a Janus coupling, constricted in the middle to an inch diameter. He attached several copper lines from the box to small, threaded nipples on the lower half of the coupling. The upward flow of the underground water could now be controlled.

Winston and Paris returned with a plastic twenty-gallon water bottle, filled with what looked like honeycombed Styrofoam covered with a black and green mold. They inverted the bottle and screwed it to the top of the Janus coupling. Jeremiah attached more copper lines and adjusted various dials. He opened a valve and the bottle quickly filled with water. He turned a dial and the water began dripping steadily back into the main line. Lastly, Jeremiah replaced the two halves of the top of the metal box and screwed them shut tightly.

"That went smoothly," he told his helpers. "Let's finish up and get out of here, before we attract any more attention."

Winston and Paris enclosed the four-foot-high water bottle in a square metal covering painted an institutional green. Black lettering on the green box read, WARNING. ELECTRICAL RELAY. HIGH VOLTAGE. DANGEROUS.

As they reloaded their equipment into the van, Paris said, "Too bad about the guards and other prison employees."

"That's always been one of the unfortunate aspects of war," Jeremiah said. "Civilians get killed."

As they drove back toward Missouri, Jeremiah dialed Laura Delaney's office number. "This is Jeremiah," he boldly told the receptionist. "The first half of my ID number is three, one, two, one, five. Tell Laura Delaney I'll give her the last four numbers when she gets on the phone."

He didn't have to wait long. "I suppose you're getting all kinds of crank calls from people who pretend to be me," he said.

"You can't imagine," Laura replied.

"I'm certain your phone is tapped, Laura, so maybe I won't reveal the rest of my ID numbers. You never know who's listening in. How about I tell you something only you and I would know. Well, maybe one other person."

"I'm listening."

"You remember last Friday night when you and Steve lay in the pasture near your pond and I stood nearby watching?" She inhaled audibly. Jeremiah understood everyone's fear of the bogeyman. He wasn't afraid of the bogeyman. He *was* the bogeyman.

"Too bad you ran away," she said. "If you'd stayed longer, Steve would have shot you."

"I'll bet he's a good shot, too."

"Have you stalked me before?"

Although she tried to remain calm, Jeremiah

sensed the near panic in Laura's voice. "Many times, Laura. You'd never guess where it first started and how many years ago that was."

"What do you want?"

"You shouldn't be in such a hurry, Laura. After all, the FBI needs time to trace this call."

"Sure, we can chat if you like. What mental institution did you escape from, Jerry?"

He laughed. Her cool exterior fascinated him, but he hoped a fire burned inside. He'd find out soon.

"Let's get down to business, Laura. The evilest of the evil are about to get their just reward and be permanently consigned to the lowest ring of hell, which is true justice. You should be here to report this wonderful news to the nation and the world."

"Where are you?"

"Near Kansas City, Laura. Grab the next flight and you'll have a fabulous news scoop."

"Will you be there, too, Jeremiah?"

"I don't think so, Laura. But when you rehash all this on *American Chronicle*, I'll call in again."

Jeremiah ended the connection and flung the stolen cell phone out the window into the Missouri River.

13

At five o'clock Pacific time, Steve sat at an airport bar, having drinks with Fleming.

"It's a nasty business we're in," Fleming said, exhaustion written on his face. "I'm just thankful the shooter didn't drill me in the forehead."

"Yeah," Steve mumbled, thinking of Kincaid's body in a coffin in a cargo hold. He didn't look forward to the solemn gathering of FBI officials and other policemen that awaited him in Washington.

"You take care, Steve," Fleming said, and then left.

As Steve drained his glass, his eye caught the television set above the bar and he saw Laura reporting live from the Leavenworth, Kansas, federal prison. Her breath hung on the cold evening air.

"What I can tell you now, if you just tuned in, is that many of the twelve hundred men incarcerated at Leavenworth have become seriously ill throughout the day, beginning shortly after lunch," Laura told the camera. "At first it was thought to be simple food poisoning and the sick were treated in the prison hospital, which has about two dozen beds. But the hospital was soon overwhelmed and now sick prisoners are being transferred by ambulance to area hospitals as far away as Kansas City, about forty-five miles southeast of here.''

The male half of the UBC news team broke in with a question, causing Laura's image to shrink into a box over his right shoulder. "Laura, is security a problem there, with so many inmates being taken outside the walls? Isn't Leavenworth a maximum-security prison?''

"Yes, it is, Reed. In fact, Leavenworth houses some of the most dangerous criminals in America. The warden, Eddie Ballard, has made a request to the federal Bureau of Prisons for additional guards. Army troops from nearby Fort Leavenworth have been assigned to accompany prisoners transported to area hospitals. I've been told the governor of Kansas is monitoring the situation here, and his spokesman said state troopers and national guardsmen will be provided if necessary.

"I should add, Reed, that no one here thinks this is a ruse invented by prisoners as a means of escaping. Apparently there are some very sick people inside the prison. The symptoms, I'm told, are abdominal pain, vomiting, and paralysis.''

The UBC coanchor, a beautiful black woman, took her turn. "Laura, are there any reports of deaths among the prisoners?''

"Wilma, I arrived here in Leavenworth about two hours ago, as you know, and we've received unconfirmed reports of deaths, but right now I'd only be speculating,'' Laura said. "We should know more after the warden's news conference later this evening.''

"Laura, you said food poisoning was initially suspected as the cause of these prisoners becoming ill. Is that still the case?'' Reed asked.

''It may be more serious than that. Attention is now focused on the water system and the possibility that it has been tampered with,'' Laura said.

Steve watched the camera pull back from a tight shot of Laura to show a beehive of activity across the road. ''As you can see behind me, there's a large group of people congregated on the grounds of the prison, near the road. Earlier we focused on an electrical transformer box near that area. A large, green metal box containing a warning about high voltage. Now it appears the box and the warning are fake.''

Laura moved sideways to stand beside a small man wearing a gray uniform, who looked simultaneously scared and pleased. As sunset approached, klieg lights illuminated them.

''This is Leonard Coe of the Leavenworth water department,'' Laura explained to the audience. ''Mr. Coe, you've been across the road with prison officials, the FBI, and federal marshals. Just what is going on?''

''Well, it looked like somethin' belonging to the power company at first,'' Coe said, scratching his head, ''but it weren't. It's attached to the water main, but it ain't nothing we put there.''

''How would you describe it, Mr. Coe?''

''Well, it looks like a big water bottle filled with chunks of dirty salt.''

''What do they suspect it is, Mr. Coe?''

He cocked his head in amazement. ''One of them federal guys, he says it looks like a big culture of *E. coli* dripping into the water main. Boy, let me tell you, ma'am, if that's the case, there's gonna be a whole lotta sick people round here!''

The camera tightened up on Laura. ''There you have it, Reed, Wilma. It looks like someone has deliberately contaminated the water system at this federal prison. I must report at this time that shortly after noon today the man now known widely as Jeremiah the Terrorist Prophet called UBC headquarters, saying that 'the evilest of the evil are about to get their just reward.' He said he was near Kansas City. Now it appears he may have been involved in this developing tragedy inside the Leavenworth federal penitentiary.''

Steve made up his mind at the bar. His flight had a scheduled stop in Denver shortly after eight o'clock, Mountain time. He probably could catch a flight out of Denver and arrive in Kansas City about 11:00 P.M., Central time. He wanted to see Laura, and if Jeremiah turned up, that would be a bonus. This time Steve wouldn't let the terrorist get away.

Just after 10:00 P.M. Laura sat in the restaurant at the airport Marriott, along with José Inglesias, her bodyguard, and Maury Gannon, the UBC cameraman who'd accompanied her to Kansas City. They ordered sandwiches and several drinks as they tried to wind down after the day's hectic pace. The news conference at the prison had ended two hours ago, although the warden revealed nothing new.

''This guy Jeremiah's a Christmas fruitcake,'' said Maury, a twenty-something news technician with a long brown ponytail and a cynical attitude. All day long it had irritated Laura to see him wearing the *J2* hat he'd bought in Dallas.

"I think that might be an accurate psychological diagnosis," she said.

"Except it's not funny to the guys inside who are sick and dying, including the guards," Inglesias added, looking around warily.

"The death toll will go much higher, I'm certain," Laura replied. "We didn't learn much from the warden and all those mealymouthed federal guys, but I think this is some kind of *serious* poison."

"I'd love to have the bottled-water concession in town right now," Maury said, grinning, and causing his companions to groan.

"Let's finish up, guys," Laura sighed. "I got to get to bed. This day started last century."

They had connecting rooms on the third floor, although Inglesias had argued to no avail with the desk clerk to move them to a safer location on the first floor.

When they arrived in front of their rooms, José took out his gun, opened the door to Laura's room, and told her and Maury to wait in the hallway while he checked out the rooms. Except for the fact that José and Maury's room had two beds instead of one, they were identical. An accordion screen could be pulled out of the wall to separate the sleeping area from a "sitting room" near a sliding-glass door leading onto a balcony.

A few minutes later, José reappeared and said, "It's okay. There's nobody in here."

"Good night, guys," Laura said.

*   *   *

Laura took a long, hot shower and put on red silk pajamas, which felt fabulous against her skin. She pulled a chair near the bed and sat looking through her book of phone numbers, fooling herself by thinking she might call her mother or one of her friends, when really she was thinking about calling Steve Wallace. Except she didn't have his home phone number. Damn, why was that? she wondered.

A man walked through the connecting door and Laura froze. It wasn't José or Maury, but a man dressed in black, carrying a gun. A man with curly strawberry-blonde hair and intense light blue eyes. The artist's sketch of Jeremiah sprang to mind and Laura grabbed for the phone sitting on the nightstand.

But he was quicker, jumping over the bed and grabbing her hand.

"Who are you?" she demanded.

"You know who I am, Laura. I'm glad you heeded my call. As promised, you got your news scoop."

He sat on the bed, between her and the telephone.

"What have you done to José and Maury?" Laura asked tremulously.

Jeremiah sneered, "They're talking things over with their Maker about now, I'd guess."

Laura put her hands to her mouth, before gasping, "You killed them?"

"I give no quarter to those who oppose me," Jeremiah snapped. "Join me or die, that's the choice I have to offer."

"What do you want from me? Why me?" She asked, distressed and near tears. She watched him place the gun on the bed. She didn't know much about guns, but she recognized the silencer attached to the barrel.

"Why? Because you have charisma, believability, and access to millions of people, Laura."

She tried to regain her composure. "What you do is news, and I report that, but I don't buy any of your philosophy, as I understand it so far."

He held out both arms, as if making a stage appearance. "You haven't heard everything yet."

"I won't let you use me. I can shut off your access to the public, at least through my show." She pressed her lips together tightly.

Jeremiah chuckled. "I doubt if Kingsley or Mel Crawford would feel the same way. Why not use your access to me to your advantage? You can be even more famous than you already are. You can hold a place of honor in New America."

"New America?"

"That's what this is all about."

She laughed shrilly. "You're insane!"

He wagged a cautionary finger at her. "Don't make that pedestrian mistake. History is replete with examples of people underestimating the underdog."

"You mean, like Hitler."

He shrugged. "Well . . ."

"You poisoned the men in that prison! Did you know that fatalities may be as high as two hundred?"

Jeremiah looked at the ceiling, frowned, shook his head, and stomped one foot dramatically. "Damn! The people who sold me that engineered bacteria said the death rate would range from sixteen to eighty-two percent of those exposed. Two hundred is on the low end, wouldn't you say, Laura? I didn't get maximum bang for my bucks."

"Engineered bacteria? What was it?"

"Botulism genes spliced onto *Escherichia coli.* Neat, huh? A common intestinal bacteria plus one of the deadliest toxins known to mankind." His smile dissolved into a pout. "But this kill rate is . . . unacceptable."

"The men in that prison were already being punished for their crimes!" Laura protested. "Who are you to decide to sentence them to death?"

Jeremiah pretended to be hurt. "I'm the Lord's spokesman, Laura! Have a little respect."

"You're one of the biggest mass murderers of the century!" she said, mockingly. "That's your only distinction."

He stood, grinned malevolently, and bowed from the waist. "Either way, let's get it on tape, if you don't mind."

She watched him jam the gun behind his belt. He took her hand, pulled her upright, and forced her to follow him.

In the adjoining room, Laura stared at José lying on the floor. A bright red stain had spread across the front of his white shirt, and his vacant eyes stared at the ceiling. The mattress on the bed nearest the hallway door had been flipped over onto the adjoining bed, revealing that many of the springs had been removed, creating a hiding place. José had probably checked the bathrooms, the closet, the balcony, but he wouldn't have looked under the mattresses. *But how had the terrorist known when to flip the mattress off and come up shooting?*

"Where's Maury?" Laura asked, tears running down her cheeks.

"He's having a prolonged bowel movement. Look for yourself."

With a sense of dread, Laura walked to the bathroom door, looked in, and saw the cameraman sitting on the stool, his pants and undershorts around his ankles. He'd been shot through the head, causing his upper body to slump sideways against the blood-splattered wall.

"Grab Maury's camera," Jeremiah said, pointing to the dresser. "I assume you know something about operating it. I have a few camera skills myself, as you might remember from my work near Atlanta."

Back in her room, Jeremiah said, "Set the camera on that table and focus it on the sofa. Turn it on and we'll film a short interview. Then we'll relax and get to know each other intimately, Laura."

A chill swept over Laura's body. She understood all too well the insinuation and the smug look. He planned to rape her later.

"I hadn't planned to introduce myself to the public yet," Jeremiah explained, "but certain events that happened today in Seattle will result in my photograph being on television, so I might as well do it right."

Jeremiah again shoved the gun inside his belt. He pushed Laura toward a sofa between the bed and the balcony. He forced her to sit beside him and put his arm around her shoulder, so she couldn't bolt.

"Ask me anything you wish, Laura. I won't lie to you or the audience." Jeremiah smiled and looked directly, confidently, into the camera lens.

Laura bit her lip, trying to decide what to do. If she couldn't escape her fate, she could make him out to be a maniac and a fool. "Why did you poison the prison water system at Leavenworth, killing all those men?" she asked.

"I, Jeremiah the Second, poisoned the water system at Leavenworth to kill all those despicable men," Jeremiah answered.

"And you feel you can play God, being judge, jury, and executioner for these men who have already had their day in court?"

Jeremiah looked directly into the camera. "As I explained when I hanged those two rapists in Dunwoody, Georgia, criminals who do evil deeds have no excuse and don't deserve to live. Thus sayeth the Lord to me. They certainly don't deserve to live at taxpayers' expense. These people are an embarrassment to God and the human race. Let's face it, America, some people aren't ready for freedom. They need direction and control. And if they don't respond to training, we should get rid of them, as we do with rabid dogs."

A whoosh of despair escaped Laura.

"Society's theories about justice, appropriate punishments, and rehabilitation are totally wrong," Jeremiah said, sternly. "You're either good or evil. You can't be a little of both. It's not that hard, people! God's giving you a choice. Take it. If you observe the Social Contract of Second Jeremiah, you have nothing to fear and eternal life to gain."

Suddenly energized, Laura had an idea about how to make him sound like a fool. "You say God has chosen you to speak for him. Is that right?"

"That's correct, Laura. Anyone who doubts me doubts God."

"What is your real identity?" Laura asked. "If you want people to believe what you say, then you should tell them something about yourself.''

''My background is as irrelevant as the early years of the first Jeremiah, or John the Baptist, or Jesus Christ of Nazareth. It's what I have to say that is important.''

''You compare yourself to Jesus Christ, the Son of God! Isn't that blasphemy?''

Jeremiah remained calm, controlled. ''I am a son of God. We are all sons and daughters of God. Who out there in your audience can say otherwise?''

''But the prophets of the Bible and Jesus didn't go around killing people. In fact, Christ welcomed among his followers thieves and beggars and prostitutes.''

Jeremiah looked directly at the camera, shaking his head sadly. ''The early Christian leaders who wrote the books of the New Testament decades after Christ's death gilded the lily, so to speak. In their zeal to make it easy for everyone to accept this new religion, they invented facts, twisted God's word, and invited the evil ones to join hands with good people. They guaranteed salvation to everyone who professed faith, even after a lifetime of heinous crimes.

''Let me ask you, members of the audience, does that strike you as the kind of thing the God of the Universe would do? No! No! No! I'm sent here by God to force you to make a choice between good and evil! To be strong, not weak. Choose evil and God will destroy you, through me. Read the real word of God in *Second Jeremiah* and know the true path to salvation.''

''You're adding to the Bible!'' Laura said, incredulously.

''It's being revealed on the Internet as we speak.

Jeremiah2.com. In new editions of the Bible, it will appear right after Revelation. For you Christians with a computer, please help spread the latest word of God.'' There was a note of rebuke in Jeremiah's voice. ''The news media could help out, too, Laura.''

''But God can't be a vengeful God! He's a God of mercy.''

Jeremiah shook his head wearily. ''Lies. Read the Old Testament carefully. God wasn't out to make converts. In fact, he communicated only with his chosen people, showing *them* the true path to salvation. What did he propose for those who opposed his people and his laws? Death, destruction, and damnation, that's what!''

''God is not generous and forgiving, then?''

''Forgiveness is something man invented as a hedge,'' Jeremiah replied, ''so he occasionally could do evil and not worry about the consequences. God didn't give Moses the Ten Commandments and say to him, 'Here, give these to the people, but tell 'em it's okay to break a few rules now and then.' No, God's rules are inviolate! Period! That's why he's God!''

''So you have a license from God to kill whoever you choose,'' Laura said.

''No, just those who break the rules. Some people worry that we have a million men in jail in America, but the truth is that millions more should be put away or, better yet, put to death. Nearly fifteen million crimes were committed last year in this country, including two million violent crimes—murders, assaults, rapes. Yet violent criminals, on the average, spend less than four years in jail. Over the last twenty years, nearly four hundred thousand Americans were murdered, but we executed only two hundred and twenty-six people. Another twenty-seven hundred murderers are whining on death row now, but the bleeding hearts eventually will force the government to let most of them live.

"The FBI should quit harassing me and do something about this evil force among us. Eight-five percent of the people are being held hostage by the fifteen percent that refuse to act in a civilized manner. No more! Henceforth we'll eliminate these people as I've done today here at Leavenworth. Then we can worry about the welfare of good, law-abiding citizens."

"It will be impossible for most people to accept this view of religion," Laura said.

"It shouldn't be. When *Second Jeremiah* is complete, it will be simple, straightforward, and undeniable. Man has made a joke of religion. Or religions, I should say. We have hundreds of religions in the world. A babble of contradictory scripture. Does this make sense to anyone of intelligence? Multiple religions are blasphemous, in fact. There can be only one true way, dictated by one true God. All other religions were concocted to soothe man's fear, or as a means for the evil ones to achieve power and wealth. Religion is used as a justification for war and conquest. In short, Laura, religion in the world today is a joke, except for the words the one true God speaks through me."

Laura jumped as the telephone rang. Jeremiah pulled out his gun, rose, and shut off the camera.

"Answer it," he said, his eyes narrowing. "But be careful what you say."

Laura walked to the nightstand, picked up the

phone, and heard Steve's voice, asking if he could come up to her room. According to the clock radio, it was 12:23 A.M.

"Hello, Mel," she replied, without missing a beat. "No, there haven't been any further developments to my knowledge." She looked at Jeremiah. "Yes, that's right. Absolutely right. See you soon."

Jeremiah opened the cylinder of the .38, emptied the shells into his hand, and put them into his pocket. He laid the gun on the table beside the camera and walked to Laura's side, forcing her to sit on the edge of the bed. He sat beside her and began to knead her shoulders with his hands. "You're all tense, Laura. We'll have to get you relaxed, won't we?"

Laura's tension increased with the knowledge that Steve would soon be there and that someone— maybe she—could be killed.

Sooner than she'd expected, Steve came through the connecting-room door, pointing his gun. Quick as a cat, Jeremiah pulled Laura in front of him.

"Let her go!" Steve commanded.

"His gun's on the table!" Laura said. She felt a knife blade against her neck and sucked in her breath.

"I'll kill her if I have to," Jeremiah said, matter-of-factly, backing toward the sliding glass door.

"No, he won't!" Laura screamed. "Then you'd kill him. He won't take that chance! Not God's *boy!*"

"I'm not afraid to die," Jeremiah replied, calmly, "but are you prepared to lose her, Steve? Yes, that's right, I know who you are."

As she watched Steve maneuver for a better shooting angle, Laura heard Jeremiah open the sliding door leading to the balcony. Then he stopped moving.

"You killed my friend in Seattle."

Obviously surprised, Steve asked, "How did you know that?"

"I know many things."

"He killed my partner. He tried to kill me."

Jeremiah laughed. "Then it was survival of the fittest and you won, Steve! It's the same game I'm playing now, and I intend to win."

"Let her go and I promise I won't kill you. You have my word."

Jeremiah laughed maniacally and let Laura go, although she felt frozen in place. Steve rushed around her onto the balcony and leaned over the railing.

"Do you see him?"

"No. Call the police!"

Laura ran to the phone, picked it up, and dialed 911 as she watched Steve swing over the balcony railing and disappear. Two gunshots rang out, causing her to drop the phone in horror.

A half hour later, Steve knocked on her door and loudly called out his name.

Laura opened the door and flung herself into his arms, holding on with all her might. "What happened?"

"When I dropped onto the balcony below, he ran out from underneath it. I shot twice. I thought I'd hit him, but he kept running around the corner of the building. I jumped to the ground and ran after him. When I got to the front of the hotel, I saw someone running along the edge of the lake toward the airport terminals. I ran after him, but he disappeared into the A terminal. Maybe he got away through the underground parking lot. The police are still looking for him."

"They were here. I told them what happened."

She clung tightly to him, her arms around his neck. She felt one of his hands pressing on the small of her back, the other at the back of her neck. When he spoke, their lips nearly touched.

"I'm sure they'll find him," Steve said. "There's no way he can get out of here on foot."

"I hope so," she said. "You don't think there's any chance he'd come back here?"

"Not really, but let's change rooms, anyway."

They let go of each other long enough for Steve to make a phone call to the front desk. Soon a bellhop helped move them to a room on the first floor. They waited another half hour for a local FBI agent to show up and stand guard outside their room.

"You take the bed," Steve said. "I'll sit up awhile."

"You must be exhausted," Laura replied. "God, I should be. It's nearly two o'clock. Mel will be calling me at six A.M., for sure. Maybe I should even call him." She thought about it, and decided she didn't want to go through another torturous description of what had happened. A more important thought intruded. "God, what about José and Maury?"

"Somebody's taking care of that."

She couldn't stay away from him; didn't want to stay away from him. Her savior. It wasn't just gratitude at being alive. She'd had the same feelings about Steve the first time she'd seen him. It was why she'd invited him to he farm, asked him to take a horse ride with her. *I want him now.*

Laura walked to Steve and stood as close as they'd been before. ''Thanks for saving me from him.''

''You're welcome.''

''Oh, Steve!'' Laura kissed him passionately, desperately. *Damned if he's going to sit in that chair all night.*

14

As events unfolded near Kansas City, another chapter of *The Book of Second Jeremiah* appeared on www.Jeremiah2.com.

THE BOOK OF SECOND JEREMIAH

CHAPTER THREE

1 Evil is Man's choice, not his destiny, nor is Man driven to Evil, so sayeth the LORD . Evil flourishes where Men ignore My commandments. In a society where there are no values and no Social Contract, Evil Men prey on Good People, who tremble in their homes.

2 Values are learned at home where parents model God's
Law for children, who repeateth what they learn.
When the model is one of love and respect, when it

encourages devotion, work, humility, and cooperation,

then exists the Goodness and Peace promised by the LORD.

3 When Children have no rules, they observe no rules.

When they know violence, they act violently.

When they know cursing, their language is foul.

When they know nothing but injustice,

they cannot act fairly in dealings with their brother.

4 Marriage is a Holy Covenant, sayeth the LORD, and the family is sacrosanct. Who are these Men and Women who ignore the marriage vows as if I were not watching and listening? Believe ye will enter Paradise who ignore My Word?

5 Sexual intercourse is allowed only within the bonds of holy matrimony and only between male and female. Promiscuity is a doorway to Evil. Lo, the LORD sayeth unto you: those who sell sex, who participate in or view pornography, will know My wrath!

6 Children born out of wedlock become wards of the state, as do those mistreated by their parents. The rights of children and society exceed those of parents who breaketh the Social Contract. A Man who declareth himself a Judge to

overrule God's law in this matter will quake at the true Judgment Day!

7 My injunction to Adam and Eve to be fruitful and multiply is not a license to pollute the earth with humanity! Practice birth control beyond that necessary to replace thyself.

8 All life is sacred, sayeth the LORD, although Man constantly devalues the life of other species. Innocent life, yea, even the seed, must always be spared, sayeth the LORD. But when a person is old enough to exercise Free Will, then the Right to Life is not absolute and can be forfeited by Evil action.

9 A prison is likened unto a receptacle for cancer cells,

which are preserved and cultivated, instead of

killed. Nay, ye cut out cancer cells, poison them, burn

them, so that the body may live and prosper!

10 The LORD also sayeth to His Prophet, Jeremiah:

Evil Men constantly trumpet their rights, while

I make note of the responsibilities they avoid.

The rights of individuality often hide an Evil intent

to avoid the requirements of a civilized society.

The right of free speech oftentimes prevents consensus,

which leads to Chaos, the handmaiden of Evil.

Those who trumpet the right of criminals are a foul wind,

for I careth only about the rights of Good Men.

11 Especially vexing, sayeth the LORD to Jeremiah, is the hero worship of modern society, wherein those least deserving, such as musicians, movie stars, and athletes, are elevated over those doing My work, including scientists, teachers, artists, and the many who labor for the collective good.

12 The LORD sayeth:

If ye must assemble in stadiums, painted and drunk,

to worship those who can run fast and jump high,

at least honor those of the animal kingdom, whose

physical gifts far exceed those granted to Man.

Fitting it would be that those acting as animals
worship those who truly are animals.

13 Television is an instrument of the Devil, when used to promote immorality, violence, sexual promiscuity, alcohol, tobacco, and drug use. A v-chip is unnecessary; simply kill those who produce such filth! In the Chosen Land, Jeremiah, acting on behalf of the people, will control the use of television.

14 The pursuit of Knowledge is the proper role for Men, since Science is My plan revealed. Education is a privilege to be earned and an obligation to be exercised, sayeth the LORD. Education can occur in many environments, including the home, and always includes instruction in the LORD's Word. Those youth who ignore education and run amok will, along with their parents, suffer the consequences reserved for the Evil Ones.

15 The life of cleanliness, orderliness, self-sacrifice, dignity, prayer, and reflection is much beloved by the LORD; the loud, boisterous, disorderly, and obnoxious are a grievous vexation to the LORD.

16 Know ye that Man's life is short, but his reward in Heaven is Eternal Life. Forsake ye this reward for money, power over others, pleasures of the flesh, and rebellion against authority?

15

As Steve and Thompson entered the White House through the north portico, Arnold Wescott, assistant to the president for national security affairs, waited impatiently, pacing the floor.

"So what the fuck happened out there last night, Peter?" Wescott asked gruffly.

"It's best if we go over it when we're with the president, Arnold."

An army colonel stood stiffly beside Wescott, who said, "This is my aide, Lieutenant Colonel Sam Douglas from the Pentagon." The gray-haired, ramrod-straight colonel smiled and nodded, but said nothing.

"Wait here," Wescott told them, as he walked to a table and picked up a telephone.

"We might be here to accept the president's congratulations for capturing a terrorist," Thompson said, in a low voice. "You should have told me, told someone, you were taking a side trip to Kansas City."

"I didn't know for certain Jeremiah would be there," Steve explained. "It was a hunch. After I telephoned Ms. Delaney and she hinted he was in her room, I could only think about trapping him before he got away. Or before he did harm to her.''

Thompson didn't buy it. ''You didn't have time to dial 911 while running to her room, or speed-dial any one of a dozen FBI numbers?'' he asked.

Worse yet, Thompson first heard the whole story about his encounter with Jeremiah from Kansas City FBI agents. Steve smiled as he recalled last night. After Jeremiah escaped, he'd forgotten about everything and everybody. He'd been fully occupied with Laura for hours.

The deputy director had called her room at 4:30 A.M. and Steve had answered the phone. After giving Steve an earful, Thompson had announced he would arrive at 7:00 A.M. local time on a private jet. They'd spent the morning trying to determine how Jeremiah had escaped, but didn't discover anything significant. Warden Ballard briefed them about the situation at the prison and they flew back to Washington.

Barely moving his lips, Thompson said, ''It also would have been nice if Ms. Delaney or her colleagues at UBC had informed the Bureau Wednesday morning about Jeremiah's telephone call hinting of a possible tragedy at Leavenworth. He was obviously in the area and remained there all day. We'd have had time to put an army division in place!''

''All right, let's go,'' Wescott announced, leading the way into the West Wing. His large head wobbled on a stick neck and his chin jutted out defiantly as he walked with a forward tilt that threatened to land him flat on his face.

Steve worried about his appearance for the audience with the president of the United States. He'd sweated through his first suit in Seattle and his second one in Kansas City. This morning it had been a choice between which one stank less.

Wescott nodded brusquely at the Secret Service agent standing sentry outside the Oval Office, opened the door, and ushered Thompson, Steve, and Colonel Douglas into the inner sanctum of power.

President Bob Carpenter sat behind

a massive desk in front of the French windows that provided a view of the famous rose garden. The president looked busy thumbing through papers and signing them.

Wescott performed the introductions. "Mr. President, this is Peter Thompson, deputy director of the FBI, whom I believe you've met before, and Steve Wallace, the agent in charge of this terrorism investigation. Of course, you know Colonel Douglas."

"Peter, Steve, Colonel," the president said, coming from behind the desk to shake each of their hands. "Let's have a seat over here." The handsome, garrulous president motioned to the sofas and chairs arranged around the fireplace, above which hung Charles Willson Peale's famous oil painting of George Washington.

"As you know, Mr. President, Director Minor is in Europe," Thompson said. "Otherwise he'd be here, I'm certain."

"Tell me all about this business in Leavenworth," Carpenter said, looking from one noncommittal face to the other. "Is this the same nut who hanged those two kids in Georgia and made a videotape of it for Laura Delaney at UBC?"

"Yes, sir," Thompson replied. "As you probably

know, he also admitted on national television to the sniper slaying of a child molester in Los Angeles.''

"How many prisoners are dead at Leavenworth?" Carpenter asked.

''Two hundred twenty-nine so far, sir,'' Thompson answered.

"And it was a biological agent? What kind?"

Thompson looked at Steve, who coughed. ''Jeremiah told Laura Delaney it was botulism grafted onto *E. coli.* He apparently was disappointed at the death rate, which he expected to be much higher.''

"I've got a press conference in an hour, timed to coincide with the evening television newscasts,'' Carpenter said. "They're going to ask me if there's any danger of this spreading."

Colonel Douglas said, "Personnel from the Centers for Disease Control in Atlanta are in Leavenworth, sir, and I've been in close contact with them. It's possible the bacteria could contaminate the entire water supply of the town of Leavenworth. Additionally, those prisoners transferred to hospitals outside the prison could possibly be a source of further infection, which makes their quarantine absolutely necessary."

"Well, we're doing that, aren't we, Colonel?"

"Yes, sir, as we speak. A botulinus antitoxin has been given to those who were exposed."

"Local authorities probably will advise people in eastern Kansas and western Missouri to boil their water,'' Wescott said. "As dangerous as this engineered bacteria is, it can be killed by boiling."

"That's right," Colonel Douglas confirmed, "which indicates Jeremiah had limited goals."

"I'm not certain I follow you," Carpenter admitted.

"If he has access to biologically engineered bacteria, he could have come up with something much more deadly," Douglas explained. "Apparently he only wanted to kill the prisoners."

Thompson leaned forward. "It's a different kind of terrorism, in my opinion. He's not randomly killing people, but rather people and institutions the public hates or is ambivalent about. In this case, crime out of control, as Jeremiah puts it. He's trying to win converts to his philosophy, his movement, whatever you want to call it. That's why he called Laura Delaney to Leavenworth. Why he hung around the area and forced her to interview him on camera."

"That was bizarre," Carpenter said. "Who could have expected that?"

Steve sneaked a look at Thompson, who remained stone-faced.

"Yet you surprised him in Laura Delaney's room?" Carpenter asked Steve.

"I was in Seattle when I first heard what was happening in Leavenworth," Steve said, knowing he should choose his words carefully. "I knew Laura Delaney was there and I knew Jeremiah had used her to broadcast his propaganda message. I knew he'd stalked her before. So I went there, although I didn't really think Jeremiah would be so bold as to remain in the area. But when I checked with Ms. Delaney, he was in her room."

"I suppose UBC will use the interview?"

"I'm certain," Wescott replied.

"Anything on that videotape we haven't talked about here?"

"Not that I know of, sir," Thompson said, looking to Steve for confirmation.

"As I understand it, Mr. President, Jeremiah restricted his remarks to a justification for his actions at Leavenworth," Steve said, honestly. Laura had told him everything when they were in the shower early this morning, but he'd been distracted.

"Peter informed me of this development as he was flying back to Washington," Wescott said, angrily, "and I immediately got on the phone to Arthur Kingsley, asking him not to sensationalize this interview, which is like asking a dog not to bark. As a concession, Arthur said UBC will flash Jeremiah's picture on the hour, the rest of the day, along with the FBI's eight hundred number."

"That will be helpful," Carpenter said. "Are you close to capturing Jeremiah, Steve?"

"I'd like to think so, Mr. President," Steve said. "We have his gun now, with the possibility of his fingerprints being on it. We hope to match it with a bullet we found at the hanging site in Georgia. We have clear videotape of him, so his physical features are no longer in question. I apparently wounded him last night in Kansas City. We found blood at the scene, and the samples are now being analyzed."

"And you also were involved in a shoot-out yesterday in Seattle, isn't that right, Steve?"

"Yes, sir."

"And the man killed there is suspected of being one of Jeremiah's men?"

"Yes, sir. We have a videotape of the two of them, and an unidentified woman, at a survivalists' expo in Seattle."

"Did you kill this man?" the president asked, hesitantly.

Steve looked briefly at the floor. "I'm not certain, sir. The investigators are still trying to determine that."

"Well, I want to commend you for all your fine work, Steve," the president said. "You're obviously on top of this case."

Steve suppressed an urge to laugh. He couldn't have scripted it better. In an effort to find a hero within the administration, the president had handcuffed Thompson, should the deputy director harbor any thoughts of taking him off the case.

"I was sorry to hear about the death of Agent Jack Kincaid," the president declared, respectfully. "I'll certainly be at his funeral." The president's sympathetic expression turned abruptly to calculation. "Back to my press conference. Is Jeremiah fronting for some foreign government or international terrorist group? Surely he didn't put together this bacteria in a basement laboratory."

"You've gone to the heart of the matter!" Wescott exclaimed, barely able to contain himself. "Jeremiah isn't some homegrown nut or vigilante. This use of a biological agent on America soil is a message from our enemies, believe me!"

"Who?" the president asked.

Colonel Douglas supplied the answer. "Any number of countries, sir. Iraq, for starters. Following Desert Storm, we discovered substantial amounts of chemical and biological agents."

"Yes, I know," President Carpenter said, wearily.

"The warehouse where Jeremiah's confederate was killed is operated by the New Covenant,"

Thompson added. "They're an international terrorist-front organization, and they sponsored the expo where Jeremiah first appeared."

Carpenter stood, buttoning his suit coat. "Anything else?"

"For whatever it's worth, sir, Jeremiah's writings might be interpreted to indicate his next targets will have something to do with the government or big business," Thompson said.

"In that case, you boys got your work cut out for you."

Wescott jutted out his prominent chin. "Downplay the botulism thing, Mr. President. Say the CDC will have a briefing later, but that there's no cause for national alarm. I suggest you be the soothing voice of reason. Invoke our democratic traditions, that sort of thing. Talk about the true meaning of Christianity. Blame this vigilante atmosphere in the nation on the right-wing fanatics that flood the airwaves with hate messages day and night. Use this issue to reinforce the need for Congress to pass a tougher antiterrorism bill."

President Carpenter digested this additional advice and, without replying, led the way into the hallway of the West Wing, where his Secret Service contingent waited.

They watched the press conference from Wescott's office. President Carpenter stood behind a podium displaying the presidential seal. A blue curtain background contained a white outline drawing of the White House. The President pointed to his first questioner.

UBC national reporter Roy Webster asked, "Mr. President, what additional information do you have about the events in Kansas, where the terrorist prophet, Jeremiah, apparently poisoned the water system at the Leavenworth federal prison with a deadly botulism bacteria?"

As Carpenter regurgitated the information they'd just provided him, Steve thought about the "Jeremiah phenomenon." Coming out of the woodwork a month ago, the killer now had a national reputation, even commanding the attention of the president of the United States. He had an unofficial title, "the Terrorist Prophet," and enough media savvy to keep his publicity balloon high in the air. Some of his fellow sociopaths, including the Dallas dynamiter, had been stirred to sympathetic action. It all amounted to a public relations coup of monumental proportions, the envy of every politician inside the Washington Beltway.

"All right," Wescott said, using a remote to turn off the television. "We got work to do, people. A new age has been ushered in today: the Age of the Terrorist in America. Someday we may look back on the Cold War with nostalgia. Forget about huge national armies slugging it out in Europe. America and the Soviet Union raining down thousands of nuclear warheads on each other. Communism is dead and the United States is the only imperial power left on earth. We demonstrated in Desert Storm and Bosnia that we can police the world, contain regional wars, and destroy doomsday weapons possessed by rogue nations like Iraq.

"But what Jeremiah represents is a new threat. What the evil forces of the world can't accomplish directly, they can do indirectly. All they have to do is tap into the racial, ethnic, and religious divisions that have been set loose all over the world. Balkanization is a fact of life and it can take seed here, too. Pretty soon we'll be founding nations at the block level!

"Jeremiah is attempting to organize a following in the United States for his idea of a theocracy, and he may have more success than we'd like to believe. If he's a puppet of the New Covenant, the next time we hear from him he may have an atomic weapon.

"I want an interagency task force formed to use everything at our disposal to run this bastard to ground and drive a stake through his fuckin' heart! You understand me!"

"I've had the same thought," Thompson said, calmly, professionally. "In addition to the White House and military intelligence, we should involve the CIA."

"I'll put a group together and get back to you, Peter. You get together with Director Minor and make certain he's on board."

"I'll brief the director when he returns, but I'm certain there's no problem on our end."

"Great, because we'll need the Bureau's cover," Wescott said, enigmatically. "Now, I need to get down to the press room and talk with the press secretary. Make certain the president didn't start any brush fires we need to contain."

Steve and Thompson walked out the east entrance of the White House, where a limo waited to take them to FBI headquarters.

"I'm certain I don't need to remind you to keep in close contact with Laura Delaney," Thompson said. "Next time she's contacted by Jeremiah, consult with me first before taking off after him."

"Yes, sir," Steve said, heaving a huge sigh of relief.

16

Jeremiah and his uncle Walter sat in a far
corner of the lobby of the five-star Intercontinental
Hotel in Prague. Jeremiah spotted them as soon as
they entered the hotel, swaggering into the lobby in
their expensive black leather coats. They might as
well have worn signs around their necks designating
them as Eastern European gangsters, he thought,
which, of course, they were.

Actually, the bald one, Zviad, was Ukrainian,
while Andrei, Walter had said, grew up near Mos-
cow. They represented the Ukrainian International
League, which had masqueraded as a sports club
when Ukraine had been part of the Soviet Union. In
fact, the UIL always had been a smuggling operation,
dealing in information, arms, and people. Through
the New Covenant, an organization he helped form
in the sixties, Walter had successfully done business
with the UIL many time before.

"Hello, Baron," Zviad said, as the two smugglers
sat opposite them. "And who is this with you?"

"My bodyguard," Walter said, affably.

Zviad, a burly man with small, darting eyes, said,
"You don't need to be afraid of us, Baron. You
know us."

"There are other dangerous people in the world," said Walter, who wore a bulky gray overcoat, not at all unnatural during a late October cold spell, a beret pulled low on his brow, a fake mustache, and thick, clear glasses designed to distort photographs. Jeremiah had learned the art of disguise from his uncle. No one would recognize him today, either, even if Czech television broadcast his photograph and compared it to his UBC interview with Laura Delaney.

"Your man talked about a big job," Andrei said. "Very difficult, very expensive." The Russian had an anemic complexion and smoked a strong, unfiltered Russian cigarette held upright between his thumb and forefinger.

"Can you do it?" Jeremiah asked.

"Ah, the bodyguard speaks," Andrei said, "and he doesn't sound like a bodyguard."

"The items would have to be delivered to the port of Odessa by the end of November," Walter said.

"Certainly it can be done, Baron," Zviad declared.

Jeremiah assumed the Ukrainian had impudently conferred the title of Baron on Walter. The gangsters had no idea of Walter's true identity.

"The *Lysander*, a freighter of Greek registry, will be in port there only from November twenty-eighth to December third," Walter instructed, writing down this information for the gangsters.

"Before we do anything, we need from you a down payment," Andrei said, in labored English.

As Walter scooted a briefcase across the carpeted floor toward Zviad's feet, Jeremiah looked around the lobby, to make certain no one had taken a special interest in their conversation.

Zviad put the briefcase onto his lap and opened it only a few inches before a smile spread across his face.

"Two million deutsche marks, as we agreed," Walter confirmed, barely speaking above a whisper.

Bribe money, Jeremiah knew, to be dispensed among the various military officials and politicians whose connivance in the theft would be absolutely necessary.

"And the rest of the money, Baron?" Andrei asked.

"In the briefcase you will find a slip of paper containing the name of a bank in Zurich and part of the numbered code of an account there. If you contact the bank and give them these four numbers and the code name New America, they will verify that the account currently has a balance of thirty-three million marks."

"New America?" Zviad asked.

Walter ignored him. "You cannot access the rest of the money without the final six digits of the account number. Those will be provided when you deliver the objects to the *Lysander* in Odessa. Not before."

Jeremiah watched the two gangsters' eyes blaze with greed. In their part of the world, inflation had so eroded the ruble and karbovanets as to make these currencies worthless. Even the dollar and the deutsche mark could be rendered valueless by a worldwide catastrophe, which was why he invested only in gold.

"Who will meet us at the port of Odessa?" Zviad asked.

"Someone from the New Covenant."

"We hear the organization has problems in America," Andrei said.

Although impressed with their intelligence, Jeremiah said, "The problem is exaggerated. Don't worry about it."

"We couldn't care less," Zviad sneered. "So long as we get our money."

As their two unsavory business colleagues walked away, Jeremiah asked, "Can you trust them?"

"Oh, yes. They're only messenger boys. The real leaders in the UIL know I have a long arm."

Walter liked to walk, so they left the hotel in the direction of the fourteenth-century Charles Bridge. When they got there, Walter slowed down his pace to admire the Baroque statues and sculptures. "Did you know that thieves stole gold ornaments from some of these statues, including an eagle from the Crucifixion?"

"The evil ones are everywhere, Uncle," Jeremiah replied, slyly.

Walter snickered. "But you are thinning their numbers in America, *ja!*"

"Considerably."

"Does this walking bother your wound?" Walter asked, with sudden concern.

"No, it's only a flesh wound to my side. It bled a lot, but it isn't serious."

"How did he get so close to you in Kansas City, this FBI agent? What is his name?"

"Steve Wallace." Jeremiah shrugged. "He's very protective of Ms. Delaney. In fact, I think they've fallen in love. He's smarter than I thought he'd be."

"I understand his devotion," Walter said, nodding appreciatively. "I watch Laura on television in Bavaria all the time. She is a beautiful woman."

Jeremiah smiled tightly. "Yes. I had hoped she would join our movement, eventually. Perhaps that still will occur."

"After you get rid of her bodyguard," Dorfler said.

His uncle's good-natured attempt to tease him about Wallace couldn't hide Walter's expression of distaste, Jeremiah noted. Walter had forever hoped his daughter, Katrina, and he would marry, even though they were first cousins. Jeremiah had never quite understood, although he had nothing against Katrina. She was just the wrong cousin.

"It makes no real difference if they identify me," Jeremiah said, changing the subject. "My real identity will always be a matter of speculation, since I was never fingerprinted as a youth."

"They can't prove anything. You are dead, *richtig*?"

"Lost in an avalanche."

"It's so sad. Even worse, your mother's birth certificate and all other official records about her family were lost after the war. There was much confusion in Germany at that time."

"There's a more pressing problem."

"*Ja?*"

"Miranda. Wallace and the FBI tracked down Vernon Monroe, obviously, which means they probably have a lead on Miranda, too."

"That is very bad! If they begin digging into her past relationships, it will lead directly to me. In a month or so, it won't matter, but now it could be very unfortunate. It could disrupt many alliances I've made over decades.''

"Don't worry, Walter. I will take care of it. Soon.''

An hour later they returned across the Vltava River and walked to Prague's main shopping and dining district on the avenue leading to Saint Wenceslas Square. Walter stopped at a favorite restaurant. "Here you can get an excellent four-course meal with impeccable service for the equivalent of twenty deutsche marks. I am a wealthy man, as you know, but I got that way by being frugal and never passing up a bargain. The UIL will learn that in a few weeks.''

They sat at a private table in a corner of the nearly deserted restaurant and talked quietly.

"You know, Jeremiah, what has happened here in the former Czechoslovakia is a justification for our plans," Walter said. "The people demanded that the country be split into the Czech Republic and Slovakia. They don't want all these artificial boundaries. They want simplicity and logic. They want to live together with their own kind. People of their own race, religion, culture, and philosophy. The Israelis, God's former Chosen People, understand this perfectly. They want to keep all the non-Jews out of their state. They'd build a wall around Israel, if they could. You have to keep out the barbarians, you know.''

"I'm not certain a return to the princely states of the Middle Ages is what God has in mind for the human race, but it certainly serves our purpose for the moment,'' Jeremiah said.

''It's the natural state of affairs,'' Walter argued. ''The Soviet Union was an unnatural creation and so is the United States. I treasure the idea that Bavaria one day could be a state itself. I'd send all the pesky Turks back home!''

Unlike Walter, Jeremiah believed in the ''master race'' concept only as a public relations tool. Carried to an extreme, it was folly. ''You are right about America, Walter. It's a more fragile republic than most assume. It doesn't take much imagination to see Florida breaking away as an independent state allied with a rejuvenated Cuba. Together they could dominate the Caribbean area. Louisiana could be an outpost of an independent Quebec, which also could gobble up Maine, New Hampshire, and Vermont, with some help from us. Mexico would love to take back the area from Texas to Southern California. *La Reconquista.* The blacks could form their own country in the remainder of the old Confederacy. The Great Plains and the Northwest are ours.''

''The old United States can exist from Washington to Boston.''

''Maybe. All that's needed to set these things in motion is chaos.''

''*Ja*, it can happen,'' Dorfler agreed fervently. ''If mutually assured destruction worked as a deterrent when the United States and the Soviet Union had a monopoly on nuclear weapons, it will also work when every nation-state or separatist movement has them.''

Jeremiah shook his head sadly. ''Too bad about Vernon. He understood the need for a separate black nation. He'd set up revolutionary cells all across the country. They would have been a helpful diversion. I hope we can still use them."

"Maybe you can find another smart, loyal nigger," Walter said.

"Perhaps."

"They cannot be part of New America," Walter added, gravely. "When they are in the minority, they are nothing but trouble. When they are a majority, they can't even rule themselves. Nowhere in the world do blacks and whites get along. It is the truth!"

Jeremiah smiled indulgently, not entirely in agreement with Walter's idea of racial purity, although the Lord would soon decree that New America be a white, Christian nation. "Let's not make all the foolish mistakes made by the Third Reich."

"Yes, I know. Don't forget, I was a teenager then. National Socialism had a good beginning. It was about racial pride, morality, equality, national strength. Hitler ruined it all with his insanities." Walter shook his head sadly, angrily. "Trying to fight a war on four fronts, including North Africa and the Middle East!"

"If he had moderated his demands and goals, he probably would have succeeded. If he hadn't driven all the Jewish scientific talent out of Germany, including Einstein and the Oppenheimers, the Nazis might have developed the atomic bomb first."

"You are right, *mein Sohn*, of course, which is why I established the Omega Project many years ago. To identify young, scientific talent around the world and try to influence their philosophical development."

Jeremiah motioned to the young waiter for more

coffee. "When they finally figure it out, Uncle, they will spend endless years arguing about our motivation."

"When I was in business and trying to figure out what my competitors were up to, I always looked for the simplest motivation. Keep in mind that most people want only three things in life, Jeremiah."

"And what would that be, Uncle?"

"Power, money, and sex. The order varies according to the individual."

Jeremiah laughed. "As usual, you are right. I would add that some people are motivated by the desire to bring order and purpose to the world. Order and purpose are everything."

"*Ja,* I understand. Most people want to complicate things. I do what I do, and I persuaded you to help me, just because I want to run things. I want to make decisions and give orders. Who says we'll do any worse than those in power now?"

Talking with Walter always had been a stimulating exercise, Jeremiah thought. *From the time I was a teenager until tonight.* "Yes, and although I'm considered to be a madman and terrorist by many in the United States, I am right. Now and forever. If we can use religion to break the back of traditional religion, most people will be better off, especially if we replace it with science as theology. If we champion the poor and downtrodden, we will amass an invincible army. If we emphasize rigid social values and rules and attack immorality and materialism, we will win the hearts of most people."

Walter nodded. "You were a great student, Jeremiah. You have surpassed the teacher."

17

Steve and Leslie Ulrich stood outside the terminal at Philadelphia International Airport and waited for local FBI agents to pick them up. Even if Thompson hadn't insisted he work with a partner, Steve would have picked Leslie to accompany him on this assignment. He believed in her ability, and admired her intelligence and intuition.

"I guess we now know why the credit card Jeremiah used in Atlanta was stolen in Philadelphia," Steve said.

Leslie nodded. "When I was here in Philly on Tuesday, before we knew about the Monroe brothers, I spent most of the day at the company that manufactures credit cards for American Express. I got together with the plant manager, some quality-control guy, a computer jockey, and the head of security. They explained to me the whole process of printing and mailing a credit card."

"And?"

"There are multiple quality-control efforts to square every card printed with every card mailed out, so they say it's impossible that Ralph Patterson's American Express card was stolen in the plant."

Leslie looked skeptical, prompting Steve to ask, "What do you think?"

"I say where there's a will there's a way."

"I've heard that before."

"Anyway, I identified three people at the plant who would have had to be in on any scheme to steal a card or cards," Leslie continued. "I also went to the postal branch where the plant delivers the cards for mailing and nosed around there most of the afternoon. Virtually anyone working the second shift the day Patterson's card was mailed could have taken it. I got a list of those folks and was checking them out when you phoned me about the identity of the guy killed in Seattle."

Elijah Potts's fingerprints revealed him to actually be Vernon Monroe. His brother, Karl, worked second shift at the Broad Street post office.

"Has Karl Monroe always worked for the post office?" Steve asked.

Leslie consulted her notebook. "Yep, since he graduated from high school ten years ago. He was four years younger than his brother, Vernon."

Steve had Vernon Monroe's background committed to memory. Jeremiah's companion at the Seattle survivalists' expo was born and raised in Philadelphia, graduated high school in 1981, enlisted in the army, reenlisted, and rose to the rank of staff sergeant. Discharged in 1987 in Okinawa. Remained in Japan, received a work visa—itself highly unusual—and worked as a translator for a Japanese real estate firm. Spoke fluent Japanese. Returned to the United States in 1992. Last known address, 1993, San Francisco. No previous police record.

"I wonder what Vernon Monroe did for the past

three years," Steve said, thinking out loud. "Where'd he live? How'd he make a living?"

"Get this," Leslie said. "Vernon Monroe never filed an income tax return since leaving the army in eighty-seven."

"I'm sure we'll find out more about him today. Hopefully it'll add to the developing picture of Jeremiah."

"Any prints found on the gun he left in Laura's hotel room?"

"Yeah, but no computer match so far. On the other hand, ballistics says it's the same gun that fired the bullet that wounded Jason Yates in Atlanta, before Jeremiah hung him."

"You still think you wounded Jeremiah in Kansas City?"

"There was a blood trail. Obviously it wasn't a serious wound, as fast as he moved."

"Still, we got DNA evidence now."

"It'd be great if he sought medical treatment and some doctor turned him in."

Leslie looked skeptical. "It's never that easy. You taught me that, Steve."

History wasn't about to repeat itself in Philadelphia. With the example of Seattle fresh in everyone's mind, Thompson had the Philadelphia agent in charge arrange for the local police Strategic Weapons Assault Team to accompany Steve, Leslie, and a contingent of local FBI agents to Karl Monroe's address in South Philadelphia, on Passyunk Avenue.

The well-cared-for brick bungalow had a living

room, dining room, kitchen, and two bedrooms on the first floor, and space for expansion in the attic. An old-fashioned slat-and-wire fence enclosed the front yard. A one-car garage sat at the back of the lot, accessible by a driveway bricked only for the tires.

The SWAT police approached from the front and the alley and took up strategic positions as Steve knocked on the front door and spoke to Sanford Monroe, father of Karl, the postal worker, and of Vernon, whose body lay in a freezer at the coroner's office in Seattle. There had been no public announcement of the dead man's identity, although the shootout had been extensively reported by the news media.

"Karl said he was gonna run errands, do some shopping, and go directly to work," the old man explained.

After agents thoroughly searched the house, Steve conferred with his colleagues. "You guys go with Leslie to the post office and wait for Karl Monroe," he said to the SWAT leader. Then he told the two local agents, "Wait out front in your car, in case he comes back here. I'll interrogate the old man myself."

"I guess you're gonna tell me what this is all about," the elder Monroe said, slightly annoyed by all the commotion.

"Sure," Steve confirmed.

The old man, who had a courtly bearing and manners to match, asked, "Would you like a cup of coffee?"

Steve declined and waited awkwardly for the old

man to go to the kitchen and pour himself a cup. When Monroe returned, he sat in a platform rocker, its brown upholstery worn to threads in places. He wore neatly creased khaki pants and a plaid, flannel shirt buttoned to the collar.

Steve sat on another easy chair, across from the old man, whom he guessed to be in his late sixties. "You have a son Vernon Monroe, born August eighteenth, 1963?"

"Yes."

"Are you married, Mr. Monroe?"

"My wife died years ago. Why?"

Steve drew a deep breath. "Mr. Monroe, I'm sorry to tell you that your son Vernon is dead. He was killed Wednesday in Seattle."

The old man set down his coffee cup on a side table, his lower lip quivering. "How'd he die?"

"He was killed in a shoot-out with FBI agents."

"Were you there?"

"Yes, I was."

The elder Monroe took out a handkerchief to cover his mouth as his thin frame heaved with quiet sobs. Steve stood and went into the kitchen, to get himself that cup of coffee and give the father precious little time to grieve the loss of his son.

"What caused all this?" Monroe asked, as Steve returned to the living room several minutes later.

"We attempted to question him about his participation in an expo this spring," Steve said.

"Expo?"

"A convention of various right-wing organizations," Steve explained. "Mainly, we're interested in a man your son was with at that convention. But Vernon opened fire on us, killing an FBI agent."

"I heard about it on the news. You mean Vernon did that?"

"Yes, sir, he did." And more. Steve's swollen, yellowish-black eye bore testimony to that, but he wouldn't mention it unless the old man asked.

Sanford Monroe rocked back in his chair and looked sadly at the ceiling. "You know, I hardly saw my son after he went into the army. Came home in eighty-five, I think it was, and then again two years ago, after he came back from Japan." He shook his head in disbelief. "Saw him twice in fourteen years. Don't hardly seem right, does it?"

"No, sir." Steve thought of his children, Kelly and Kyle, and feared they, too, would grow up and forget him, especially now that he saw them only two or three times a year. He had great empathy for the man whose son he'd killed.

"Why'd you bring all those gunmen today," Monroe asked, suspiciously, "just to tell me my son is dead?"

"Mr. Monroe, the man your son associated with is extremely dangerous. He's killed several people already and we had to take precautions, especially since we didn't know the situation here."

The old man blew his nose, put away his handkerchief, and took a drink of his coffee. "I ain't gonna pass judgment on you, Agent Wallace. I know you got a job to do, and I'll help you any way I can."

Oddly, Steve felt a kinship with the old man. "Mr. Monroe, you said Vernon was last here two years ago. Did he say what he did, where he lived?"

"No. I asked all those questions myself, but he just said he was still in the commercial real estate business, like when he lived in Japan, and that he traveled a lot. Lived out of hotels, he said.'' The old man shook his head. ''Didn't sound like much of a life to me, but he had money. Yes, sir. He had a lot of money and he was generous to me and his brother.''

''Your other son, Karl, was he close to his brother? Did they see each other more often, that you know of?''

''Could be,'' Monroe guessed. ''Not while Vernon was in the army, of course, but maybe after he visited here in ninety-three.'' He leaned forward, as if to impart a confidence. ''A couple of times after that, Karl took some time off work and left town for a few days. Wouldn't tell me where he was going. I thought it might be a woman, you know, but he coulda been visiting his brother somewhere.'' The father sat back, inhaled deeply, sadly, at the thought his sons might have excluded him. ''To tell the truth, I had that feeling then.''

Steve shuddered, again hoping he would never be in the old man's shoes. ''Mr. Monroe, I want to be honest with you. Other FBI agents are now questioning Karl. Is there anything else you can tell me about Vernon? You say you don't know where he lived or what kind of work he did, other than his statement that he was in the real estate business. Did he ever give you a phone number or an address where you could contact him in an emergency? Did he ever send any letters you kept?''

The old man pondered the questions for a moment and rose laboriously. He went into another room, causing Steve to tense and stand. But Monroe came back with a shoe box, which he handed to Steve. They sat side by side on a sofa.

"Vernon wasn't much of a letter writer, but every letter I received from him since he joined the army is in there. And a few photographs. You can take your time looking at 'em, but I hope you don't carry 'em off. That's about all I got left."

The twenty or so letters covered a fourteen-year period. Steve scanned them as rapidly as possible, not seeing anything that jumped out at him, but thinking he'd photocopy each one, anyway. He picked up a stack of about seventy-five photographs. Three rolls of film to cover a decade and a half. He turned several over to discover writing on the back.

"Did your son write on the back of these photos?"

"No, I did that," the old man said, laughing. "Vernon wasn't much of a letter writer, but he would call now and then. He'd talk for an hour on the phone to me and Karl. I'd ask him about those photos and he'd tell me the circumstances. I'd write the facts on the back, so I could look later and remember everything, you understand?"

Steve examined each photograph carefully. When he saw one of Vernon and Jeremiah, Steve sucked in his breath. "Who's this?"

Monroe took the photo, turned it over, and peered through a pair of bifocals. "Well, that's Vernon's friend Jerry. Can't remember anything else Vernon said, except this was taken in Tokyo in eighty-nine." The old man searched his memory. "Vernon said something about this Jerry being in the import-export business, I believe. That's about all I can remember."

Steve thumbed through the remaining photos as

rapidly as he could, setting aside one that pictured Vernon, Jeremiah, and a woman who, as near as he could remember, resembled the woman sitting at the expo table in Seattle.

"Who's this woman?"

Again Monroe took the photo and turned it over. "Her name is Miranda. I remember talking to Vernon on the phone and asking if that was his gal, or Jerry's, 'cause they look . . . well, they all three look close in this photo, don't you think?"

Indeed he did. They appeared to be the three musketeers, in fact—a closeness conveyed by their smiles and the way they had their arms around each other.

"Where was Miranda from? What did she do for a living? What do you know about her? What was her last name?"

The old man chuckled, his grief temporarily assuaged by this nostalgic journey down memory lane. "Well, Agent Wallace, I recall that she was from Chicago, yessir, 'cause she had a Polish name. Let me see, I wrote it here on the back. Dumbroski. That's what it sounded like, anyway."

Steve separated out the photo and placed it alongside the one of Jeremiah and Vernon. They looked at the remainder of the photos together, one man eagerly seeking to revive memories, the other looking for pieces of a puzzle that would flesh out the picture of a terrorist.

Steve discovered one last photo of the three of them, on the deck of a home. "Where was this taken?"

"Oh, I remember that one well," Monroe declared. "They were at Ocean City. New Jersey. Not more than an hour's drive from here. I told Vernon I could come down sometime when he was there. It was Jerry or Miranda's beach house, as I recall."

"Do you know exactly where this house is?" Steve asked, breathlessly. "Did you ever go there?"

"No, I never did." Monroe took off his bifocals, wiping them with his handkerchief, as tears ran down his cheeks. "Vernon never did ask me to come visit."

18

Laura watched the studio monitors, choking back tears, as this edition of *American Chronicle* began with a memorial to José Inglesias and Maury Gannon. It consisted of photographs and film footage when possible, comprising the highlights of their lives.

A panel of experts on religion, government, and law enforcement viewed her forced "interview" with Jeremiah and offered diverse opinions, most couched in jargon and legalese. A more lively audience discussion followed as Laura stood at the front of the set, recognizing those who wanted to talk.

"I think Jeremiah's blasphemous, pure and simple!" said a heavyset, dour-faced woman.

"Some of these verses make sense to me," a well-dressed young man admitted. "It seems like Jeremiah is just repeating what's already in the Bible. The difference is, he says we all have a choice to do good, and that society doesn't have to put up with evil people who choose to do otherwise."

"Do you agree with him?" Laura asked.

The young man shifted from one foot to the other. "I agree with the philosophy, although I don't approve of him killing all those prisoners.''

An elderly man raised his hand and walked to a centrally located microphone, his breath labored by the effort. ''I was surprised to hear how much it costs to keep a prisoner at Leavenworth for a year. Over sixteen thousand tax dollars. More than my annual retirement income. Most of 'em don't deserve to ever get out. Can't we do something else with them?''

A thin, middle-aged woman said, enthusiastically, ''I like everything in God's new book about values! That's the kind of society I want to live in. We don't have to put up with evil, you know.''

A dark-haired man with a beard took a handheld microphone from a staff member and intoned in a deep voice, ''Killing is against God's law. God will judge evil in *his* time. The problem with having a maniac like Jeremiah make these judgments is that next he may start killing blacks, or Jews, or homosexuals, or anybody who disagrees with him.''

A man with a tanned, deeply lined face said, ''I support the idea of society setting hard and fast rules and not letting people be citizens if they can't follow the law. Maybe it's not right to kill lawbreakers, but why should they have more rights than the rest of us who obey the rules?''

A woman sporting a big smile and wearing a bright yellow print dress said, ''God is love, and He loves us all, good and evil. Our rewards and punishments will occur on Judgment Day.''

At the end of the show, Laura announced the results of a UBC scientific poll of five hundred viewers taken during the telecast. ''Nearly eighty percent strongly opposed Jeremiah's actions at Leavenworth,'' Laura said, ''although sixty percent have a positive reaction to the terrorist's new 'command-ments' on the Internet.''

Privately Laura despaired over the statistics indi-cating that one in five people thought it okay to mur-derously attack prison inmates. And a clear majority agreed with Jeremiah's ''philosophy'' regarding the struggle between good and evil. *This guy is tapping into a deep national vein of fear and frustration,* she thought.

Trent Dillman. Graduating senior, class of 1980, Lincoln High School, Sioux Falls, South Dakota. Tight, blond curls cut close to his head. Well-formed face, clear complexion, nice smile. Dark suit, narrow lapels, white shirt, dark tie. All-American kid, by appearance, Laura thought.

Elsewhere in the yearbook that had been mailed anonymously to UBC, Laura found photographs of Dillman as a member of the wrestling and gymnas-tics teams, as well as the marching band. Several people also anonymously called UBC's 800 number, and Laura agreed with their assessment that Dillman resembled a younger version of Jeremiah. Mel Craw-ford sent her on assignment to check it out.

As the airliner approached the Sioux Falls airport, Laura looked out the window at the street grid, out-lined by stubby trees apparently afraid to grow too tall and suffer the effects of the fierce winter winds that sweep the prairie. In this small city of only a hundred thousand souls, a ten-story downtown build-ing stood out as one of the largest structures on the prairie for hundreds of miles.

A cab took her to an east-side residential neighborhood consisting of small, rectangular ranch houses, indistinguishable from the thousands like it around the nation. Laura rang the doorbell at the house of Trent Dillman's only living relatives, Richard and Karen Dillman, his uncle and aunt.

At first no one answered the door, and Laura prepared to leave, but just then an old, massive Buick pulled into the driveway.

"You people are damn sure barkin' up the wrong tree," Richard told Laura, without any animosity. "We saw that guy on television, didn't we, Karen? Didn't look a damn thing like the Trent I remember."

A frail woman in her sixties, Karen hugged a worn gray sweater to ward off the biting cold. "Jeremiah's got the same curly type hair, but it's more wavy than Trent's was. Besides, how can you tell? Jeremiah's a man, Trent was just a boy."

His hands stuffed deeply into the pockets of a denim jacket with a red and black plaid lining, Richard laughed. "Hell, Trent's been *dead* since he was a boy!"

"When did he die?" Laura asked, wishing they'd invite her inside where they would all be more comfortable on this gray, raw day. Yet they continued to stand on the sidewalk. *Why don't they want me inside their house?*

Richard rubbed his gray beard stubble. "The court declared him dead in eighty-seven, but he disappeared the fall after he graduated from high school. 'Bout this time of year, too, wasn't it, Karen?"

"Yes," she said, squinting back in time. "It was October, I do believe."

"He disappeared in Austria?" Laura asked, looking at research notes provided by a producer.

"Yep. Near Innsbruck. Damn fool kid! He shouldn't a been traipsing around Europe in the first place, let alone snow-skiing." Richard swung his arm around to encompass the open horizon. "Hell, you don't see any mountains around here, do you? What did he know about snow-skiing?"

"Did he go to Europe by himself?"

"He went with that Schropa kid," Richard spat, disgustedly. "Davey made it back okay. Sells insurance down on Minnesota Avenue. But I guess you know that."

Karen gave her husband a shush-now look. "Ms. Delaney ain't from around here, Richard."

Richard looked confused. "Really? Where you from?"

"Washington. She's on one of those television shows."

Richard Dillman squinted around a prominent nose. "I ain't ever seen you before."

Laura wanted to wrap up the interview before she froze to death. "Are you Trent Dillman's only living relatives?"

Richard thought on that question for a moment. "Yep, round here, anyways. You see, Trent's dad, Gus, was my brother. We were the only two kids in our family, and our folks been dead for years. Gus died two years ago himself. Lung cancer. I stopped smoking myself right after that, didn't I, Karen? Frieda, who was Gus's wife and Trent's mother, she died when the boy was, what, Karen, ten?"

"Eleven."

"And Frieda was from Germany!" Richard announced, as if that were a sin. "Gus met her there in the fifties when he was in the army. Frieda didn't have no relatives. They was all killed in the war.''

Karen looked at the sidewalk, using the toe of her shoe to nudge a small rock into a crack. ''That's what Frieda told everybody, but I remember talking to her once and getting the impression she had brothers and sisters over there who were still alive.''

''How did Frieda die?'' Laura asked.

''Breast cancer,'' Karen replied, sadly. ''She was only thirty-five.''

''Now, we may have some distant relatives in Ohio,'' Richard continued, indulging an obvious tendency to ramble. ''On Mom's side of the family. That'd be the Caruthers.'' He laughed with amazement. ''Hell, I ain't seen none of them since I was a kid.''

Downtown, Laura waited until

Davey Schropa finished talking to a customer and then introduced herself. ''I'm Laura Delaney with UBC.''

''I watch your show all the time,'' Schropa said. ''Come on in.''

His office had wood paneling halfway up the wall and then glass to the ceiling, giving the insurance agent a clear view of anyone coming through the front door.

''You're one beautiful woman,'' Schropa said appreciatively, sitting behind his desk.

''Thanks.'' She hoped he wouldn't start drooling. Nevertheless, Laura crossed her legs slowly, to keep Schropa from thinking too far ahead. ''We've had a lot of calls from the Sioux Falls area ever since UBC broadcast my interview with Jeremiah.''

"I know, I know. The same ones been calling me. Sure, there's some resemblance, but hell, Trent's been dead for fifteen years!''

"Tell me about the trip the two of you took to Europe after high school.''

Schropa snickered, as if he were still a teenage prankster, which fit Laura's general impression of him. The insurance agent had rosy cheeks, a receding hairline, and the beginnings of a potbelly.

"We backpacked from youth hostel to youth hostel. It was something Trent and I talked about from the time we were sophomores and there was this Dutch exchange student in our high school.''

"Did you visit this Dutch kid when you were in Europe?''

"Yeah, in fact, we did. We flew into Amsterdam where he lived. Stayed with him about a week, as I recall. We'd saved enough money for the airline tickets, but I don't think we had a hundred dollars between us beyond that.''

A hundred dollars? How had they planned to pay their way? "Were you guys into the drug scene?''

"Gosh, no! You mean, like selling drugs for traveling money? Back in those days we were mainly beer drinkers, although we did smoke some hash in Amsterdam.'' Davey looked apprehensively through the glass panels at his secretary. "It was legal then, there in Amsterdam, you know. Say, you ain't gonna put any of this on the air, are you? My wife never misses *American Chronicle*. Ain't this conversation what you refer to as, ah . . .''

"Off the record, Mr. Schropa. Absolutely. I'd go

to jail before I'd tell anybody." Except Steve. She
smiled seductively at Schropa.

"Oh, good."

"Where did the two of you go when you left Amsterdam?"

Schropa struggled for the recollection. "Belgium,
northern France. Paris. We didn't stay there long,
though. The French are not the friendliest people in
Europe. We hitchhiked to Germany where we met
some German kids about our age near Wiesbaden.
There's a U.S. Army post there, I think."

"And you hung out with them?"

"Yeah, they were"—Schropa searched for the
right word—"vagabonds. Bums, I guess." He
laughed at the memory. "They moved around, crash-
ing here and there, with other kids, university students, people we'd meet in bars. Most everyone
spoke English. We were having a *real* good time."

Laura suppressed a smile. Schropa seemed an un-
likely candidate for Jeremiah's army. "How long did
you stay in Wiesbaden?"

"Ten days or so, until about the end of August, I
think. Then our German friends decided to go on the
road, first to Heidelberg and then Nuremberg. We
stayed in Nuremberg the rest of August and Septem-
ber."

"Stayed with whom?"

Davey massaged his chin. "Lots of people. We
even slept outside, at first. There's a big parade
ground and an old abandoned Nazi stadium on the
outskirts of the city. Lotsa kids used to crash there
at nights. Course, the German cops frowned on that,
and you didn't want them to catch you. They'd beat
the hell outta you! Anyway, we met some new

people and they had a ratty apartment just outside the old walled city. That's where we stayed most of the time." He paused, frowned.

"What's the matter?"

"Oh, nothin'. You just got me thinking. Some of the German kids were older, in their early twenties, and they were a tough group. Lots of radical political ideas. Anyway, I stayed away from that scene and concentrated on the girls." A big smile spread across Schropa's face. "One particular girl."

Laura smiled warmly, as if she couldn't wait to hear about his teenage love life. "You remember her name?"

Davey responded with conviction. "Sure do. Mona." A concerned look came over his face, as he asked again, "My wife ain't gonna hear about this, is she?"

Laura ignored Schropa purposefully. "What about Dillman? Did he hang out with these radicals?"

"I see what you're getting at," Schropa guessed. "Yeah, he did, but it don't mean anything. Trent's dead!" The insurance agent leaned toward Laura to make his point. "What? You think he got radicalized in Germany and faked his death so he could come back here fifteen years later to be a terrorist?"

Laura stared at Schropa until he frowned and looked away.

"Just what were Dillman's political ideas in those days, when you two were bumming around Europe?"

"Hell, I don't know. Our folks were all Republicans, so I guess we were, too. Look, Trent was just a teenager. He liked the radical Germans. Thought it was a kick to hang out with them. Not because of their political ideas, but because they were wild, daring. Trent liked danger.''

So does Jeremiah, Laura thought. "What kind of dangerous things did you do in Nuremberg?''

"It ain't important. We were just kids sowing our wild oats.''

Laura put on her best vulnerable-woman look. "I'm just doing a job, Davey. Help me out, please.''

"Well, it was nothing big, anyway,'' Schropa admitted. "The guys Trent hung out with rolled people for money, sold black-market cigarettes. They might have smuggled stuff in and out of Czechoslovakia, just for spending money. It ended, anyway, when Trent met some girl whose parents had an apartment in the old walled city of Nuremberg, and a chalet in the southern part of Germany. About the first of October, he went south with her. A couple of weeks later there was an early snow, high up in the mountains, and they went skiing. That's when he got himself killed.''

They'd met people with money, Laura thought. His mother's relatives? "How did he get killed?''

"They think he got off the ski trail and fell into a ravine. When word got back to Nuremberg, I called Trent's dad and he flew into Munich. I met him there and we went to Innsbruck and talked to the police and embassy people and everyone, but they couldn't find Trent's body. Eventually we came home. They never did find him, even in the spring.''

"Who went skiing with him?''

"His girl and her friends, but on that last run Trent got separated, as I understand it.''

"This girl he met, she wasn't a relative, was she? Did Trent say anything to you about meeting his mother's relatives in Germany? Did his dad know these Germans?''

Davey scoffed. "No, no, no. She was just a German girl.''

"You don't remember her name, do you?''

Davey looked blank. "Katherine, maybe, but I'm not sure. You could find out easily enough. Check the court records.''

Laura closed her notebook, indicating she had no more questions.

Schropa imparted a final confidence. "You know, Trent didn't have any life insurance. Now, that was a big mistake! I tell the high school seniors now that I can write them a term life policy for a little bit of nothing. Later they can convert it to whole life and start putting something away for an emergency. Ms. Delaney, you mind if I ask you about your life insurance coverage?''

19

Just before the 7:00 P.M. closing time, Steve parked the car in front of McClintock Realty and he and Leslie went inside. Steve asked for the owner and soon found himself shaking hands with Gerald McClintock, a roly-poly fiftyish man with an engaging smile who insisted they call him "Rooster."

"You folks lookin' to buy or rent?" Rooster asked, hands on hips, leaning back with his mouth slightly open in anticipation of a sale. Suspenders held his pants in place beneath a prominent belly.

"We're lookin'," Steve replied. "Could we go into your office?"

Inside, with the door shut, the realtor asked, "You two married?"

"No," Steve replied, taking out his ID. "I'm Agent Steve Wallace of the FBI and this is my partner, Agent Leslie Ulrich." Leslie also showed her ID.

"My, my," Rooster said, clasping his hands behind his head as he rocked back in his chair. "The FBI. Well, what can I do for you folks?"

"First, I need to emphasize that we're conducting a murder investigation and that this conversation is confidential,'' Steve said, delivering part of the truth.

"I understand completely."

Steve laid the photo of Jeremiah, Miranda, and Vernon on the realtor's desk. "Do you know these people or recognize the house?" Steve considered the photos he'd discovered at Sanford Monroe's house a good enough lead to justify the ninety-minute drive to Ocean City, New Jersey.

Rooster rocked forward, put on a pair of bifocals, and peered at the photo. "Nope, don't know 'em. And there ain't enough of the house showing to identify it." He looked over the bifocals at the two FBI agents and smiled. "But I can tell you a couple of things."

"Okay."

He turned the photo around. "See this here? That's what we call a 'hurricane door.' It's recessed into the exterior wall of the house. You can barely see the handle in this photo. The door slides out on a track and covers up these glass patio doors during a storm. Most of 'em are made of a lightweight steel that can withstand winds up to a hundred and twenty miles an hour."

Rooster rocked back in his chair, mouth open, eyes gleaming as he waited for a response from Steve or Leslie.

Leslie made a guess. "It's facing the ocean?"

"Bingo," Rooster replied, lurching forward in his chair to again stare at the photo. He opened the drawer to his desk, took out a magnifying glass, and examined it closely. Then he laid down the glass and rocked back, looking from agent to agent.

Steve took the glass and looked, and then handed both items to Leslie.

"See that blue plaque on the wall behind them?" Rooster instructed. "You can make out most of the letters, but not all of 'em. People down here are prone to name their beach houses. Sea Watch, Ocean View, things like that. Or they have their family name up there." Rooster rocked forward, taking the photo and glass from Leslie. He focused on the plaque. "The Cho—Can't see the rest." He sat back and looked at the ceiling. "Let's see. Could be *The Chowder Sea*. Maybe those folks really like their clams!" With that he let loose a rollicking laugh that left him red in the face and coughing.

Steve thanked Rooster and repeated his confidentiality request. Outside, in the car, Steve again looked at the photo, thinking "The Chosen Few" could be engraved on the plaque. The title of the book written by John James, aka Jeremiah the Terrorist Prophet.

"What now?" Leslie asked.

Steve looked at his watch. It was nearly eight o'clock, fourteen hours after he and Leslie had flown out of Washington, D.C. They'd need a vehicle with four-wheel drive to travel the eight miles of beach above and below Ocean City, using binoculars to locate the beach house. Best wait until sunrise, he thought, while the fall vacationers slept in on Saturday morning and they had the sun at their backs.

"How about dinner?" Steve suggested.

"I'm starved," Leslie replied.

"I'll call Thompson and then we'll find a place," Steve said, remembering to keep his boss fully informed.

*   *   *

Four-thirty came way too early as the alarm jolted Steve awake. He had just stepped out of the shower when someone knocked at his motel room door. He looked through the peephole at a man in a suit. "What do you want?"

"I'm FBI agent Thomas Nowicki, from the Atlantic City office."

Steve quickly dried, put on clean underwear and socks, slipped on his trousers, and took out his gun. Then he opened the door and Nowicki walked in.

"Let me see your ID again," Steve asked, examining it carefully. "Did you talk to Thompson?"

"No, but my boss did." He handed Steve a card. "You want to call him at home, go ahead."

Outside, Nowicki introduced Steve to three other agents. They had come in a car and two four-wheel-drive Jeeps, the kind that looked perfectly natural on the beach, whether used by seashell hunters or surf fishermen. In fact, two of the agents wore jeans, boots, flannel shirts, sleeveless down-filled jackets, and caps. Fishing poles fitted into slots on the front bumpers of the Jeeps looked like large, dual radio antennas.

In the still dark parking lot, Steve explained their mission. He and Leslie would ride in separate trucks, each driven by one of the disguised agents. Leslie and her partner, Agent Mark Rohm, would drive to the south end of the island and start back north at sunrise. Steve and his driver, Agent Ronald Ingersoll, would proceed from north to south until they met. Nowicki and the other FBI suit would patrol the coastal highway in their sedan. They'd all stay in touch by car phone, although all had walkie-talkies tuned to the same channel should they wind up on foot for any reason.

"I already talked to the local sheriff," Nowicki said, in a "New Joisey" accent. "They're ready to provide backup, but there's no use involving them now."

Inside the Jeep, Steve found a thermos of coffee, along with still warm bacon-egg-and-cheese sandwiches wrapped in foil. "Where'd you get these?" he asked Ingersoll.

"Seven-Eleven up the road," the agent replied. "It's gonna be damn cold on the waterfront."

They drove north nearly to the toll bridge leading over the Great Egg Harbor inlet before turning down a street leading to the ocean. They drove boldly around the barrier at the end of the street onto the beach. A reddish-yellow glow lit up the eastern horizon as they parked, waiting for it to become light enough to see the houses through binoculars.

"You know for certain this house is around Ocean City?" Ingersoll asked.

"No. That's just the address I was given."

Ingersoll offered a skeptical assessment. "That means it could be anywhere from here to Cape May."

"That's the optimistic viewpoint. The guy who sent this photo to my informant"—which was what Steve chose to call Sanford Monroe, for simplicity's sake—"could have said the house was in Ocean City when it's really south of San Francisco."

At daybreak Ingersoll drove south along the beach, while Steve focused binoculars on the seashore homes, searching for the telltale hurricane door and the blue plaque. Violating the law, they drove through the dunes several times when breakwaters blocked their way. Leslie called on the car phone to say that she and Rohm were headed north.

Single-family homes on large lots predominated north of the city. As they neared Ocean City proper, the homes gave way to retail establishments and a boardwalk that began at St. James Avenue and extended south to Twenty-third Street. Due to several rock breakwaters, an amusement park, and a pier, they couldn't drive on the beach in this area. So Steve walked the boardwalk and communicated by walkie-talkie with Ingersoll, who drove the Jeep on parallel streets, many with Monopoly board names.

Just as they maneuvered the truck back onto the beach near Twentieth Street, Steve received a call from Leslie, who'd spotted the house about two miles south of them.

They sped down the beach and parked beside Leslie and Rohm's Jeep. Both Steve and Leslie rolled down their windows. "It's the three-story house with the blue trim," she said.

He focused the binoculars on the house Leslie pointed out. South of the city, the houses changed in construction from single-family homes to two- and three-level multifamily dwellings, most built on pilings and tightly packed together. Many of these structures had ocean-side decks on several levels, complicating their task.

The clearly readable plaque of the first-floor deck gave it away, since the glare of the morning light obscured the hurricane door handle. No lights were on in the house, which looked desolate and vacant, more so because of its weathered, gray wood exterior. A widow's walk enclosed by a protective railing circled the third level.

"You stay here, pretend you're fishing," Steve said to Ingersoll. He got into the Jeep with Leslie and Rohm, and said, "Drive to the street in front of the house."

On a bay-side street several blocks north of the house, Steve and Nowicki stood beside the Ford. "I suggest we leave your guy right here in the car, and send Rohm in his Jeep south several blocks. That way we got the house triangulated, no matter which way they run."

"You and I and the broad are going to take him down, assuming he's here?"

"Yeah, you got a problem with that?"

A vinyl fence surrounded the bottom part of the house. Through an open driveway gate they saw a dark green Mazda parked in one of the spaces between the pilings.

Nowicki had a search warrant, but Steve didn't plan to give Jeremiah or anyone else advance notice of their presence. Probable cause would have to do. Leslie jimmied the lock on the door leading into a recessed concrete foundation.

Inside the support column, they crept up a spiral staircase to a landing and door. Leslie swung the unlocked door open quickly but quietly, and went to the right. Nowicki followed the swinging door to the left, covering the area of the house facing the ocean. Steve went between them and crouched against the wall, his gun pointed upward.

A first-floor living room overlooked the ocean and

led to the deck where the Three Musketeers had had their photograph taken. By whom? Steve wondered. Karl Monroe?

Not having found anyone in the first-floor dining room, kitchen, or den at the front of the house, Leslie led the way up another spiral staircase, which opened to the second level. Here they discovered an ocean-side recreation room furnished with a pool table, giant TV screen, video game machines, and several bean bag chairs. The hallway leading to the front of the house had a door on each side and one at the end, all three closed.

Walking as if on air, the three agents each selected a door. They opened them simultaneously, each prepared to issue a call for help should they discover an occupant. No one occupied the two bedrooms or the screened porch, where Steve looked out at the street and saw Rohm's Jeep parked two blocks south.

The top floor consisted of a master bedroom opening onto the widow's walk, and a small storage room. The unmade bed looked slept in and felt warm, but if Jeremiah and his girlfriend had been here, they'd left earlier. Maybe there had been a second car, Steve thought.

"Okay, let's get busy," he said, "starting with this level. We'll work our way down and out."

Nowicki proceeded to bug both rooms and a telephone. Leslie dusted various items for prints, which she then lifted with a special tape before wiping off the dust and restoring each item to its original condition.

Steve looked through a two-drawer file cabinet in the master bedroom closet. It contained typical documents, including the mortgage, life insurance policies, car registration and title, health insurance information, phone and utility bills, credit card files, tax returns, a will, bank and savings accounts. All were in the name of Miranda Dombrowsky, presumably the woman photographed with Vernon Monroe and Jeremiah.

As Steve photographed these papers with a special camera that focused at close range, he heard a noise that caused him to jump. He looked up to see that both Nowicki and Leslie had drawn their guns.

"Where'd it come from?" Steve asked.

"Outside, I think," Leslie replied.

Steve already had looked through the glass porthole at the top of the door leading from the bedroom to the widow's walk facing the ocean. Besides, from his position on the beach, Ingersoll would have seen anyone out there. Steve kicked open the locked, double-keyed door and cautiously stepped out onto the widow's walk, followed by Leslie and Nowicki.

The body of a woman wearing only panties dangled over the edge of the house, facing the rising sun. Her wrists had been lashed to the iron railing with rope, so that she had the appearance of having been crucified. Steve grabbed her long, auburn hair and pulled her head back. One look at her face told him it was Miranda Dombrowsky, and that she was dead.

"Oh, my God, look!" Leslie said, pointing toward the water's edge. A body lay beside the Jeep. Through binoculars Steve saw it was Ingersoll.

"Look at this," Nowicki said, holding out a sniper rifle that Steve recognized as a Heckler & Koch, equipped with a silencer.

As Nowicki shouted into the walkie-talkie, they

raced toward the bottom of the house and out into the street, where the dark-colored Ford had screeched to a stop.

"I can't raise Rohm!" Nowicki shouted.

Steve looked down the street where the other Jeep had been parked. It was gone! "Stay here," he said to the others, and jumped into the car driven by Nowicki's partner. They rocketed down the street for two blocks and Steve jumped from the car even before it stopped. Rohm's body lay in the ditch to the side of the road. Steve rolled him over and saw his throat had been cut, deeply, almost to the spinal cord.

Steve stood, looking in every direction, as he fumbled for his cell phone. He dialed Thompson's number in Washington while shouting at the agent in the car, "Call the local police! Hurry. He can't be far away!"

Within a half hour state police helicopters searched the area from the air. At roadblocks established between Atlantic City and Cape May, state police stopped all traffic and compared a faxed photograph of Jeremiah to all occupants of all vehicles.

But as dark approached, the massive containment effort failed to turn up the terrorist.

"We don't even know if he was in the house," Steve told Leslie. "Someone else could have killed Dombrowsky."

"Maybe. What now?"

Steve shook his head. "I guess we go home."

20

Steve sat in his office with the door closed, reviewing the case with Leslie. "He was there, I know it," Steve said, as much to himself as her. "He saw us coming. Spotted the Jeeps on the beach, whatever. He shot Ingersoll with the sniper rifle with the silencer on it."

"They're comparing the bullets taken from Ingersoll's body to the one that killed Raymond Doyle in Los Angeles."

"They're probably the same."

"Dombrowsky's neck was broken."

"The thump we heard was when he dropped her body over the side of the railing. He'd already shot Ingersoll. During the time it took me to kick down the door, he'd somehow scrambled down the side of the house."

"He ran along the beach side of the houses and came up behind Rohm."

"I still don't understand how he got off the island without someone recognizing him."

"He could be very good at disguises. He could have had help. He could have driven to a marina, got into a boat, and sailed up or down the coast until he was around the roadblocks. They weren't stopping boats on the ocean.''

"Yeah, anything's possible." Especially since they found Rohm's Jeep abandoned in the middle of the city. "There are dozens of explanations. Unfortunately, Thompson doesn't buy any of them. The only reason I'm still in charge of this case is that the Atlantic City office had operational control in Ocean City."

"Until we get canned, or you tell me different, I'm still digging for facts, and we got a couple of things going for us."

"Please tell me some good news."

"We got Karl Monroe under lock and key. He's already admitted stealing the American Express card Jeremiah used in Atlanta. He's knows he's possibly facing the death penalty as an accessory and he's talking a mile a minute."

"Let me guess. He doesn't know anything we don't already know."

Leslie shrugged, conceding the point. "Still, his testimony would be important at any trial."

"Let's hope we get Jeremiah in our gun sights again and there won't be a need for a trial."

"Did you know I was a basketball player in college?"

Steve frowned and looked at Leslie, trying to fathom the reason for this abrupt change of topics. "Yeah?"

"University of Tennessee."

"The lady Volunteers. One of the country's great college basketball programs."

Leslie blushed. "We went to the Final Four twice when I was there. Won it once."

"I can't believe you kept this to yourself. Does anyone here know?"

"Thompson. I thought the guys in the squad would just turn it into a joke. You know. Wanting to watch me dribble or something like that."

Steve smiled ruefully. "Look, I know it's been hard on you. What can I say? The FBI is trying to overcome a long history of racism and sexism in its ranks."

"I understand. Incidentally, thanks for all the faith you've put in me. Guys like you make it tolerable."

"Now I understand why you put everyone to shame in the physical fitness evaluations."

"Well, I didn't just bring it up so you'd give me all these compliments, which are appreciated nonetheless. The thing is, after thinking about it, and doing some investigating, I know about Miranda Dombrowsky."

"How?"

"She was a personal trainer," Leslie said, "and worked with several well-known female athletes, although recently I understand she'd been concentrating on the private business sector. You know, working for corporations who want to get their fat cats into shape."

"Do we know any of her clients?"

Leslie paged through the contents of a file folder and handed Steve a piece of paper. "Here's a partial list of them, past and present. You might recognize some of the track and field stars and the professional ice skaters. Actually, one of her clients was a teammate of mine at Tennessee, who also ran track. I thought Dombrowsky looked familiar. I may have seen her on campus once. I checked around and she had a good reputation as a first-class trainer. Her most famous client, of course, was Emma Dietze.''

''The German tennis player?'' Steve asked.

''Yes, the one who was killed.''

Steve remembered the tragedy. Dietze burst onto the international professional tennis scene by winning Wimbledon at age eighteen. The next year she won the first of two grand slams, also claiming titles in France, America, and Australia. Then she bought a palatial house in Palm Beach, Florida, although retaining her German citizenship.

''Four years ago Dietze was stabbed to death by a mugger outside a trendy West Palm Beach restaurant,'' Leslie said. ''The killer was never captured and the case is technically still open.''

Steve stood and walked to his window, where he could see out over E Street. ''I talked with Laura Delaney last night for just a few minutes. They got out ahead of us on the public calls about Jeremiah. There's at least the possibility he might be one Trent Dillman of Sioux Falls, South Dakota.''

''Where's this guy now?''

''Officially dead. Unfortunately, he was never fingerprinted, so it's really a dead end. But here's the one thing Laura told me that's now interesting. His mother was German.''

He waited for Leslie to connect the dots. ''The New Covenant that's promoting Jeremiah probably originated in Germany,'' she said slowly. ''Dietze was German. Dietze had a connection to Dombrowsky, who ran with Jeremiah.''

''It might explain why he killed her.''

''He was afraid she'd point us in the right direction.''

"Follow up on it, Leslie."

"We can only take this so far. We should be poking around in Germany, which is a little beyond our jurisdiction."

Steve screwed up his face. "I know. We're probably gonna lose jurisdictional control of this whole investigation, but if we know more and understand more than everyone else, we'll still be in control."

"Is that something out of the agent's unwritten manual of operation?"

"Page twenty-three."

Steve left his car in the FBI's underground parking garage and took a cab to the condo near the Pentagon, where he met Laura. It took them only a few trips to carry his personal belongings to Laura's Land Rover.

As they drove toward the farm, Laura said, "You've burned all your bridges now, big boy. If this doesn't work out, you'll be homeless."

Steve laughed, feeling so comfortable with Laura he couldn't imagine it not working out. Even though they'd known each other only a few weeks, and only became lovers beginning that night in Kansas City, he felt like he'd known her all his life. Once, he'd have sneered at such romantic idealism.

"So what's going on in the investigation?" she asked.

"Is this Laura Delaney, inquiring reporter, asking?"

"You're still mad I got onto the Trent Dillman thing first."

"Hardly, although the German connection is interesting. There're only about ten thousand other people in the country who're certain Jeremiah's living next door, or just around the corner.''

''Yeah, and I'm one of them. They didn't have him lurking around in their pasture, or stalking them.''

''Seriously, I assume you're going to continue traveling and digging up stories about this guy, like you did in Dallas and Leavenworth.''

''You bet. The UBC news department is salivating at our ratings, now that we've been accepted by the public as the network with the most news about the terrorist.''

''Just remember, these news events are a great way for him to set a trap for you.''

''I remember.''

''You need another bodyguard. A good one.''

''There's an applicant for the job.''

''Who?''

''Maria Inglesias. José's wife.''

Steve met her at the farm and decided to find out if Maria could do the job. They needed a bodyguard. He wanted to sleep with Laura at night, not sit up in a chair watching her.

''Let's take a spin around the property,'' Steve said.

''Good idea,'' Maria responded, putting on a jacket over a shoulder holster holding a 9-mm Beretta.

''Don't worry about me,'' Laura said, trying unsuccessfully to be sarcastic. ''I'll just move your clothes into the house, Agent Wallace. Like a good little woman.''

Steve chuckled as they walked toward a Ford pickup parked at the side of the house. He got behind the wheel and saw a Heckler & Koch MP-5 submachine gun lying on the seat between them. Probably the same weapon her husband had carried. They drove down the hill toward the road.

Laura's farm comprised a quarter section, or about 160 acres bounded on two sides by roads: the north-south state highway on the east side of the property and the east-west blacktop leading by the front gate toward the mountains. At the western end of Laura's property line, Steve turned right onto a wheel-rutted fire trail that ran alongside a white post-and-board fence that completely encircled the property. Two hundred yards up this trail to the north, he stopped near the small pond where Jeremiah had crept to within a hundred feet of he and Laura the night they lay on a blanket under a full moon.

Maria followed as Steve climbed over the fence and walked into a dense thicket of pine trees standing between the fence and the pond's dam.

''Jeremiah was here several weeks ago,'' Steve said.

''José told me all about it,'' Maria admitted.

''I'm sorry about your husband.''

''Me, too,'' she said, drawing herself up proudly. ''But life goes on. If you're worried about my woman's emotions affecting my job, don't. I'm a professional, too, and I want this job.'' Her eyes narrowed. ''Maybe I'll get a chance to deal with that bastard myself!''

She seems tough enough, Steve thought. And

deceptive-looking. Many would take the Latin beauty to be a model.

She unslung the submachine gun from her shoulder. "See that No Hunting sign over there?"

Steve followed her pointing finger until he located the yellow sign posted on a tree up the road about thirty yards.

Holding the gun at waist level, Maria emptied a short clip at the sign, which took only seconds since the submachine gun fired at a rate of eight hundred rounds per minute.

They walked the fence line until they were opposite the tree, which stood on the west side of the fire road. Steve counted fifteen holes in the sign, a phenomenal accuracy firing from waist level at that range.

"I'm just as good with the Beretta," Maria said.

"You've convinced me. It's Laura's decision, but as far as I'm concerned, the job is yours." As a backup, he planned to have one of his people always shadowing Laura.

"You moving in here?" Maria asked.

"Yeah." He didn't figure he owed her an explanation.

"I was just asking so I don't accidentally shoot you at night. José and I guarded people before who had spouses, lovers, kids, friends, parents. It's part of the package. One thing you can count on is my loyalty. I don't talk out of school."

Steve nodded, understanding her subtle language. He liked her. As they walked back toward the truck, Steve stepped on something metal, and stopped. He used the toe of his shoe to kick back the grass covering a two-foot-square iron grate recessed several inches into the ground. It obviously hadn't been removed in a long time.

"What's that?" Maria asked.

Steve shrugged, looking in the direction of the small pond and then through the trees and across the fence. A culvert ran beneath the fire road and emptied into a small creek angling across Laura's property.

"Possibly some type of drain for the lake," Steve guessed. "An overflow device, maybe."

"You want me to check it out, Steve?"

He shook his head. "It's not important."

He and Laura had a long, leisurely dinner, played a game of Liverpool rummy, talked, and listened to much of Laura's eclectic CD collection, ranging from rock to country to jazz and blues. Before they knew it the clock chimed ten, and they climbed the stairs toward *their* bedroom.

Steve took off his shoulder holster and hung it over a knob on the bed's headboard. He watched Laura's eyes move from the gun to him.

"Did you bring handcuffs and that blackjack thing?" she asked earnestly, and then broke out laughing.

They took turns using the bathroom, and Steve emerged wearing a pair of midnight-blue pajamas, which he ordinarily didn't wear to bed. He'd selected the color since it seemed to complement his black hair. Somehow, he wanted their first official night together at the farm to be a memorable one.

Laura emerged in a new cherry-red teddy, which left nothing to·the imagination.

"Wow!"

"This is just the costume. The performance will knock you flat."

"Yeah, but I have great recuperative powers."

"Really? In that case, I'll applaud you."

An hour later, they lay spooned together in bed, looking out the moonlit window.

"Is this what the FBI brass meant when they said you should take care of me?"

"Not exactly."

"You're doing a helluva job, G-man. I'm gonna try to get you a raise."

"You won't have to try hard, Laura. Tell me one thing. Why me? You could've had anyone in the world."

"Then consider it a compliment. Actually, I was worried that you'd never get laid again."

"I worried a lot about that myself."

"Seriously? Don't judge me on the basis of my looks, any more than you should draw unwarranted conclusions about someone who's fat and ugly. Beneath the surface, I've been lonely for a long time. Looking for the right guy. Don't tell me you're not him?"

"I am. Someday, if you like, I'll say 'I do.'"

21

Laura's next assignment took her to the Illinois State Fairgrounds on the northern edge of Springfield. Ordinarily deserted during November, one Saturday nearly four thousand people filled a twenty-five-thousand-square-foot arena near the front gate to hear Adam Doyle of the New Covenant.

Knowing her celebrity might cause her to be recognized, Laura wore a black wig, knit beret, and a calf-length winter coat, all of which she kept on inside as she and Maria found seats in the bleacher section. Other spectators had filled most of the folding chairs on the area floor near the speaker's platform.

Doyle began speaking into the microphone, producing a shrieking sound the audio engineer quickly adjusted.

"The growing power of the Internet is obvious here today," he said, setting off a buzzing in the crowd. "I want you to know that not one single dollar was spent to advertise this event, other than posting a notice on Jeremiah2.com. I understand there are people here today from as far away as Saint Louis, Chicago, and Des Moines."

Laura scribbled in a notebook. Later, when she called her camera crew and technicians in, she wanted a list of questions to ask Doyle and selected members of the audience.

"I'm Adam Doyle, the manager of the New Covenant, an import-export business located in Seattle. We helped establish this Web site and maintain it. That doesn't mean my organization or I endorse everything Jeremiah says and does, in the same way you probably don't like everything the president of the United States says or does. What I endorse is my right—and your right—to debate any issue or event or movement that arises in our society. That's how a democracy operates."

That line got a lot of applause, causing Laura to look closely at those seated around her. To her surprise, she detected a genuine enthusiasm. *Who are these people?* she wondered.

"Any visitor to this Web site can view Jeremiah's photograph and learn what federal law enforcement officials know about him. You can read magazine and newspaper articles and editorials about his activities, and see a schedule of upcoming television talk shows about Jeremiah, including UBC's *American Chronicle*. You can also read and download the latest chapters of *The Book of Second Jeremiah*."

Laura smiled. She'd have to report back to the UBC brass that Doyle gave the network free publicity.

"I don't know Jeremiah," Doyle continued. "Never met him and don't know where he is, thank you."

The audience laughed and Laura considered that

Doyle had about exhausted his necessary list of disclaimers.

"But I do like what Jeremiah has to say in the three new Bible chapters he's revealed," Doyle said. "I must tell you that the FBI has given my company fits about setting up this Web site, but we think that's our right."

That comment generated spontaneous applause, Laura noted.

"Jeremiah's writings usually appear elsewhere on the Internet," Doyle said. "We just incorporate them into Jeremiah2.com.

"Truthfully, I agree with most of what he's said on television. We are under attack by an army of criminals. People are totally responsible for their actions. We do live in a modern-day Sodom and Gomorrah. Our society lacks value and direction. The excessive materialism of our economic system is depressing. Government is so unresponsive that most people in America have given up on it. It seems obvious to me that we need change."

That summary of Jeremiah's teachings got Doyle his biggest hand so far, causing Laura to write furiously, thinking she had to ask him who wrote it.

"Chapter two of *The Book of Second Jeremiah* talks about a New America, where a social contract will be enforced," Doyle said. His voice dropped to a whisper. "Wouldn't you like to live in an America where you didn't have to lock your doors at night, where you could walk anywhere you wanted to without fear, where you could allow your children and grandchildren to play without constant supervision?"

Then he shouted, startling even Laura. "Where you didn't have to worry about your children's minds being polluted with all the filth that's printed and broadcast in this country!''

Some in the audience stood, clapping, whistling, and shouting out their approval.

''But it's not right to kill the evildoers in our society,'' Doyle said, in a disheartened tone. ''That's one of the Lord's commandments. Jeremiah may be God's instrument of justice, but you and I aren't.''

Laura looked around her. People nodded glumly. Most were older, white, with perhaps a majority of females, which Laura found incomprehensible.

''Wouldn't it be nice to live in a New America where we could simply *expel* evil people?'' Doyle said, joyously shouting out his message. ''Where we could kick out those people with criminal records, or anyone who refused to obey the laws and rules of a civilized society? People who engaged in immoral behavior. People who won't work! People who take advantage of others. The loud, boisterous, disorderly, and obnoxious people the Lord mentioned to Jeremiah in chapter three of *The Book of Second Jeremiah*.''

A chant started among those seated on the folding chairs: ''Yeah! Yeah! Yeah!'' Laura imagined that New America would be a dreary place populated by these look-alike zombies.

Doyle held up his arms to quiet the audience. ''We let people flood into old America without any controls and can't figure out why we have so much poverty and crime and unemployment. Wouldn't it be great if you had to *earn* your way into a New America by your good works? Just like you have to earn your own grace, as it says in the Bible. Wouldn't it be great if you could only stay in New America if you observed the rules and manners of a civilized, Christian society?''

Once again the audience responded enthusiastically, and Laura spotted several animated individuals she planned to interview later and find out their background and motivation.

"You've about heard enough from me," Doyle said. "I'm just like you. I'm interested in the idea of a New America. I wanted you all to know there're many other people out there just like you.

"What can we do? We can continue to study and meet in cyberspace. Pass on discussion documents into the mainstream of our society. Continue to expand our ranks. We'll definitely have more meetings like this all over the country—wherever people want to come and listen to me, or anyone else, talk about these important issues."

Doyle held up his arms again, signaling for silence. "In Quebec, our neighbor to the north, they're talking about forming a new nation of less than eight million people! That's what it takes. Do you know the population of Israel? Let me tell you. *Ten million people.* We have three hundred million people in the United States. Don't you think there's three to five percent of our population who want to live a different life?"

Laura watched people parade single file out of the two tunnels leading beneath the bleachers. They circled the arena floor, carrying signs on sticks that read: VICTIMS' RIGHT, NOT CRIMINAL RIGHTS . . . JEREMIAH II . . . NEW AMERICA FOREVER . . . STOCK MARKET BULLSHIT . . . THE ONLY GOOD POLITICIAN IS A DEAD ONE. It caused her to remember the Dallas street vendor, and she regretted not wearing her "Jeremiah Sucks" T-shirt.

"The next time you drop into our Web site, a file will be opened for you and your neighbors," Doyle said. "You can register your name, address, and telephone number if you're interested in helping form a New America. We can do that, you know. Our constitutional rights include freedom of speech and freedom of movement. If people want to form a society based on Christian values, who would oppose that? You think about it. Thanks for coming! There're refreshments in the back and there'll be entertainment for the next hour, beginning with gospel singers. Enjoy yourself and get to know your neighbors."

Having shed her disguise and summoned her camera crew, Laura sought out Doyle and shoved a microphone in his face. "You say you don't know Jeremiah personally, but you sold him a booth at a survivalists' expo in Seattle, didn't you?"

Doyle had a sick smile on his face, although he tried his best to appear jaunty. "How'd you get in here, Ms. Delaney?"

"It's a public meeting, isn't it? This is a state-owned facility. Are you saying we can't be here? Do you have something to hide?"

"Of course not."

As he talked, Doyle walked through the crowd, trying to get away from her. At the back of the arena a group sang, "Rock of Ages, cleft for me. Let me hide myself in thee."

She wouldn't let him hide from her. "Did Jeremiah tell you to organize these meetings? Have you met him? Where? Did he tell you what to say here?''

Doyle abruptly stopped retreating and appealed to the crowd around him. ''Ms. Delaney, this is why people hate the news media so much. You're always trying to stir up trouble. Always trying to create a controversy where there isn't any. Isn't that right, everyone?''

Laura ignored the growing number of people around them and spoke in a smooth, confident voice. ''Isn't the New Covenant for which you work really a terrorist-front organization?''

''See what I mean!'' Doyle protested, in a squeaky voice.

''Who's the founder of the New Covenant? Is it an individual or group in Germany? Do you know Trent Dillman of Sioux Falls, South Dakota? Wasn't his mother from Germany?''

That got his attention, Laura saw, to her delight. Surprise and then horror planted themselves on Doyle's face. Laura pressed on, wielding the microphone like a scalpel. ''You talked about your constitutional rights and the rights of this audience to discuss any subject and to move around freely. But isn't what you're talking about here very close to treason?''

Doyle literally jumped up and down on the concrete floor, jabbing his finger at her. ''She's trying to intimidate us! Her and her network. The United Broadcasting Corporation. They do this all the time. Disguise themselves. Sneak into places where they aren't welcome and then accuse God-fearing people like us of being traitors!''

''I don't like the looks of this,'' Maria whispered into Laura's ear. Laura now paid attention to the sizable crowd surrounding them. They didn't look happy and accommodating.

"But this is good," Doyle said, gaining confidence. "It's an example of what you won't see in New America. These liberals in the news media got too much power. They're power-mad, in fact. Always trying to stir up trouble. Get you folks to fighting among yourselves. Make you afraid to say what you really feel. When's the last time you saw Laura Delaney do an *American Chronicle* show about hardworking Christians who pay too much taxes? You didn't see that show, and if you did, she'd just be making fun of you all for being ignorant and intolerant. That's what the liberal news media thinks about God-fearing white folks. Ain't it true?"

"Damn right!" someone said, and Laura turned to see a face dark with anger pressing toward her. Someone jerked the microphone from her hand and shoved the cameraman to the floor, his camera hitting the concrete with a shattering sound.

"Let's get out of here!" Maria said, helping Laura up and shoving her toward an exit. When someone blocked their way, Maria swung a forearm, knocking the man backward.

Outside the arena, Laura took the cell phone from her pocket and dialed three numbers.

"Who're you calling?" Maria asked.

"The police." Now she had the lead-in to her story, Laura thought. In one of their first public meetings, Jeremiah's followers had used the same violent tactics as their leader. She just hoped they could salvage the film in the broken camera, if they could find the camera.

22

The interagency task force formed to capture Jeremiah held its first meeting in the FBI building, in the fifth-floor, lead-lined "submarine" room, otherwise known as the Strategic Information Operations Center.

Arnold Wescott, the president's national security adviser, opened the meeting. "Officially, this group does not exist. No paper will emanate from this group. Unofficially, we're here to cooperate in locating and capturing the terrorist known as Jeremiah."

Steve understood. As a result of federal legislation and executive orders, the FBI had authority to conduct domestic security investigations and keep the results secret. The Bureau could even contract secretly with private intelligence-gathering sources. In short, they could provide cover for the task force. By contrast, at the White House and the Pentagon, the clerical, security, and maintenance staffs likely were on the payroll of the *Washington Post*, the United Broadcasting Corporation, and other news organizations.

Wescott introduced those sitting around the table,

including his aide, Lt. Col. Samuel Douglas, Steve, Thompson, Geoffrey Hauser from the CIA, and Malcolm Leuwellen, a Justice Department lawyer with a patrician bearing.

"Steve, bring us up to date," Wescott ordered.

"We've amassed a lot of physical evidence, all of which will be useful in court, if Jeremiah is arrested and tried."

"A trial would be a good forum to debunk all the myths arising around this guy," Leuwellen said.

"We can tie Jeremiah to the New Covenant, which as you know may have originated in Germany among rightist groups," Steve continued. "There's one interesting lead about Jeremiah's real identity, which, if true, ties his mother to Germany. Continuing down this road, Miranda Dombrowsky, who Jeremiah may have killed in New Jersey, can be linked to Germany through several clients, notably Emma Dietze, the tennis star killed in Florida. Whether this all means anything, we don't know at the moment."

"Whatever it means, it will relate primarily to motivation and organization, as well as Jeremiah's base of financial support," Thompson said. "Meanwhile, the FBI is putting most of its resources into anticipating his next target and catching him in the act."

"You've had several good chances," Wescott said, acerbically.

"Yes, we have, Arnold," Thompson replied. "And we've learned from our mistakes. This guy's no lone gunman. There's no way he could have escaped from Kansas City or Ocean City without a significant network of support."

"Jeremiah's also attracting a following among the general public, as Laura Delaney's recent televised report from Springfield, Illinois, demonstrates,'' Wescott said.

"Let's get back to the European connection," Hauser said, as he lit a cigarette without asking anyone's permission. "We got a team in place that can follow up these leads. If they mean anything, we'll find out."

"Good. Along that line, Colonel Douglas has some photos for us to look at," Wescott said.

Douglas, dressed in a business suit, wordlessly took out a handful of photos from a slim briefcase and placed them in the center of the table.

"Take a look, gentlemen, and pass them around," Wescott said, "but remember that these photos go home with Colonel Douglas."

One by one the photographs came into Steve's hands. All involved the same four people, either all together or in pairs.

"Colonel Douglas, tell us about these photographs."

Douglas held up the photos one at a time. "These two men going into this hotel in Prague are midlevel functionaries in the Ukrainian International League, a onetime sports organization that is now involved in a host of illegal activities in central Europe."

Wescott interrupted to provide details. "Specifically, bribery and extortion, aimed both at Ukrainian businessmen and politicians. The UIL also engages in smuggling, bringing into the Ukraine scarce Western goods. They smuggle out the two things a former Soviet state possesses that are prized by the rest of the world: intelligence and weapons. We've feared for some time this might include nuclear weapons. Go on, Colonel Douglas."

The Pentagon intelligence officer held up a photo for all to see, which pictured the two Ukrainians with two other men, one a tall, elderly gentleman who wore a beret, thick glasses, and a bulky, gray overcoat. He had a mustache. An oblique picture of the other man revealed he wore a black overcoat and thick glasses, and had oily black hair.

"The four men met together briefly in the hotel lobby," Douglas said.

"And afterwards?" Steve asked. "Where did they go? Did you follow them?"

"Military intelligence didn't take these photographs," Douglas explained. "Obviously we can't be everywhere in the world at all times."

"Really," Hauser said, mockingly.

Douglas smiled genially. "So we buy from freelancers, some of whom specialize in photographing hotel guests. It was only after examining the photographs carefully that we were able to identify the UIL men, whose names are Zviad and Andrei, by the way. It set off some alarms at the Pentagon."

"And the other two?"

"We scanned their photos into a computer program that strips off their disguises," Colonel Douglas said. "We only had a profile shot of the one guy, and that yielded nothing. But the older man bears some resemblance to Walter Dorfler, a wealthy German businessman with ties to neo-Nazi groups."

Steve looked skeptically at the computer sketches. "It's less than compelling evidence."

"Nevertheless, another German connection seems more than coincidental," Wescott said.

"Our agents in Europe will check out Dorfler,"

Hauser said. "We also have assets within the UIL. We'll find out what they're up to."

"The administration is in contact with people we trust inside the Russian and Ukrainian governments," Wescott said. "Security will be increased at all sites where there are nuclear weapons."

"Are we overreacting here?" Leuwellen asked. "Grasping at straws. Maybe Jeremiah is simply delusional. God knows we've had our share of religious fanatics in recent years who've attempted to put together a following. I agree this guy has a lot of skill and luck, but most serial killers do. There's no reason to believe he's part of some huge international conspiracy. Peter's on the right track. Stick with standard investigative tools, get a step ahead of Jeremiah, and catch him."

Like everyone else, Steve looked at Wescott. The presidential adviser's famous chin jutted out defiant and his large head wobbled unsteadily. "Maybe so, Malcolm. Maybe so. I've put my neck on the line not only because of my intuition that Jeremiah's something more than a religious fanatic, but also as a result of a lifetime of studying trends in our country. You know what I see?

"I see a melting pot that no longer makes stew. It has quit boiling and the ingredients are starting to separate out. Not only have we given up on integrating people of different colors, cultures, and religious backgrounds, but we've got thousands of groups that have circled their philosophical wagons around some central belief, whether it's religion, abortions, guns, sexual orientation, whatever, and they don't want anything to do with anyone who believes differently.

"This is a dangerous situation. Much more dangerous than people like you think."

"I was just offering my opinion," Leuwellen responded, stiffly. "I assume that's why you asked me here."

"Actually, no, but let me continue," Wescott said. "The United States is ripe for a charismatic demagogue like Jeremiah. When he sends Adam Doyle out into the middle of America to give his 'living without fear' speech, more people are listening than we'd like to imagine. They've had enough of crime. They yearn for a simpler time when America was a more innocent place. When all their neighbors were white and Christian, preferably Protestant. When they felt like they had a say in things. Now, you might say that's also a myth, Malcolm, but people love myths. And they can be mesmerized by a guy who's good at making them up."

Wescott might be right, Steve thought. Ironically, the divisions in this room mirrored those in the country. Some people saw Jeremiah as a threat; others didn't. Some actively enlisted in his campaign, while others paid no attention at all.

"Tactically, I don't see how it will work," Hauser said. "Getting people to come to meetings is one thing, but becoming a soldier in a secessionist movement is another. There've been many leftist movements around the world with broad public support, but they've seldom converted that into military and political power."

"If this guy's as smart as I think he is, he'll keep his philosophical and theological supporters separate from his soldiers," Wescott said. "For one thing, it makes it harder to attack his movement, because there are innocent, although misguided, citizens involved. If all his followers were simply mercenaries, we'd simply kill them."

"The Civil War decided the issue of secession in America," Leuwellen said, in a pontifical manner.

"Well, that war might have gone differently if the Confederacy had nuclear weapons," Wescott snarled, "which is why our effort in Europe is extremely important."

"All these efforts are important," Thompson said, in an obvious attempt to smooth ruffled feathers. "Which is why all of us in this room need to work together."

"Thank you, Peter. Now, what I really want from the Justice Department, Malcolm, is for you to put the word out to every crook in the land under indictment that full pardons are available for any information leading to Jeremiah's capture."

"For any crime?" Leuwellen asked, incredulously.

"If some murderer or molester has information about Jeremiah, I'll get him out of jail and buy him a villa in the Caribbean," Wescott spat back. "Furthermore, I'm going to see to it personally that a countercampaign is launched on the Internet. We're going to consistently disrupt access to a particular Web site. All those on-line jackasses discussing Jeremiah's *teachings* will get a letter questioning their sanity and patriotism. We may even cause a little trouble at their place of work, or inject the IRS into their lives."

Leuwellen shook his head in disbelief. "I'd just as soon not be hearing this."

"And I'd better not ever hear it back!" Wescott snarled.

Like Thompson, Steve felt it prudent to sit back and listen. Certainly the FBI wanted to avoid any commitment or indiscretion that would haunt them later.

"As you all know, fund-raising is one of my talents," Wescott said. "I'm currently in the process of forming a national organization tentatively called American Patriots, which will function as a truth squad to counteract Jeremiah's various deeds and pronouncements. He's not going to go unchallenged anymore, as he has to date. Some of you may recognize this technique from recent political campaigns, where it's been used successfully to turn around public opinion.

"Finally, money talks and bullshit walks! American Patriots also will soon announce a reward for information leading to Jeremiah's capture. I can tell you now the amount will be a million dollars!"

The CIA man whistled, and Steve saw Thompson smile.

"It's peanuts compared to the damage this bastard can do," Wescott said.

"May I be so bold as to ask who will comprise the membership rolls of the American Patriots?" Leuwellen inquired.

The national security adviser glowered at the government lawyer. "People of power and wealth who prefer the status quo to revolution!"

Wescott had one more piece of advice for Thompson and Steve. "I suggest you boys call in all your markers in an attempt to find this guy. Use anybody and any means possible. Your country will appreciate it."

23

Leaving his hotel in the World Trade Center complex, Jeremiah walked east on Liberty Street in the direction of Wall Street, marveling at the sea of humanity scurrying this way and that, as if they really knew what they were doing and where they were going. He considered them rats in a maze, running a preprogrammed route.

Millions of people lived and worked in the towering, undistinguished concrete and glass buildings that sat on a narrow, fragile island, which might sink into the ocean if even one more square yard of concrete were added to its surface. If one building fell, the domino effect would surely flatten all the others, creating a heap of rubble. That would be a fitting monument to what New York represented, Jeremiah thought—overcrowding, filth, gross materialism, immorality, anonymity, inequality, injustice.

He walked south on Trinity Place, coming shortly to a black, iron gate located in a block-long brick wall that rose six feet above the sidewalk. Jeremiah opened the unlocked gate and bounded up the stairs into the Trinity Church cemetery.

The terrorist cut through the graveyard, jaywalked

across Broadway, and walked east along Wall Street past the members' entrance to the New York Stock Exchange, a symbol in his mind of American decadence.

Nevertheless, Jeremiah blended perfectly into the environment, dressed in an expensive suit tailored at Gieves and Hawkes on London's Savile Row and carrying a financier's standard leather briefcase. His hair and eyebrows were still dyed black, as they'd been in Prague, and he carried a teakwood cane hooked over one arm as a distracting prop. Hopefully people would remember it and nothing else about him.

He turned a corner and headed toward the visitors' entrance to the stock exchange at 18 Broad Street, in the eight-story, neoclassical Post Building. The terrorist stopped to admire the ninety-two-year-old building, with its granite facing, second-story portico, and pediment decorated with stone sculpture.

Inside, Jeremiah fell in line behind a group of high school kids and their teacher queuing up in front of a metal detector. Besides an expensive pen, his briefcase contained a hundred thousand dollars in cash. Carrying that amount of money into the exchange wasn't illegal, or unusual, he knew.

Jeremiah went first to the visitors' gallery on the mezzanine level for one last look at the trading floor before his guide arrived.

The trading floor extended from the Post Building through three stock exchange buildings to 11 Wall Street, where it ended in an area called "the garage."

The trading floor looked jerry-built, with many

steel cables extending from ceiling anchors to numerous figure-eight-shaped "trading posts," where market specialists worked. At each trading post the cables attached to a multitiered metal framework which had "arms" suspending stock-price monitors over the floor, creating the impression of a giant metal insect.

At high-topped desks along the perimeter of the trading floor, clerks talked on the telephone and wrote trade orders on pieces of paper they gave to traders in brightly colored smocks, who implemented the orders by screaming and communicating in a sign language only they could understand.

As Jeremiah contemplated the scene, the noisy, pubescent crowd of fuzzy-cheeked boys and chatty girls appeared. Jeremiah listened to the elementary economics lesson voiced by the young high school teacher, herself barely removed from childhood.

"This is where people buy and sell stock," she said. "A stock certificate is actually title to part of the company. You buy stock, you own a part of the company."

"How much?" asked a girl.

"Depends on how much stock you buy," the teacher explained.

"Okay, say I buy ten shares of stock. Do I own ten percent of the company?"

"Of course not! The company may have sold millions of shares of stock."

"Exactly how much stock does a company sell?" asked a studious-looking boy wearing thick glasses. "Who makes that decision?"

"It varies," the harried teacher replied. "It's not important. What you need to know is that if you buy a certain amount of stock, you own shares in the company. Isn't that great, students?''

Jeremiah saw the kids reflect looks ranging from boredom to disinterest.

"If you buy the stock, say, at ten dollars a share and it rises in value to fifteen dollars, then you've made a fifty-percent profit,'' the teacher continued.

"So if you bought one share, you made five bucks, right?''

The teacher smiled at her pupil. "Correct.''

"Big deal,'' a hulking kid said. "You gotta have money to make money. I already knew that.'' He and his buddies then turned away from the lesson in disgust.

"Why are these people wearing different-colored jackets?''

. " 'Cause they're dweebs.''

"Why is all the paper on the floor?''

"So janitors have something to do at night, asshole!''

The teacher signaled vainly for quiet and then elevated her voice above the mayhem. "When you buy stock, the company uses your money to make improvements in its product or service to make greater profits,'' she said, gaily. "At the end of the year, they may pay a dividend for each share of stock. Like a Christmas bonus.'' The teacher smiled, pleased with her effort.

"How much?''

"That depends on the company, how they did during the year, how much stock you own, and how much of a dividend they declare.''

"Jeez, you can't get a straight answer from her, can you?''

"Who can understand all this shit, anyway?"

"Who cares! I don't know anybody who owns stock. My old man puts his spare change into the lottery!"

The young teacher seemed impervious to criticism, Jeremiah thought. "And if you own stock, you can go to the stockholders' annual meeting and vote on issues," she said.

"Does each person get a vote?"

"No, votes are determined by the amount of stock you own."

Some kid laughed. "She doesn't know *anything*."

"She's a teacher!"

"Who are those people?" another student asked, pointing downward through the glass to the floor of the exchange.

"They're traders, and they're buying and selling stock for people," the teacher replied.

"How do you know whether to buy or sell? I mean stock prices yo-yo, right?"

The teacher looked momentarily confused. "Yo-yo?"

"Go up and down."

"Like in and out," one student said, making an obscene gesture with his fingers. "You can get screwed, too."

"That's enough of that kind of talk," the teacher said, sternly. "Mainly, whether you buy or sell depends on the advice you get from your broker, or your own research."

"So most people don't really understand what's going on? For them it's a gamble?"

"All business activity is a gamble, to some extent."

"If you bet money and can lose or win, that's gambling."

The teacher sighed. "If you look at the displays in this room, maybe you'll understand better. Also, if you pick up one of the telephones, you'll hear a short history of the stock exchange."

The kids rushed to get to the telephones first, but most put the receiver back in the cradle after listening only a few minutes to a dry statistical account of how three thousand companies listed on the exchange offered for sale 154 billion shares of stock valued at over six trillion dollars.

As the high schoolers moved on to another stop on the tour, an elderly security guard approached Jeremiah. "Kids say the damnedest things, don't they? These kids understand perfectly. This is a big gambling pit run primarily for the benefit of the casino, which is also known as the New York Stock Exchange. Most people can't get up the ante, and if they do, they're at the mercy of people jerking around stock prices."

"I gather you don't have a lot invested in the market?"

"My take-home pay from this job barely pays the rent and allows me to eat at McDonald's once a week. And I ain't about to let these guys gamble with my retirement money."

"Doesn't hardly seem fair, does it, Mr. Pollard?"

"Nope. I'm just happy to finally be able to do something about it."

Pollard took Jeremiah to the fourth floor of the Post Building, where brokerage firms, lawyers, government regulators, and communications companies had offices. The guard walked to a vacant office and unlocked the door. Forty boxes had been stacked in the middle of the room in four equal rows, creating a bomb nearly four by eight feet in size.

"No trouble getting the boxes up here?" Jeremiah asked.

"None," the guard replied. "I traded around to get on the second shift and helped the guys from the moving company bring 'em up the service elevator last night."

Jeremiah knew the boxes contained a total of two thousand pounds of RDX, or cyclonite, a powerful military-grade high explosive stolen from a navy depot in San Diego. Its rate of detonation was 28,125 feet per second, or 25 percent greater than that of dynamite. The firing train consisted of an electronic timer/battery connected to an electric blasting cap.

Jeremiah knew the explosive potential of this bomb greatly exceeded that of the four-thousand-pound witch's brew of fertilizer and fuel oil used to blow up the Murrah federal building in Oklahoma City.

He handed the briefcase to Pollard, who in exchange gave Jeremiah a seven-inch Beretta weighing less than two pounds, which nevertheless had a thirteen-round magazine filled with 9-mm shorts. It fit nicely into Jeremiah's back pants pocket. He hoped he wouldn't need it to get out of the building, but better safe than sorry.

"The money's all there," Jeremiah confirmed. "A hundred thousand dollars."

Pollard hefted the briefcase, smiled, and laughed.

"It's nice for a change to get paid big money for work you love!"

As Pollard left the room, Jeremiah walked to the pile of boxes and opened one on top, exposing the cylinder-shaped timer/battery. He twisted the pointer to show twenty-five minutes and then pulled on the lanyard, freeing the safety pin.

In the hallway Jeremiah positioned himself directly in front of a security camera placed high on the wall near the bank of elevators. He used his fingers to flash a code: three, one, two, one, five, one, nine, four, two. Then he took a red cloth banner out of his coat pocket and unfurled it for the camera. The black lettering read: SECOND JEREMIAH 4:15.

Across the street from Liberty Plaza, a small park catty-corner from the World Trade Center, Jeremiah approached a bank of pay phones located in front of a pizza parlor. He dialed a number at the United Broadcasting Corporation in Rosslyn, Virginia, and after the recorded voice-mail message concluded and the beep sounded, he said, "Laura, this is Jeremiah the Prophet announcing that the stock market is going to crash in"—Jeremiah checked his watch—"eight minutes."

As Jeremiah entered the lobby of a hotel attached to the World Trade Center, he *felt* a rumble coming from the direction of Wall Street. It reminded him of the time he'd watched aerial bombing in Afghanistan, courtesy of the Soviet army. During that war of liberation, he'd first become aware of Laura Delaney, NBC foreign correspondent. Later he got a close-up look at her during a state dinner in the Kremlin. She'd been on his mind ever since.

Jeremiah had a bellhop get his bags out of storage and hail a cab. He told the cabby to go up the Westside/Henry Hudson highway and take the Holland Tunnel to the Newark Airport.

The sad, wailing sound of many sirens—police cars, fire trucks, and other rescue vehicles—filled the air.

"Jesus, wherever that is, I hope we don't run into it," the cabby said, over his shoulder.

"Don't worry, we're going the opposite direction," Jeremiah replied, confidently.

24

Laura sat alone in her office watching television reports about the blast that had caused the collapse of the New York Stock Exchange's Post Building. She turned down the TV volume and replayed the voice-mail message in which Jeremiah had predicted the stock market would soon "crash."

She felt scared and sick at her stomach. She immediately called Steve at the FBI, but he wasn't in, and no one could tell her his whereabouts. For all she knew, he could be on his way to New York. She left a message, confident he'd call.

Laura turned her attention back to the television. The steel girders of the Post Building remained standing, but a mountain of concrete, steel, and wood had collapsed onto the first-floor trading pit. Huge holes had been blown in the sides of several adjacent structures, causing the collapse of entire floors. People trapped in these buildings waved frantically at a news helicopter, which provided an aerial view of the damage, including billowing smoke that could be seen miles away.

A camera view from the south end of Broad Street showed that debris had landed as far as three blocks away, even knocking over the statue of George Washington that stood at the corner of Wall and Nassau streets.

Mel suddenly burst into her office, waving several pieces of paper. "We just received a fax of chapter four of *The Book of Second Jeremiah*. It's a justification for the bombing of the stock exchange. He did it! I had one of my assistants check Jeremiah2.com. They don't have this chapter. We got an exclusive!"

Laura pushed the replay button on her voice mail so Mel could listen to Jeremiah's message.

"Unbelievable," Mel said.

"Yeah, we're the exclusive terrorist news network. Do you think Jeremiah will want a consulting fee? A residual from the rebroadcast of programs about him?"

Mel ignored her sarcasm. "Here's another idea. I'm always thinking. I got hold of one of our reporters in New York and told him to find out which company installed the security cameras at the exchange. You know why? The cameras are monitored internally by the exchange's security guys, but a copy is being made elsewhere, just in case of an accident like this."

"Accident?"

"If we can get hold of today's security tapes, I'm certain we'll see Jeremiah in the building. Jesus, Laura, this the stuff Peabody and Polk awards are made out of!"

Laura stood, disgusted at her old friend. "Mel, do you understand what has happened here? It's more than a news event. That bastard blew up the New York Stock Exchange! Hundreds, maybe thousands, of people are dead and injured. I don't give a shit about his justification. Most of those people were innocent bystanders. People just like you and me, Mel.''

"Jesus, Laura, give me a break. I understand, but the fact is he did it. It's the biggest news story of, God, I don't know how long. It's clearly the most deadly terrorist attack on American soil of all time. Every news organizations in the world's gonna be all over this story for the next year. Maybe longer.''

"Did it occur to you we're being used, Mel? Do you think it was an accident he did this on a Tuesday, in the early afternoon? He tips us off and dumps the fax in our lap. We got just enough time to put it all together in an award-winning edition of *American Chronicle*, set to air tonight at eight P.M. I'm glad at least it was the first Tuesday after Thanksgiving. Maybe some people who work in that area took an extended vacation.''

Mel slumped into a chair, a pensive look on his face. "I hear you, Laura. I just don't know what else to do except run with what we got. Do what we do. You're not suggesting we not use this stuff? Ignore what happened?''

Laura didn't answer his questions. "I'm sure we can count on him calling in during the show. I'm not kidding, Mel. It's like he was a special correspondent. Journalistic ethics may be just another oxymoron in Washington, D.C., like military intelligence and political savvy, but it bothers me that we're giving this guy a platform! Don't you see, Mel? Without us to broadcast his murderous spree, he wouldn't be killing people! There'd be no point! We're accomplices here, for Christ's sake!''

She watched Mel shake his head, as if he couldn't believe his ears.

"Jesus, Laura, you've climbed mountains and braved machine-gun fire to get a story. You sound like one of those government lawyers who tried to get a restraining order against the network and prevent us from broadcasting the hanging of those two teenagers."

"Well, maybe they had a point!" Laura snapped.

"No, they didn't!" Mel yelled, confidently. "UBC could disappear right now and Jeremiah won't go away. He'd just find another outlet. What about the Internet? The public has a right to know what's going on. And believe me, Laura, in case you've forgotten about the essence of our business, there are plenty of journalists—unethical though they may be in your mind—who are just waiting to take over from us. Waiting for us to fuck up. He doesn't need us, Laura. We need him!"

Laura bit her tongue. "I'm gonna forget you said that, Mel. But don't worry, I'm not going to walk out. Not tonight, anyway. I'll get up there in front of the cameras and perform for everyone. This is one evening you can be assured I'll read all the shit you put on the TelePrompTer. I don't want my personal stamp on this show. And when it's over, I'm taking a couple of weeks off to think about my career options. I make a lot of money working here, Mel, but it may not be enough in this case."

Mel stood, holding his hands out front. "I'll leave you alone, Laura. I understand what you're saying. I just hope you see my side." He paused. "Friends still, huh?"

She knew they'd still be friends when this blew

over, but for the moment she just stared at him sourly until he left and closed the door.

American Chronicle began its broadcast that evening with live footage of the on-going rescue and cleanup work at the New York blast site, where artificial lights had turned night into day. Mel had been right. Every journalist and photographer in the world seemed to have descended upon New York City.

"UBC and *American Chronicle* obtained a copy of a security camera videotape taken several hours preceding the blast," Laura told the audience, "which occurred today at twelve-forty-two P.M. eastern standard time. You'll see Jeremiah the terrorist standing in front of the camera flashing a series of numbers, which correspond to those he painted on a wall in Los Angeles when he first began his terrorist campaign several months ago. The banner he's holding refers to a verse from chapter four of the so-called *Book of Second Jeremiah*." Laura had lied to Mel. She wasn't reading the TelePrompTer material verbatim. The words "terrorist," "terrorist campaign," and "so-called" were her impromptu additions.

"We received a fax in our studio of the entire chapter," Laura continued. "Of course, we have no proof of its authenticity. Anyone could have made it up and sent it to us. With that disclaimer, I'll read the verse contained on the banner: 'Man must devise a new economic system to advance to the next stage of civilization, sayeth the Lord to his Prophet, the Second Jeremiah. The inequitable distribution of wealth and the inefficiencies of an artificial economy based not on God's values and plans for mankind, but rather on greed and profit, createth social and economic problems that hinder human advancement.' "

After a commercial break, Laura directed the viewing audience to a live report from the blast scene by UBC reporter Roy Webster, who stood on Broad Street just outside police lines. Fire trucks, other emergency vehicles—even a crane—lined the street.

"This is Assistant Fire Chief Lorenzo Reyes," Webster said, moving to the fireman's side. "Chief, UBC has just reported evidence that Jeremiah the terrorist is claiming responsibility for this bombing. Do you know how he did it?"

"No, Roy, not at this time. It'll take bomb and arson experts days, maybe weeks, to determine that."

"But given your experience, just by looking at the scene, what can you tell us?"

The fire chief shrugged. "It was some type of explosion, but I don't know what kind of material was used."

"Can you give us an estimate of casualties?"

"Not really. I'd guess a thousand people or more worked in the Post Building, although I don't know for sure. There weren't many survivors."

"I've heard rumors the adjacent buildings are in danger of collapse," Webster said, "and that people are still trapped in these buildings."

"That's true," Reyes said. "I gotta go now."

Webster squared up in front of the camera. "In a tragedy like this, there are a thousand personal stories." Webster motioned and a young man walked into the scene. "This is David Scruggs, whose wife,

Ginger, works in the Post Building for a communications firm. David, what did you think when you first heard about the explosion?''

"I prayed my wife wasn't dead," David said. "I took the subway from midtown down here, but they wouldn't let me get close to the building. I walked all around the area and was about to give up when I turned around and saw Ginger.''

Webster motioned a woman into camera range. "This is Ginger Scruggs. Ginger, where were you when the explosion occurred?''

"My boss sent me to a meeting over at the World Trade Center.''

"How do you feel knowing your friends and colleagues probably are dead?''

The woman hugged her husband, tears gushing from her face. "Lucky. We're just so lucky. I don't know why.''

The show continued with interviews of other survivors, relatives of those still missing, bomb and terrorism experts, and politicians promising various remedial efforts. Several organizations claimed responsibility, including an infamous Palestinian terrorist cell, despite Jeremiah's verifiable claim of authorship.

Financial analysts reassured investors that records for the day's trading at the stock exchange shouldn't be difficult to reconstruct, since the majority of buy/ sell orders originated outside the exchange and were only being implemented by the traders.

"Most companies listed on the NYSE are expected to suspend trading in their stock for the rest of the week," Laura reported. "In the meantime, we've learned of plans by federal regulators and industry officials to resume trading next week. One plan reportedly under consideration involves a temporary trading of New York Stock Exchange issues on either the nearby American Stock Exchange or NASDAQ, the computerized over-the-counter exchange. The details of this complicated task are not available now.''

As she waited for another commercial to end, Laura suddenly hated her job, even as she performed it by rote, remembering all the hard-learned lessons: Remain seated most of the time; use facial, not hand, gestures to convey emotions; always smile and strive for intimacy with the camera; remember that audience surveys reveal that 93 percent of the message getting through to viewers is conveyed by body language and voice tone. Only 7 percent of surveyed viewers listened to her words. *What's wrong with these people?* she wondered. What was wrong with her for participating in this charade? Everyone in America needed to sit down and talk. To pay attention to the words.

Next, *American Chronicle* cameras filmed events in the White House Press Room where President Carpenter read a statement deploring the violence and pledging an all-out effort by the FBI to bring Jeremiah to bay, as well as any individuals or organizations aiding him. The president announced plans to attend a memorial service in New York on Friday and hold a news conference afterward.

Standing outside the White House, Arnold Wescott, the President's national security adviser, declared a reward fund. "Laura, I want to inform your audience that a private organization, American Patriots, has announced a ten-million-dollar reward for information leading to the capture of Jeremiah the terrorist," Wescott said. "I repeat, that's his capture only, not his conviction for the various crimes he's committed."

Then, the dreaded call came. Laura put Jeremiah on the loudspeaker so the audience could hear their conversation.

"How are you this evening, Laura?" Jeremiah asked, his voice calm, almost serene.

"Obviously you did this bombing," Laura said, distastefully, refusing to use his name. "Why?"

"The stock market is a symbol of what's wrong with our economy, which concentrates wealth in the hands of a few and forces everyone else to do their bidding. Had I not destroyed the market, the manipulators would have continued to artificially alter stock prices for their own benefit.

"The average per capita income in the United States is under twenty thousand dollars. Forty percent of families live on less than twenty-five thousand dollars a year. Yet the top twenty percent of privileged Americans earn nearly half of all wages paid. Top company executives earn one hundred thirty-five times as much as the average worker's pay. Worse yet, those in the top five percent own or effectively control eighty percent of the nation's commercial real estate, stocks, and bonds.

"For more than half of all Americans who do the real work of our society, the stock market is irrelevant. These are the forgotten Americans I represent.

"The gross inequality in the sharing of wealth is a sin in the eyes of God, who made all people in His image. Individuals containing the spark of God cannot and should not be categorized into income levels. Good people are equal in the sight of God throughout their lives, and socially acceptable physical and intellectual labor is to be equally rewarded. So sayeth He, Supreme Ruler of the Universe. Individuals achieve distinction in the eyes of God by their good deeds, nothing else.''

Laura replied, scornfully, ''The U.S. economy has never been stronger. Most people who want to work have decent-paying jobs and opportunities to do better and earn more. Many, many Americans have greatly increased their wealth by investment in the stock markets individually, or through mutual funds or retirement accounts. America is still the land of opportunity. Our economy is the envy of the rest of the world.''

''Then the world's values and America's values are not God's values, which are revealed in the Bible, including *The Book of Second Jeremiah*.''

''You obviously continue to claim that *you* speak for God.''

''I do. So says He, so say I.''

Laura punched a button on the phone, abruptly ending the call and the FBI's effort to trace it, which she figured wouldn't be successful, anyway. She looked into the camera, barely able to contain her anger, and said, ''It's obvious we're dealing with a madman who has no respect for human life. We can safely conclude that he doesn't speak for God. We have to report the news here at *American Chronicle*, including the horrible news, but I'm one journalist who questions whether we should continue to give this mass murderer a bully pulpit. Perhaps you in the audience should let us know what you think.''

The studio audience applauded Laura's speech loudly as the show went to a commercial. When the show resumed, with only a few minutes left, various experts and selected members of the audience gave their reaction to the bombing and Jeremiah's new verses, copies of which had been distributed to the audience at the beginning of the show. The ambivalence that had greeted Jeremiah's killing of criminals at Leavenworth didn't carry over to his actions in New York, which nearly everyone condemned.

One caller compared Jeremiah's latest verse to communism. He speculated that agents of the former Soviet Union might be behind this terrorist campaign in America.

After the cameras quit whirling and the studio lights dimmed, Mel stood in front of Laura's desk. ''I don't think your editorial comment was wise,'' he said.

''Maybe not, Mel, but frankly, I don't give a damn.''

Laura and Steve drove in the darkness toward their farm in the foothills.

''I'm thinking about quitting, or at least taking a leave of absence,'' Laura said.

''That's up to you.''

''I don't need the job. I got oodles in the bank. I own the farm outright. I got you. What do you think?''

''I think we should go home and make love.''

''I mean about my job,'' Laura said, although his offer revived her spirits.

"From what you told me, Mel has a point."

"Maybe you should sleep with him tonight," Laura replied, but she wasn't really mad.

"Television didn't create Jeremiah and he wouldn't disappear if TV quit reporting his activities. He'd find another publicity avenue. He'd be happy if talented opponents like you abandoned the battle. He won't. He's in this until he wins, or gets killed or locked up."

"You're right, of course."

"And he won't leave you alone, even if you barricade yourself at the farm."

"What's he want?"

"He's become obsessed with you, Laura. There isn't any logic to it."

"How can I fight back?"

"You rule the airwaves now, Laura. UBC will do whatever you tell them. There's a backlash against Jeremiah right now. He's trying to pit economic classes against each other. Exploit that. Do a series of shows about everything that's right in America. At the same time, pursue this Trent Dillman angle. The German connections. Why did he kill Miranda Dombrowsky? Look into the Emma Dietze murder. There's something important there. If you reveal this guy as nothing more than a calculating terrorist, you end his appeal."

"God, you're such a stud I always forget how smart you are. Let's hurry home so you can FBI me."

"What!"

"Fondle me, bite me, get intimate with me." Laura laughed boisterously and strained against her seat belt as she tried to "FBI" Steve.

25

Immediately following the *American Chronicle* show, the fourth chapter of *The Book of Second Jeremiah* appeared on the Internet. Someone with a valid student code used a computer in the University of Illinois library to distribute the chapter file to members of a user group discussing articles and books critical of American capitalism. The Jeremiah2.com Web master later added it to the terrorist's official Web site.

THE BOOK OF SECOND JEREMIAH

CHAPTER FOUR

1 The greatest Evil is the dirty stain of greed that poisons the mind of Man, sayeth the LORD to Jeremiah.

2 The description of Satan and his followers also applies to the marketplace and market manipulators: cunning, deceitful, corrupt, unfair, manipulative, impersonal, wicked, prideful, dishonest. Capitalism rewards those who scheme

and penalizes those who do real, honest labor,
with their hands or with their minds.

3 The LORD sayeth:

Dishonesty is the hallmark of the marketplace,
and no man, in buying goods or services,
or selling the products of his labor,
hath not been misled or cheated.
4 The Stock Market is a tool whereby
the rich get richer
through their manipulation of production and prices;
it has no relevance for most working
people whose wages
barely purchase the necessities of life.
5 Capitalism hath no social principle and
assumes man
is incapable of social good, only private
gain.
Capitalism makes wealth the main de-
terminant of Man's
Worth, which is contrary to God's
teachings.

6 Remember that Christ said not to lay up
treasures on Earth, and that a camel could easier
pass through the eye of a needle than a Rich Man
enter the Kingdom of God.

7 Men confuse what they need with what they want.

The marketplace encourages materialism and

unnecessary consumption, turning Man from his true goals of

reverence, obedience, and cooperation. Guilt-induced

holiday buying sprees, including the celebration of Christ's

Birthday, are akin to the worship of false idols.

8 Hear this well, sayeth the LORD, for it is a fundamental truth: Wealth can only be created by man's physical or intellectual labor; therefore, such Wealth cannot be owned by another, any more than one man can own another man's body or soul. I did not create Men to be slaves, sayeth the LORD!

9 All necessary labor and the Wealth produced takes place in a cooperative environment, where Men are dependent upon each other; hence, all Wealth is of equal value, and to be shared equally, so sayeth the LORD.

10 Necessary work is any labor associated with the production of goods and services serving basic human needs, including: food, clothing, housing, utilities, approved forms of transportation, health care, education, scientific inquiry, and research.

11 Much work is unnecessary, sayeth the

LORD, including that associated with the entertainment industry and the manufacture and sale of products and services that appeal to the vanity of Man. Perfume and facial paint, jewelry and fashion clothing, will not gain ye entrance into Heaven!

12 Eliminating unnecessary service work and other inefficiencies of the marketplace will free Man for necessary work and increase the efficient production of Wealth, thereby creating more free time for those who serve the collective good.

13 People who form a civilized society may invest in the State the right to allocate labor and establish work priorities and consumption goals, sayeth the LORD.

14 Who decideth that one Man's labor in this world of interdependence is less worthy and deserving of a lesser reward, asketh the LORD? Everywhere, the Man who labors with his hands or mind is subservient to the Facilitator who Evilly manipulates, lies, and cheats, but produces nothing. These middlemen include the money changer, paper trader, insurance man, salesman, advertiser, public opinion manipulator, bureaucrat, and politician.

15 Man must devise a new economic system to advance to the next stage of civilization, sayeth the LORD to his Prophet, the Second Jeremiah. The inequitable distribution of wealth and the inefficiencies of an artificial economy based not on God's values and plans for Mankind, but rather

on greed and profit, createth social and economic problems that hinder human advancement.

16 Money is a symbol of Greed and unnecessary in the computer age, sayeth the LORD. Return to the barter system used by the original twelve tribes of Israel. Coin and paper can be replaced by a system of credits and debits that reflect Man's labor and needs. It shall be called the Wealth Exchange.

17 If a Man has a specific marketplace talent, give thanks to God, don't rob your fellow man of his due in a limited system of rewards. A businessman's partner is his employee; both are servants of the People. All are children of God.

18 Private property is a right of all people; rents are another tool of oppression by the wealthy, a means by which the Greedy steal from their brother. The land is to be held in trust by the State for the equal use of all Men, so sayeth the LORD.

19 The worldwide marketplace, concerned with endless

consumption of largely unnecessary goods and services,

directly contributes to overpopulation because of its

never-ending need for labor and consumers. In turn,

this causes migration of poor people and clashes of cultures.

In an overpopulated world of limited resources,

a Rich Man stealeth from his brother,
making him poor.

20 People denied their fair share of society's
Wealth are justified in using any means possible
to overthrow the oppressive marketplace and establish economic justice, so sayeth the LORD to
his prophet, the Second Jeremiah.

21 The Wealth Exchange will eliminate the
Cult of Money and economic and social classes;
it will promote the rule of law, reward hard work,
and ensure social cooperation. It will set Man to
his proper work, which is the worship of God and
the quest for Knowledge. So sayeth the LORD of
the Universe!

26

The general's wife bitched nonstop about not breaking this, not scratching that, as they loaded her family's household goods onto the moving van. Zviad didn't like manual labor, anyway, especially outside in the bitter cold of December.

Zviad and Andrei, loyal members of the Ukrainian International League, masqueraded as private moving company employees. Two airmen from the Ukrainian air force base just outside Pereyaslav also helped load. The man ostensibly in charge was Sgt. Viktor Komarov, whom Zviad had bribed several weeks ago to help them with their real mission on base.

"Remember, Sergeant Komarov, you must be at our new quarters in Odessa by eight A.M.," the general's wife carped. "No later! I want everything moved into the new house before noon. Do you understand?"

"Yes, ma'am," the sergeant replied. "Bitch," he said beneath his breath as the general's wife walked away.

Within a half hour, they'd finished, and Sergeant Komarov dismissed the two airmen. "Go to the mess hall and get something to eat," he said. "I told them you'd be late."

Zviad and Andrei smoked a cigarette with the burly sergeant. Zviad recalled his first meeting with Komarov in a bar on the edge of town. The sergeant was drunk and wanting to fight someone when Zviad asked him to step outside. Before the scary-looking sergeant could hit him, Zviad handed over a bundle of one hundred thousand deutsche marks, a small fortune in this part of the world. The equivalent of twenty years' salary for the thirty-five-year-old Komarov, who'd stared dumbly at the wad of bills and immediately sobered up.

"It's only a down payment," Zviad had said. "I'll give you another hundred thousand marks when the job is done."

"What do I have to do? You want me to kill someone? I can kill a couple of generals for this amount of money. Maybe the whole general staff."

"We want to steal something from the air base." His bosses at the UIL had decided a master sergeant like Komarov could better accomplish the task than an officer or a civilian. And at a cheaper price.

"Anything! What is it you want? A jet fighter? That's possible, you know."

Anything was possible in a desperate situation, Zviad knew. Even though the rich black soil of the Ukraine made it the breadbasket of the old Soviet Union, producing an abundance of grains, sugar beets, potatoes, and livestock, jobs were scarce now and most people barely scraped by.

The Ukraine had been a natural military staging area for the Soviets, behind the shield posed by the Warsaw Pact nations. But now that the newly independent Ukraine sought accommodation with the West, it couldn't afford a large military force. Komarov would soon join the legions of the unemployed. Zviad knew it, and so did the sergeant.

The next day they'd talked about details and Zviad had suggested the down payment be used as bribe money, and the final payment as Komarov's profit. Later tonight that payment would be made.

"Come with me," Komarov said to Zviad. "Andrei, you drive the van. Back it up to the bunker where I stop."

Komarov drove a military jeep across the base and stopped outside a Quonset hut near a concrete bunker half buried underground. As the wind cut through his body, Zviad hoped Komarov's plan would work. It wouldn't be easy getting off an air base surrounded by barbed wire, land mines, and guard towers. Guards with dogs walked the perimeter of the base four times during an eight-hour period. If anything went wrong, they'd soon be in the brig, or dead.

Inside the hut, Komarov asked the sergeant in charge, "Are the guards taken care of?"

The sergeant looked suspiciously at Zviad. "Only one. The other refused to talk about it."

"He is adamant?"

The sergeant shrugged. "He is stubborn."

Komarov shrugged also and handed the other sergeant a standard-issue bayonet. "Use this."

"Not me!"

"Yes, you. He will let you get close to him."

"What will you do with the body?"

"Put it in the moving van. We'll wrap it in a rug. In the morning you can report him missing without leave." Komarov reassured his fellow noncommissioned officer, "It happens all the time anymore, especially when they don't pay us on time."

The other sergeant looked skeptical, Zviad thought.

"It makes you an extra four thousand marks you won't have to pay the guard," Viktor hinted.

The sergeant considered that logic and began nodding his head with confidence. He put on a heavy coat and left the hut. Zviad handed Komarov another cigarette as they waited. The sergeant returned within minutes, nodded at them, and removed his coat. He sat at his desk and resumed his paperwork, as if nothing had happened.

They rolled the dead guard inside one of the general's wife's expensive Persian rugs and placed it among the furniture. Inside the bunker, Zviad and Andrei loaded the bombs with Cyrillic markings on the side onto wheeled carts and rolled two of them out of the bunker, while Komarov kept watch. The hydraulic lift attached to the back of the van easily hoisted the five-hundred-pound bombs inside.

"Do you think these bombs will be used for negotiations, like the Baron said?" Andrei asked.

Zviad shrugged. "Who knows? Someone will use them someday. It's a wonder the Soviets didn't drop them on the Germans, the French, the Americans. I don't have anything against those people."

"I have distant relatives living in America."

"I just want the one hundred fifty thousand marks they promised us for this job."

"That's not much of the Baron's down payment."

"No, most it goes to UIL big shots. Of course, there are government and military officials, and people at the port authority to bribe. It's the way things are here, Andrei. If we're ever going to be rich, we'll have to find another way."

Komarov locked the van doors, attached an official metal seal, and drove toward the base exit. They stopped at a sentry post and Komarov handed his orders to the guard.

"I'm supposed to look in back," the guard said.

"Okay by me," Komarov said, nonchalantly, "but we'll need to call the general so he can authorize breaking the seal. He gave me strict orders about that, because the last time he moved, some things were stolen. So you call him at home."

A sour look passed over the guard's face and he handed back the papers. "Move on, Sergeant Komarov."

Zviad let out his breath as they passed through the gate. His hands shook as he lit a cigarette.

Andrei, who sat in the middle, said, "That was close."

"What would you have done if he called the general?" Zviad asked.

Komarov laughed. "You think I'm dumb! The guard is a good actor. In case someone was listening, he has a good excuse. He's already been paid."

It would take them about seven hours to drive the four hundred kilometers to Odessa, Zviad calculated, where the bombs would be transferred to a UIL truck about 3:00 A.M.. He and Andrei could then sleep during the day and later celebrate a job well done. Odessa had many good nightclubs and lots of willing women.

They drove through several small towns, where Zviad figured the people dreamed about a better life under capitalism. What they should worry about, he thought, wasn't money but irradiated water they drank from the Dnieper River, which received water from the Pripyat River, which flowed through Chernobyl, a nuclear ghost town for at least the next hundred years.

Zviad glanced nervously into the side mirror. After they'd traveled about fifteen miles, he saw it again. Car or truck lights.

"Someone is behind us," he said to Komarov, who checked his mirror.

"So what? It's a public highway."

"Yes, but I think they've been behind us ever since we left the base. At first they didn't have their lights on."

"You're just jumpy," Andrei said.

"They got behind us soon after we came out of the gates. I'm certain. I thought I saw the moon reflect off a car. They only turned their headlights on when we approached the first intersection."

"Relax," Komarov said, smiling.

"We don't have the other hundred thousand marks with us," Zviad said. "The League people we're going to meet have it."

Komarov's eyes narrowed as he glared at Zviad. "You think I would be so stupid as to rob the UIL? How long would I live after that?"

Then it can only be the Baron's men, Zviad thought. The New Covenant. If they killed the three of them and took the bombs, the Baron wouldn't have to make the final payment of thirty-three million deutsche marks. Sergeant Komarov might not cross the UIL, but the Baron would.

Zviad thought about their route, which would take them through two more small towns, Kagarlyk and

Tarasca, before they came to the major highway that went directly to Odessa. He knew this road well and there was a long curve up ahead where they could turn onto a side road and get behind the car tailing them. Besides, they needed to dump the guard's body, anyway.

"Turn off here," Zviad ordered as they approached a bend in the road. "We'll dump the guard's body."

It took less than five minutes for them to open the double-wide van doors, roll the guard out of the rug onto the ground, and reseal the door. They had barely turned back onto the highway when they met a car coming toward them.

"That car!" Zviad said. "See if it doesn't swing back around behind us."

Zviad kept his eye on the side mirror and noticed Komarov did the same on his side of the truck. "Well, I'll be damned," Komarov said. "You were right, Zviad. He turned around. Who are they?"

"Someone who wants to steal the bombs."

"I've got a surprise for them," Komarov said, a steely look in his eyes. Suddenly he swung the big van into the passing lane and applied the air brakes, causing the car to roll alongside the truck. Zviad looked out his window right at the driver.

Komarov immediately swung the van back into the right-hand lane, sideswiping the car and forcing it off the road. Zviad saw the car leave the road, travel through the ditch, and fly out the other side, where it crashed into a tree.

They left the van idling at the side of the road, with its warning lights flashing. All three ran to the smoking car and looked inside. Zviad opened the driver's door and felt his neck for a pulse. Both front-seat passengers were dead, but the man in back moaned and wiped blood from his face.

"What do you want to do now?" Komarov asked. He patted a holster holding a 9-mm Makarov. "We can kill the one in the backseat and be on our way."

Zviad thought furiously. "No, our bosses will want to know about this. We need him alive so they can question him. Let's see if this car will run."

It wouldn't, so they tied up the bloody man and put him in back of the van. Then they continued to drive toward Odessa, and no one else followed them.

About 3:30 A.M. they pulled over at a twenty-four-hour rest stop, where many trucks idled while their drivers slept, used the rest rooms, or ate in the restaurant.

Andrei and Zviad's superiors had made arrangements for a UIL truck to be there at the rest stop, so they could exchange the money for the bombs. They didn't want Komarov to know their final destination in Odessa. The exchange of the one hundred thousand marks for the bombs went smoothly. Zviad and Andrei transferred the bloody man to a car waiting for them. They planned to follow the UIL truck to the freighter, where someone from the New Covenant would give them the rest of the account numbers for the thirty-three million marks being held in a Swiss bank account. Then they'd decide what to do with the bloody man.

Zviad soon heard a rumbling sound from the rear of the car, which began to shake and wobble. He pulled over on the shoulder, stepped out into the cold night, and looked disgustedly at a flat tire, caused, no doubt, he thought, by the horrible condition of the pockmarked road. He coughed angrily, his throat burning from too many cigarettes, his eyes bloodshot from lack of sleep. He ordered Andrei to change the tire while he watched the bloody man.

Within fifteen minutes, they were back on the road and shortly came to the port. Zviad didn't know the *Lysander*'s exact location, but he drove in what he thought was the right direction, searching for the UIL truck. He turned onto a dirt road, crossed several pairs of railroad tracks, and drove through an open gate. Between a huge crane and a large metal building on the right, he saw water.

He drove around the corner of the metal building and saw the league truck, its back doors wide open and the bombs gone.

"This does not look good," Andrei said. They approached the truck cautiously, their weapons drawn. The windows of the cab had been shattered with automatic-weapons fire, killing both men up front. Whoever had stopped the truck then sprayed the cargo area with gunfire, Zviad figured. The bullets easily ripped through the thin metal, also killing the three league men in back.

"They'd have done the same to us if we'd been here," Zviad said. "This has to be the work of the New Covenant! They put men in back of us and here at the port, so they could steal the bombs!"

"Since we weren't killed, the league will think we knew about this and faked the flat tire," Andrei said, his hands shaking as he lit a cigarette. "They might even think we have the bombs."

Zviad thought for several minutes and said, "Get in the car."

"Where are we going?"

"I'll tell you later." They might actually never see home again, but if his scheme panned out, Zviad wouldn't care, because they'd be rich.

27

With guns pointed in the air, Steve and Leslie stood in the hallway of an apartment building near Tompkins Square, waiting for four SWAT members from the New York City Police Department to break in the door of unit 202, where Ronald Pollard, a security guard at the New York Stock Exchange, lived.

When the door splintered open, Steve followed on the heels of the black-clad SWAT members, who soon had Pollard spread-eagle on the floor. One SWAT policeman pointed an assault rifle at Pollard's head and another kept a knee in the security guard's back while he cuffed him.

"The place is clear," a third SWAT guy said, emerging from a hallway. "Nothing back there but a bathroom and bedroom."

"You sure you brought enough storm troopers to capture an old man?" Pollard gasped, as they jerked him to his feet and pushed him into a kitchen chair. Pollard's thin, white hair stood on end and his faded blue terry cloth robe gaped open to reveal a white undershirt and boxer shorts.

"We can handle this now," Steve said to a uniformed police sergeant. "Why don't you station two guys in the hallway and two more in the first-floor entryway until we're done questioning this guy."

"This is what's wrong with America," Pollard continued, regaining his breath and composure. "The police are always harassing innocent people, which is easier than taking on the real criminals. You guys scared of 'em?"

Steve pulled a dining room chair into place in front of Pollard and sat down. "Mr. Pollard, I'm going to read you your rights, so listen carefully." While Steve read the Miranda rights from a card, Pollard continued to complain sarcastically about his treatment.

"Mr. Pollard, do you know the terrorist known as Jeremiah?" Steve asked, as Leslie operated a compact video camera that fit nicely into a pocket of her FBI windbreaker.

"Damn right I know him!" Pollard blurted, surprising Steve.

"How do you know him?"

"Learned about him and his teachings on the Internet!" the old man said loudly. "Got a Mac right over there." He nodded in the direction of a computer sitting on his dining room table. "You'd be surprised at the rage people are feeling. They're pissed at the way things are going in this society! You can't stop it!"

"Did you help Jeremiah bomb the New York Stock Exchange?"

"Yep!" the unshaven, pallid security guard admitted, defiantly. "I helped 'em bring in the explosives the night before. They couldn't've done it without me!"

"Who are they?"

Pollard leered at Steve and Leslie. "Just ordinary people like me."

"Why'd you do it?"

"Because Jeremiah's right about those stockbrokers and big shots at the exchange. They're just screwin' people outta their hard-earned dollars! Jackin' around prices and lining their pockets so they can live in a mansion in Jersey or Connecticut. They ain't got nothing to do with the real America. They don't work. They're leeches! But they walk right by the workingman like he doesn't exist! Guards, janitors, kitchen help. All the people that wait on 'em. Treat us like we were dog shit on their shoes! Fuck 'em! They got theirs, huh!"

Steve stood, a puzzled look on his face. He hadn't expected such an easy confession, although ample evidence linked Pollard to the bombing. The security tapes showed him meeting Jeremiah in the visitors' gallery about an hour before the blast. Both had gone into a fourth-floor office, and Pollard had come out later carrying a briefcase.

"You must know Jeremiah signaled to a security camera that he was involved in the bombing. Didn't it occur to you those same cameras would show the two of you together?"

"I'm proud of what I did," Pollard said. "My plans are to stand trial for helping blow up the stock exchange. I want a public lawyer! I want a big trial down at Civic Center, covered by television and the *New York Times*. Hell, I want Laura Delaney to interview me for UBC!"

Steve shook his head in annoyance and looked at Leslie, who tried to restrain a smile.

"You said you met Jeremiah on the Internet. Did he come by your apartment?"

A maniacal look seized Pollard's eyes. "When I figured out what the movement was all about, I signed up on the Internet. Told 'em I'd help, do anything! Somebody called me and asked a bunch of questions." Pollard cackled. "They was real interested in where I worked. Then Jeremiah called and asked if I'd help blow that damn place up. I said, 'Hell yes!' " Pollard drew himself up proudly in his chair. "And by God, he come by and talked to me like I was somebody! I don't have to describe him for you incompetent assholes, do I?" The old man sneered at Steve and Leslie.

"I'm gonna tell you everything, but nothin' I say is gonna lead you to him, for God's sake! You think he's that dumb? Sure, you might net some more small fish like me, but they won't give a shit, either! We're already the rejects of society. Look at this apartment. If you plan to walk around this neighborhood, Agent Wallace, you'll need that gun."

"Not everyone that lives here becomes a terrorist."

"That's 'cause they ain't got no guts, or they're just too shell-shocked to act. Me, I got nothing to lose. I got nowhere to go except the graveyard. You can't do nothin' to me that ain't been done already! But I got even and now I'll be famous!" He lowered his voice to impart a confidence. "Know what? When New America is set up, there'll be a prisoner exchange. There'll be plenty of people wanting to get from one side to the other. You think you're gonna send me up the river for the rest of my life, don'tya? No, sir! I'm gonna be a hero in New America!''

Steve calmly endured the tirade, which Leslie videotaped. Then he showed Pollard a photo of Jeremiah, Miranda, and Vernon Monroe. "You know these people with Jeremiah?" he asked.

"Nope."

"Not even the woman?"

Pollard looked closer. "Don't know her."

"What would you say if I told you Jeremiah broke her neck?"

"I'd say he was done with her."

"It shows you how he treats his friends," Steve said, harshly. "He didn't help you get away, did he?"

"I didn't need any help beyond the money he gave me," Pollard replied, defiantly.

"He paid you to help him blow up the stock exchange!" Steve said, distastefully. "I thought you were a loyal soldier of the new movement which abhors money."

"When in Rome . . ."

"Where's it at?" Steve asked. "The money? How much were you paid to help kill and wound nearly two thousand innocent people?"

Pollard laughed, shaking his head. "You ain't gonna find that money. I got it hid real good. And another thing, FBI man, there ain't no innocent people in America!"

Leslie interrupted, trying a gambit. "You have to know something of use to us, Mr. Pollard. It could cut down your jail time. If it was important information, you might not even go to jail."

"What are your orders for the future?" Steve asked.

The old man roared until he began to cough, and Steve recognized the angry, defiant look of the true believer.

"You think I'm part of his inner circle! I don't know what the hell Jeremiah's gonna do tomorrow, except I hope he keeps killing the crooks, the big shots, and the politicians!"

Steve jumped on that last reference. "Politicians? Jeremiah has never mentioned them as targets. Did you talk to him about it? Does he have another job for you?"

Pollard snorted. "You didn't read *The Chosen Few*, didya?"

Actually, Steve finally had finished the "Blue Book," which indeed contained many disparaging remarks about representative government.

Pollard's expression changed abruptly and he appeared worried, compliant. "Check my E-mail if you like. Maybe there's a message for me from Jeremiah or somebody else in the movement."

Intrigued, Steve walked toward the Mac and looked it over helplessly.

"Just turn it on and then I'll show you how it works," Pollard offered.

"You stay where you are," Steve ordered, looking at Leslie. "You know how to operate one of these?"

Leslie set the video camera on the table. "Got one at home. This'll only take a minute."

As she sat in front of the computer, Steve stepped into the short hallway leading to the bedroom, looking around warily but keeping an eye on Pollard.

When the old man fell to the floor, Steve knew something was terribly wrong.

The explosive device inside the computer blew Leslie back nearly eight feet, against the far wall. Steve avoided being hit by shrapnel only because he stood around a corner of the hallway.

He ran to Leslie's aid. She had on a flak jacket but suffered extensive head wounds, although there wasn't much blood. Steve looked into her eyes and spoke to her, but Leslie didn't respond. He could barely feel her pulse.

Chaos reigned around him. The explosion brought the SWAT police back and they had Pollard braced against a wall.

"Call an ambulance!" Steve shouted, trying to be heard above the angry voices. One of the black-clad SWAT members pummeled Pollard.

When he saw a policeman dial 911, Steve picked up Leslie and left the apartment, running the stairs to the first floor. Getting her to the paramedics even two minutes earlier might make a difference.

He stood on the curb, hearing sirens in the distance, silently urging them on. He saw his cold breath hanging on the air, but not Leslie's. He sank to his knees, cradling her with one arm, as he blew into her mouth and used the heel of his other hand to begin CPR.

The EMTs arrived and took over, but at some point one of them looked helplessly at Steve, who knew, even as he helped load Leslie into the ambulance. His partner and friend, and one of the best college basketball players in America, had been killed by one of Jeremiah's henchmen.

* * *

A replay of the nightmare in Seattle followed, as Steve waited for the conclusion of a local police investigation and the release of Leslie's body by the coroner. He returned to Washington on the US Airways shuttle and arrived shortly after midnight at Reagan National Airport, where Laura waited along with Director Minor, Deputy Director Thompson, and a large contingent of FBI agents and law enforcement officials.

Laura clung fiercely to Steve, who insisted they go outside to the tarmac while an honor guard transferred the coffin to a hearse.

"Oh, God, it could have been you!" Laura sobbed, refusing to let go of his hand.

"I know."

"I'm terribly sorry, Steve," Thompson said, his face ashen. "I know how close you were to Leslie."

Steve turned abruptly, facing Thompson but speaking to all the other agents within hearing distance. "Did you know she was an athlete? One of the best basketball players in America? Did you know who she was?"

"Yes, I did," Thompson replied, in a calm, low voice. "And when she came to me a year ago with her resignation in hand, I reminded her of who she was and the challenge she faced."

As a limo drove them across the Potomac toward FBI headquarters, where Leslie's body would be kept in the morgue pending funeral decisions by her parents, Thompson spoke to Steve and Laura.

"Ordinarily I wouldn't talk business at a time like this," he began, "but time is of the essence. You remember the task force meeting, Steve, and Wescott's concern. Well, those fears have come true. I don't know all the details, but the CIA reports that two atomic weapons were stolen from an air base in Ukraine.''

"You can tie Jeremiah to that?"

"There may be no connection, but we have to be prepared just the same. We're not going to have much time to mourn Leslie. We need desperately to find this guy."

"Tell me what to do," Steve said, tight-lipped.

"We'll keep doing what we've been doing," Thompson replied. "My remarks are as much for Laura as you."

"You want me to report this theft of the nuclear weapons?"

Thompson looked out the windows at the nation's monuments. "Yes. I've talked about it with Wescott and others. The people have to know how serious this situation is. Maybe then we'll get the leads we need to find and arrest this guy."

28

Hans Dietrich Hoffman sat at a table in a corner of a *gasthaus* sipping beer and waiting for his midmorning appointment. At a table across the room near one of the windows overlooking the street, four old men played cards.

Hoffman immediately recognized the Ukrainian when he opened the door. The bald gangster wore the same leather coat he'd had on when CIA free-lancers had photographed him in Prague. Hoffman waved at Zviad and asked the waiter for another beer.

Zviad sat, looked around anxiously, and asked, in broken English, "You are with the American CIA?"

Hoffman replied, rudely, "I'm here, aren't I?"

"But how do I know you are with the CIA?"

Hoffman took the photo from his suit-coat pocket and handed it over. "This is you and your friend recently at the Hotel Intercontinental in Prague, is it not?"

The beady-eyed Ukrainian examined the photograph as if Hoffman had made it appear magically. "This man we were talking with is from the New Covenant," Zviad said. "I can tell you some very interesting things about that organization."

Hoffman, who knew all about the New Covenant, did as he'd been instructed and placed Walter Dorfler's photograph on the table.

"*Ja*," Zviad said. "That's the Baron."

Although surprised, Hoffman registered no emotion. "What else do you have for me today?"

Zviad drank from his beer and again looked suspiciously around the *gasthaus*. "Very valuable information, but it will cost you."

"How much?"

"Two million U.S. dollars, deposited in a Swiss bank account."

Hoffman laughed derisively. "That's a lot of money."

Zviad stared intently at Hoffman. "How much would your bosses at the CIA pay to learn that two nuclear weapons have been stolen from somewhere in the old Soviet Union and shipped out to sea on a freighter?"

Hoffman restrained his growing excitement. "That's old information. Now, if you knew their location, that would be valuable information."

Zviad nodded and smiled. "When the money is deposited in this account I have opened in Geneva"—the Ukrainian shoved a slip of paper across the table—"I will do this for your CIA: I will tell them the name of the ship the bombs were loaded onto and the port it sailed from. I also know a lot of details about the theft, including who did it, how it was done, and many of the people who were bribed. Would that be worth two million dollars?"

Hoffman smiled, thinking it was a bargain price. "Possibly. Anything else?"

"Yes," Zviad replied. "I can give you a guy who

can tell you more about the Baron and the New Covenant.''

"What guy?"

"One of the ｜ ｕp of New Covenant thieves, who planned to kill us while their buddies hijacked the bombs. But we turned the tables on them and captured one of them. I call him the bloody man.''

"Why?"

"Because he broke his nose in a car crash. Also he bleeds from the other end, too. I cut off one o his nuts.''

"You what!"

Zviad leaned closer to relate the gory details. "This guy said he was from the New Covenant and just following us to make certain everything went all right. He said he didn't know the guys who shot up the truck and took the bombs. I knew he was lying, so when we got here in Germany, I cut one of his balls off. You know, like they do the small bulls in the spring. You just slit the sack down the middle and pull one out and cut off the sperm cord.''

Hoffman shuddered at the thought. "And he tells you the truth to avoid losing his other testicle?"

Zviad smiled and nodded vigorously at his intelligent student.

"And is this . . . bloody man . . . with you today?"

"Yes, my partner watches him, but I don't think he can run away!" Zviad laughed uproariously at his own joke.

"When could you hand him over?"

"Soon," Zviad promised. "As soon as my Swiss bank account is full of American dollars.''

"Walk with me," Hoffman requested. He stood and put ten deutsche marks onto the table. They stepped outside into a *biergarten* closed during the winter. Off to the northeast stood the old castle built in the Middle Ages as part of a wall surrounding the old city of Nuremberg. As they walked west, Hoffman flashed a hand signal and a black Mercedes pulled alongside. Two burly men jumped out and pushed Zviad into the car. Hoffman knew they would interrogate the Ukrainian, using methods far more sophisticated and antiseptic than Zviad's, although not necessarily more effective. They'd probably pay him and his partner the two million. The CIA wanted to be known as an organization that paid its spies and defectors well, especially for valuable information.

A few blocks from the *Hauptmarkt*, Hoffman located an apartment building, accessible off a cobblestoned street. Walter Dorfler's family home was in Munich, but they knew he kept an apartment in Nuremberg for his mistress, Deirdre Schultz, who often accompanied him on business trips.

An imposing iron security gate barred entrance to the courtyard of the three-story, U-shaped building.

"*Entschuldigen Sie, gnädige Frau*," Hoffman called out to a woman sweeping an inside walkway. "Can you tell me if there are any apartments to rent."

"No," she replied, coming closer to the gate. "We are full, but there is a waiting list. You should come back tomorrow at ten when Herr Krause is here."

"Ah, yes, thank you. This looks to be a respectable neighborhood. Are there good people living here?"

The woman frowned at Hoffman's obvious stupidity. "Yes, of course, this is a very respectable place.

Several well-known people live here, including Walter Dorfler. Do you know of him?''

''Yes, Dorfler the industrialist. I'm a journalist and have interviewed Herr Dorfler in the past. Is he home?''

''*Nein*. He is away on business, I think.''

Hoffman walked across a stone bridge over the Pegnitz into the Lorenz district of the city, passing by the impressive Gothic towers of Saint Lorenz Catholic Church. On a nearby building an optimist had spray-painted the message: *Nie wieder*. Never again. Hoffman the pessimist considered the only relevant questions to be where and when.

Nuremberg already had paid the price. Here the Nazi party revived the idea of a German Third Reich and held parades in the *Hauptmarkt*. Rallies at the Zeppelinfeld southeast of the walled city had attracted more than a million of the party faithful.

The Allies rained their vengeance on Nuremberg from the air in early 1945 and later that year held trials in the city for the worst of the Nazi criminals. But his fellow countrymen had rebuilt their beloved city, although some of its inhabitants held on to ideas from the past.

Hoffman walked down Adlerstrasse to the headquarters of *Neu Deutschland*, a Catholic, anticommunist, anticrime, anti-immigrant organization, opposed first to the Federal Republic and then to reunification of East and West Germany. As near as Hoffman could make out, they wanted a return to autocratic German principalities. He had long considered them to be strictly regional in nature and of little interest to the CIA. But maybe not.

*   *   *

Hoffman leaned against a building and smoked a cigarette as he waited for his colleagues to finish their business with Zviad. Although he lived in Stuttgart on the edge of the Black Forest, Hoffman had been on assignment for several days, first traveling to Bayreuth and now here.

In Bayreuth, the hometown of both the nineteenth-century composer Richard Wagner and Emma Dietze, the international tennis star, Hoffman had talked to the parents of Johanna Gerhardt, Emma's best childhood friend.

Hoffman carried with him to Bayreuth a copy of the photograph of Jeremiah, Miranda Dombrowsky, and Vernon Monroe. His CIA handlers wanted him to flesh out a suspected link between Jeremiah, Dombrowsky, and Emma Dietze.

The Dietze family always had been publicity-shy and wouldn't talk to Hoffman, who seduced the Gerhardts with the bogus promise of a photo spread of them and their daughter in *Der Spiegel,* a renowned German magazine. Hoffman's cover for years had been that of a freelance writer.

Over coffee and strudel, Hoffman persuaded the Gerhardts to show him their family photo albums, which proved a treasure trove. The CIA had a detailed biography of Emma Dietze, but Hoffman had been shocked to find a photograph of Emma, Johanna, Emma's first cousin, Katrina Dorfler, and an unidentified teenager whose photograph he'd seen before in an American high school yearbook. Trent Dillman, of Sioux Falls, South Dakota.

"Do you know this young man?" Hoffman asked, pointing.

Both Gerhardts examined the photograph. *"Nein,"* Frau Gerhardt said. "But I think he was an American visiting the Dorflers in Munich. Walter has many friends in America, you know."

One in particular? Hoffman wondered. If Jeremiah was Dillman, which seemed increasingly likely, he had a decades-old connection to the Dorfler family. Walter and Dillman's German mother, Frieda, were probably brother and sister. Hoffman had persuaded the Gerhardts to allow him to copy the photograph of the four young people, promising to return it promptly.

Hoffman knew Dorfler got his start after the war as a young executive with the Bavarian Motor Works in Munich, eventually becoming president of the company. He also became a major stockholder in both Adidas and Siemens, two other internationally known German companies.

"Herr Dorfler lives in Munich, I know, but where is his daughter, Katrina?" Hoffman had asked the Gerhardts.

"She lives in Nuremberg," Herr Gerhardt had said, "where she works for *Neu Deutschland.*"

Dorfler had flirted openly with many fascist groups, but Hoffman had been unaware until now that he had any proprietary interest in *Neu Deutschland*, as suggested by his daughter's employment.

Hoffman dropped his cigarette on the sidewalk and snubbed it out as his CIA colleagues arrived by car and parked across the street. He went into the bank building and walked up the stairs to the second floor.

He entered the offices of *Neu Deutschland* and asked for Katrina Dorfler, knowing she wasn't there since they'd had her apartment and office under surveillance for several days. *The whole family probably has gone underground*, he thought. Hoffman left a manila envelope for Katrina, however.

The envelope contained a copy of the photograph of Katrina, Emma, Johanna, and Jeremiah, and a note that read: "Katrina, I need your help. Miranda was killed by the FBI. I suppose Walter told you. I have come back to Nuremberg and must talk with your father, but I find his apartment is under surveillance. Can you help me? You know only I would have this photograph. Meet me at our favorite restaurant before seven tonight. Love, Trent."

At the end of the day, when the *Neu Deutschland* office closed, CIA agents followed each of its staff members. Shortly after 6:00 P.M., Katrina appeared at the apartment of a co-worker. She stayed only briefly and then drove back into the walled city to a Greek restaurant near the southwest gate, possibly the "favorite restaurant." She parked her car and went inside, but exited shortly thereafter.

As she walked toward her car, the Mercedes pulled alongside her and stopped. Hoffman got out and said, "Jeremiah asks that you accompany us."

"Who are you?"

"A friend of New America."

"He said he'd meet me here."

"The plan has changed. Security precautions."

"Why should I trust you?"

Hoffman shrugged. "I'll tell Jeremiah you wouldn't come."

With only a brief hesitation, Katrina Dorfler naively got into the backseat and Hoffman slipped in beside her.

They drove northwest from the walled city to the suburb of Fürth, and only when the driver entered the American army post did Katrina understand what had happened to her. Hoffman restrained her as she tried to open the door and jump out.

They drove to the American hospital where wounded troops, downed pilots, and hostages from America's imperial adventures had been taken for decades, to be medically treated and debriefed before being flown home. Today a patient would undergo drug intervention in one of its treatment rooms.

One of the American team members stood behind Katrina's chair, his hands placed firmly on her shoulders. She had black hair, a good figure, and an interesting face, Hoffman thought. As she watched the syringes being prepared, he saw panic in her face, although she said nothing. That silence and her overall proud bearing indicated to Hoffman that she understood her fate and accepted it.

After various chemicals flowed into her blood vein via an intravenous line, a balding U.S. Army major wearing combat fatigues began the questioning.

"Do you know the terrorist called Jeremiah?"

"Yes."

"When did you meet him?"

"In the summer of nineteen-eighty."

"Where?"

"Here, in Nuremberg."

"Did you live here then?"

"No."

"Where did you live?"

"In Munich, with my mother."

"But you were visiting your father here?"

"Yes."

"Who introduced you to Jeremiah?"

"My father."

"Was Jeremiah an American?"

"Yes."

"What was his name then?"

"Trent Dillman."

The major smiled triumphantly and looked at the others, including Hoffman, who chewed gum furiously.

"Are you related by blood to Trent Dillman?"

"Yes, he is my first cousin."

"Did Trent Dillman meet you first, or your cousin Emma Dietze?"

"I introduced Trent to Emma."

Everyone in the room shook their heads in amazement.

"And did Trent Dillman travel with you and your father to your family chalet in Garmisch that fall in 1980?"

"Yes."

"And did your father and Trent Dillman fake his death in Austria in October of that year?"

Her body tensed, she frowned and shook her head, but the chemicals penetrated her defenses. "Yes," she admitted.

With Dorfler's money and influence, that hadn't been difficult, Hoffman thought.

The major threw in a wild-card question. "Were you in love with Trent Dillman?"

"Yes."

"Where did Trent Dillman go, after he was thought to be dead?"

Katrina looked confused.

The major rephrased his question. "Did Trent Dillman stay with your family, studying with your father?"

"Yes."

"For how many years?"

"Five or six."

"Then he returned to the United States?"

"No."

"Where did he go?"

"To the Far East. China, Russia, and Japan."

"And then he went to the United States?"

"Yes, where he lived with Emma until she was killed."

The major looked at the video camera. "Did your father and Jeremiah plan a terrorist campaign to be carried out in the United States?"

"Yes."

"For what reason?"

"To break it apart."

"And is it their plan to use nuclear weapons in their terrorist campaign?"

The drugs could only make her tell the truth, Hoffman knew.

"I don't know."

"Where is your father?"

"I don't know."

They hadn't told her everything, Hoffman thought. The CIA now had its evidence, although none of it could be made public or used in court. Dorfler was Jeremiah's controller. They'd hatched this plan over decades. It involved the eventual use of nuclear weapons, presumably to force the American government to allow the existence of a secessionist state within its borders.

Now that we know everything, can we do anything to stop it? Hoffman wondered. At any rate, his role was over. He wondered where they'd send him next.

29

Jeremiah watched through the window of his oceanfront villa as the nearly nude woman walked across the concrete apron of the swimming pool, the clicking of her high heels amplified in the stillness at dawn, when the sun had barely peeked above the Atlantic Ocean horizon. Even the usually noisy seagulls had their heads tucked under their wings.

She wore a white cowboy hat, white bikini bottom, a white pistol-and-holster set, and white boots. Red was the complementary color of the hatband and the intricate design on her holster set and boots. The threads in the tassels dangling from the nipples of her bare breasts were red, white, and blue.

He watched as she stood in front of the door of a nearby villa, adjusted her hat and boobs, and knocked. Presently a middle-aged man with disheveled gray hair and sleep on his face opened the door. He brightened considerably at the sight of this beautiful messenger.

Jeremiah saw the woman begin a song-and-dance routine, which he couldn't hear clearly, although he understood the procedure. Then she reached for the holsters, but came up not with pistols but banded one-hundred-dollar bills. The man in the villa accepted the cash, a conversation ensued, and the woman went into the villa and closed the door.

Later that afternoon, Jeremiah saw the man again, this time on the hotel property located across the intercoastal waterway where the original hotel stood. Built in the 1920s in a Spanish architectural style, the hotel's perfectly manicured grounds included tall palm trees and flowering bushes, as well as an elaborate maze of enclosed walkways and secluded courtyards. Guests could walk to a nearby championship golf course.

Jeremiah mingled with a crowd attending the inaugural cocktail party of the Safe Use Tobacco Institute convention, held each December in Florida at the Boca Raton Ocean View Hotel and Resort. Guests gathered around a pool adjacent to a two-story convention center.

Clay Howard, Speaker of the House of Representatives, and three dozen other congressmen had accepted invitations to the convention. In fact, Jeremiah also saw Howard's early morning visitor, who had on more clothes, although her mission hadn't changed. "Cigarette girls" such as her circulated among the tobacco lobbyists and their mostly male guests, providing smokes and anything else a gentleman might want.

Jeremiah walked about freely without fear of being recognized. A makeup genius had added wrinkles and age to his face and dyed his hair white. He wore white golfing shoes, green pants, and an oversized shirt that accommodated a prosthetic device that gave him the appearance of having a humped back. He walked with the aid of a cane and had a large, old-fashioned hearing aid looped over one ear. He'd rented a real seventy-year-old woman to play the role of his wife this afternoon. Few people paid them any attention as they hobbled from group to group, listening to the various discussions. Anytime someone spoke to them, Jeremiah pretended not to understand a word.

As Jeremiah listened, Howard talked with three tobacco lobbyists, all of whom smoked either cigarettes or large cigars.

"Mr. Speaker, you represent a tobacco state."

"The great state of Mississippi," Howard answered.

"Then you know how all this restrictive legislation is killing our business and throwing people out of work."

"There're things that can be done if you boys just keep providing grease for the machinery," Howard said, drawing deeply on his cigar.

"But the majority of people seem to support this legislation," another lobbyist said. "Especially laws to restrict advertising directed at teenagers."

"If teenagers don't take up the habit, we're dead over the long run."

"You boys got to look to other markets. The American people don't want you giving them lung cancer, but they don't give a shit about the Chinese, for example."

"And there's five times as many of them!"

"Mr. Speaker, what we need is language in trade

agreements forcing the Chinese and other countries to open up their markets to us.''

Howard looked around the pool. ''Well, I'm with you boys and so are a lot of my colleagues. Hell, there's twelve committee chairmen here from the House and the Senate. You treat them right and they'll take care of you.''

Tomorrow SUTI's annual golf tournament would be held, Jeremiah knew. Invited guests, which included members of Congress, the administration, cabinet officials, and carefully selected journalists, received a new bag of clubs upon reporting for their first tee time. He'd been told a side pocket contained cash: for first-timers, usually ten thousand dollars; for someone as important as Clay Howard, as much as a hundred grand. As the Speaker of the House could attest, that wasn't the end of the free gifts, either.

The nearby two-story convention center contained meeting rooms, an exhibit area, and a great hall that could be arranged for speaker meetings, luncheons, and a kick-off dinner and dance. One side of the great hall opened onto a swimming pool and outdoor bar.

Various organizations annually rented booths to display their products and dispense information about ''safe'' tobacco use. Jeremiah tottered through the exhibit hall, looking at the tobacco company booths, which provided information about manufacturing techniques designed to make smoking more healthful. Others detailed their many ''good neighbor'' activities at local, state, and national levels. They had established soup kitchens to feed the poor, funded a new scientific research building on a college campus, and sponsored a major NASCAR event.

Research organizations made available at their exhibits copies of ''scientific'' studies funded by SUTI that ''proved'' tobacco use was perfectly safe. Polling organizations made available the results of opinion surveys (again, funded by SUTI) that documented the profound enjoyment many people derived from using tobacco products.

Jeremiah viewed the convention program posted on a central bulletin board. Speakers or panel discussions would address such topics as how to deal with the biased, liberal news media; plans to expand foreign sales of tobacco products; advertising messages that worked; and, most important, legislation pending in Congress that could be helpful or harmful to the industry. In fact, Speaker Howard would hold forth on that very subject this evening, right after dinner in the great hall.

After Jeremiah's "wife" disappeared out a side door, the prophet approached the exhibit area registration desk, where a young woman sat. With a shaky hand he presented several papers, including a receipt acknowledging his payment weeks earlier of one thousand dollars to rent exhibit space over the three-day convention.

''Filters Recycling Company,'' the registration clerk said. ''We're glad to have you exhibiting here for the first time.''

''My pleasure,'' Jeremiah said, loudly.

''Let me show you to your exhibit site.''

She led the way, and Jeremiah shuffled along behind. In the exhibit area, Jeremiah's young assistant stood beside a cart loaded high with boxes. Even in these perilous times, security at the convention primarily targeted party crashers and other unauthorized guests, including photographers trying to snap a candid shot of some cigarette girl sucking up to a bigwig.

Wearing an approved exhibitor's badge, Jeremiah's helper had parked a van in an unloading area off the hotel's driveway, unloaded the boxes, and rolled them through an unlocked door leading into the convention center.

"How's this work?" the young woman asked, as Jeremiah's assistant began unloading boxes stamped with the word BUTTWIPE.

"Huh? Oh, how's it work. Butts Used Ten Times Will Increasingly Preserve the Environment. BUTTWIPE."

"You mean reusing the filter paper requires less logging of trees?"

"Something like that. Here's one of our butt cans."

"What do I do with it?"

"What? Oh, you snub your butts out in this can, snap it shut, and put it in one of our mailers." Jeremiah adopted a stern look. "No lipstick-smudged butts, young lady."

The young woman looked skeptically at the address on the mailer: BUTTWIPE, c/o The Smoke House, 1600 Pennsylvania Avenue, Washington, D.C. She shook her head and left.

Four boxes contained the exhibit materials, and the other nineteen boxes the RDX left over from the San Diego burglary that provided the military explosives used to blow up the New York Stock Exchange. Explanatory labels had been attached to these boxes: "Pool Chemicals, for Use by Certified Technicians Only."

Jeremiah's assistant pushed the cart across the hallway into the great room, where the wait staff prepared for this evening's dinner, speech, and dance, scheduled to begin at 7:00 P.M. He watched his assistant put the boxes into the storage space underneath the stage, placing them on several long carts that ordinarily held dining chairs. A radio-controller battery would spark the explosion.

"Check the boxes now and then to make certain no one gets curious," Jeremiah said. "About seven, walk away three or four blocks and set it off."

"Okay, boss."

Jeremiah ambled toward the water taxi that would take him to his oceanfront villa, where he planned to pack and check out.

A half hour before the blast, Jeremiah used a pay phone in Fort Lauderdale to call a computer in Little Rock that called Laura at UBC headquarters in Virginia.

"You're early; the show doesn't start for another two and a half hours," Laura said.

"Is it about me?"

"It certainly is. We're going to parallel your activities with those of Adolf Hitler. You remember him? He wrote a book outlining the Third Reich that would last a thousand years. Kinda like your book and Bible verse. He rounded up criminals and nonwhites and those who didn't agree with him and put them in concentration camps, where they were burned and gassed. He used bombs on other nations."

"No, no," Jeremiah said, trying to sound exasperated. "New America will be a theocracy, not a fascist or communist state. You people just can't get beyond your traditional bugaboos. Look to the Old Testament leaders, such as Joshua and David, for appropriate parallels. I am not out to conquer lands and people, but rather I am here to lead the true believers to the promised land."

"Like that murdering nut Ronald Pollard?"

Jeremiah laughed into the receiver. "Pollard did have his idiosyncrasies. Too bad Steve doesn't know something about computers."

"Don't bother to call in tonight," Laura snapped. "I won't take your call."

"I have a much better story for you. Representative government is something I won't allow in New America. It's just another way for the rich and the self-appointed aristocracy to line their pockets and screw the people."

"Who elected you God's spokesman?"

"In New America we'll have direct democracy over the Internet."

"You're going to jail, not New America."

"Another bomb is set to go off," he whispered into the phone.

"What? Where?"

"In Florida. I'd suggest you get a UBC helicopter up in the air between Miami and West Palm Beach. That way you'll have exclusive coverage of the blast itself, which I guarantee you will be most spectacular."

He heard Laura's voice quake. "Who are you killing this time?"

"People who deserve it even more than the evil people who were the objects of my previous demonstrations."

"Can you be more specific?"

"See if you can figure it out, Laura. Their lives are in your hands." Jeremiah hung up.

30

Jeremiah purposely hadn't given her enough time, although Laura had immediately called Steve.

"It wasn't your fault," Steve said the next day. "He was just being cruel and heartless. We tried frantically to identify the target and had actually zeroed in on the SUTI convention, but it was too late. If anyone's to blame, it's the congressmen who went to great lengths to hide their attendance."

Still, Laura felt guilty about the deaths of nearly five hundred people. Among the thirty-one dead congressmen were twelve committee chairmen—the so-called "Cardinals of Congress"—the House Democratic whip, the assistant Republican majority leader in the Senate, and the Senate chaplain.

Thanks to quick action by Mel Crawford, a UBC news helicopter filmed the blast. Laura knew Mel thought it another UBC coup, but he had the good taste to not tell her that.

"What do you think about the president's response?" Steve asked.

"I think it's necessary," Laura said.

President Carpenter had declared a national emergency. Citing his oath of office as requiring him to "protect and defend the Constitution of the United States," Carpenter promulgated martial law in the District of Columbia, and positioned federal troops at key points in Washington, as well as at various approaches to the city, just in case Jeremiah planned other political assassinations.

Many governors followed suit and activated the National Guard, stationing troops around government facilities, military posts and installations, and financial institutions.

"It's this business about suspending habeas corpus that has people all worked up," Steve said. "It was last done at the start of the Civil War."

"Congress didn't hesitate, though. For the next six months you guys can arrest and detain indefinitely anyone suspected of committing or supporting terrorism," Laura said. "You don't even have to bring charges in court."

"I already feel the power," Steve joked. "But an appeal has been filed with the Supreme Court."

"My sources tell me the Court's going to shelve that appeal for exactly six months. Everyone wants Jeremiah caught, whatever the price."

President Carpenter invited Laura to the White House for an exclusive interview to be broadcast at the beginning of Thursday evening's *American Chronicle*. Other news organizations protested this show of favoritism, but Laura knew the White House read poll results. A majority of Americans looked to Laura and UBC for the definitive news coverage of Jeremiah's activities.

The opening camera shot from the pillared colonnade outside the Oval Office showed President Carpenter sitting behind a walnut desk. Photographs of his family had been placed on a credenza in front of a window framed with gold curtains and flanked by the American and presidential flags. Dressed in a dark suit and a red-white-and-blue-patterned tie, the president sat at an angle so he could speak directly to Laura, seated to the side of the desk. Two cameras would film the interview from different angles.

Laura had given a great deal of thought to the interview. While she might preach journalistic integrity and responsibility to Mel Crawford when it served her purpose, she knew that journalists, in conducting interviews, indulged their personal and political beliefs, whether unconsciously or by design. The very nature of the interview process could make it either an inquisition or a fireside chat, depending on the questions and the attitude of the interviewer.

This evening Laura had a twofold agenda. She wanted Carpenter to be successful—to be presidential and to rally the nation to his support. And she wanted to debunk all the myths surrounding Jeremiah.

"Mr. President, thank you for speaking to us this evening," Laura began. "As you can imagine, the American people are greatly concerned about the steady escalation of terrorist activities over the past three months, especially the bombing of the New York Stock Exchange, and now the bombing of this convention in Florida where so many of our congressional leaders died. Jeremiah seems intent on undermining the economic and political foundations of the United States.

"Isn't it also true that your administration has uncovered evidence that Jeremiah may be attempting to smuggle two atomic bombs into the country, presumably to be used for blackmail purposes?"

Carpenter, obviously champing at the bit throughout this introduction, eagerly responded, "Laura, our intelligence services have confirmed that two nuclear weapons were stolen recently from a former Soviet air base in the Ukraine. The Ukrainian government already has arrested dozens of individuals involved in the theft."

"And were these bombs smuggled out of the Ukraine?"

"Yes, they were."

"Do you know their present location?"

"No, we don't," Carpenter admitted, while projecting confidence. "But we will find them, and the American people need have no fear that these nuclear weapons will ever enter America. We will take the same extraordinary measures to intercept them as if they had been fired at us from abroad. Furthermore, any nation that aids these terrorists in any way will be considered to have launched a nuclear attack on the United States."

Laura looked concerned. "Mr. President, what does that mean?"

Carpenter stared menacingly at the camera. "If a foreign country helps deliver these bombs to American soil, directly or indirectly, I will order our military forces to respond in kind. The United States always has reserved the right to use nuclear weapons to defend our national sovereignty. I might add that our military forces worldwide are currently on their highest level of alert."

Laura smiled, pleased with his response. "All right, sir, let's attempt to pinpoint any foreign involvement in Jeremiah's terrorist campaign. I'm informed that the FBI suspects Jeremiah is really one Trent Dillman of Sioux Falls, South Dakota, who allegedly died nearly fifteen years ago during a skiing accident in Austria. Can you confirm his identity, Mr. President?"

"I can, Laura. Jeremiah and Trent Dillman are one and the same."

"Can you tell us the relationship between Trent Dillman and Walter Dorfler, a well-known German businessman with ties to many right-wing organizations?"

President Carpenter inhaled slightly as he prepared to unravel a complicated mystery. "Walter Dorfler is Trent Dillman's uncle. We have irrefutable evidence linking Dorfler to the theft of the two nuclear weapons in the Ukraine. He also appears to be affiliated with the New Covenant, an international organization linked to many terrorist causes. In fact, he may have founded that group."

"So Trent Dillman, who became Jeremiah, spent fifteen years conspiring with his uncle and other fascists about this terrorist campaign in the United States."

"Yes. These facts certainly put the lie to Jeremiah's allegation that God inspired him to form a New America. Jeremiah is nothing more than a calculating terrorist and murderer attempting to organize a cult following and establish a breakaway state. Anyone who believes him, supports him, or follows him is a fool and a traitor."

Strong words that not all of the president's advi-

sers support, Laura knew. But true, nevertheless. "Do you know the whereabouts of Walter Dorfler at this time?"

"No, Laura. Dorfler has disappeared, but the German government is cooperating in every way possible with the United States to apprehend this man. And, I must add, there is no evidence whatsoever to link Dorfler with anyone in the German government."

Laura pressed the point. "Is there any evidence linking Jeremiah to any other foreign government or a terrorist organization operating with the blessing of a foreign government?"

"Not any *clear* evidence," Carpenter emphasized, "but I can assure you the CIA and military intelligence are investigating all such leads. If any linkages are found, the United States will immediately confront the government in question. It will be very interesting to find out exactly where Jeremiah has been all these years he was pretending to be dead. We know one of his close friends, Vernon Monroe, spent many years in the Far East."

Well done, Laura thought. The president's words would surely put the fear of God into the Chinese, North Koreans, and others. "When we come back, Mr. President, I want to talk some more about the New Covenant."

When the commercial ended, the camera came up on Laura chatting amiably with the president. Befitting this somber occasion, she wore a dark blue suit highlighted by a simple strand of pearls. By design, her lipstick and red earrings completed this subtle patriotic ensemble.

"Mr. President, you've linked Trent Dillman, aka

Jeremiah, to the German fascist Walter Dorfler, who, as you said, may have founded the New Covenant, a terrorist support group that has been very active in the United States. In fact, they've extensively publicized Jeremiah's campaign by indirectly establishing and maintaining a Web site on the Internet, Jeremiah2.com. What is being done about this organization?''

Carpenter's face clouded over. ''Several weeks ago we raided their offices in Seattle, and the information gained by the FBI in that raid greatly aided us in identifying Jeremiah and linking him to Dorfler and the stolen atomic bombs.''

''Will the FBI now arrest anyone connected with the New Covenant?''

''Anyone directly connected, yes, including Adam Doyle, who apparently heads the organization in this country.''

Laura briefly touched her chin with her hand, indicating a dilemma. ''The problem seems to be that so many people have innocently contacted this Web site and discussed on-line Jeremiah's various ideas and pronouncements. Some even attended town meetings sponsored by the New Covenant. Are these people guilty of aiding and abetting terrorism?''

''That's a very difficult question, Laura, and the answer depends on what they actually did.'' President Carpenter looked as if he were about to teach a class on democracy and politics. ''You see, if you're a Ronald Pollard and you get on the Internet and say you'll do anything to help Jeremiah achieve his goals, including allowing terrorists to carry explosives into the New York Stock Exchange, then you've obviously committed a crime.''

"Yes," Laura prompted.

"If you get on-line through your computer and say those stockbrokers deserved to die in that explosion, that's deplorable, but it's also free speech in a democratic society."

"But should these people fear arrest and detention, as would be possible through Congress's suspension of habeas corpus?"

"Not unless they engage in violence or treasonous acts," the president said. "In a democracy, you can say what you please and vote for any candidate or political party you choose, but you can't shoot, hang, bomb, maim, or kill people, or threaten to violently overthrow the government." He paused and added, "And good, decent Americans shouldn't even lend tacit support to such violence."

"Let's continue discussing this whole issue of democratic dissent," Laura said. "First, Jeremiah has made great use of the Internet, which is largely beyond the control of the United States government, isn't it?"

"Absolutely!" Carpenter replied. "There's no greater evidence that we live in a global village. Internet communications can arise anywhere in the world and be transmitted anywhere there are telephone lines, regardless of national borders. We need an international convention to regulate the content of the Internet in the same way the Federal Communications Commission regulates the content of shows on your television network, Laura."

"But right now, there's nothing our government can do to prevent Internet users from continuing to promote Jeremiah's cause," Laura asserted. "Even if the government disrupts Jeremiah2.com, some other organization or person can publicize Jeremiah's Bible verse and his various exhortations from another site on the Internet.''

"That's true," Carpenter conceded, "but we're going to be carefully monitoring Internet activity and contacting people we believe have overstepped the bounds of propriety in this critical time."

Laura shook her head. "That's what's bothering a lot of people about this suspension of habeas corpus. They fear it will allow a witch hunt designed particularly to stifle democratic dissent."

"That's simply not true, and the courts and Congress will not allow it. We have too long a tradition of democracy in this country."

"How large a following do you think Jeremiah has nationally?" Laura asked, the concern in her voice both obvious and heartfelt.

"This character may have strung together a loose coalition of religious extremists, racists, anarchists, fascists, and others on the fringes of society," Carpenter said, with distaste, as if he were speaking directly to those very members of the viewing audience, "but they're not going to carve out a New America on this continent. Not unless they plan to defeat the military forces of the United States on a field of battle." Carpenter smiled tightly and nodded once for punctuation, as if to put the fear of God into Jeremiah's "supporters" while soothing the fears of the general public.

"Mr. President, I understand a private organization called American Patriots has announced a reward fund to be paid for information leading to Jeremiah's arrest. That fund has now been doubled once again to twenty million dollars. Can you tell us who make up the American Patriots?''

''My office will release a list of names tomorrow, Laura. Basically, contributors range from citizens contributing five dollars to major corporations donating tens of thousands of dollars. What they have in common is a love of the United States, as it is.''

''Mr. President, is there anything else you have to say to the nation this evening?''

Carpenter squared away behind his desk to look directly into the camera's lens. ''I ask you, the American people, to remain calm. There is no reason to panic. We are faced with a crisis, but our nation's very existence and our individual freedoms have been challenged many times before. The enemies of the United States have learned that once the fury of the American people is aroused, the forces of evil opposing us are always routed and destroyed. That will also be the case with Jeremiah the terrorist, and his supporters at home and abroad. Freedom is at stake, and in this fight you and your government are one and the same. We will bring to this battle every weapon at our disposal.

''If you have any information to help us catch the terrorist Jeremiah, or if you know anything about the stolen nuclear weapons, please call the eight hundred number appearing on your television screen. Through the grace of a loving and forgiving God, we will find the mass murderer called Jeremiah and bring him to justice. God bless America. Thank you and good evening.''

*   *   *

After a commercial, Laura appeared alone outside the Oval Office, the night lit brightly by television lights.

"In an exclusive and extraordinary interview tonight on UBC, President Carpenter shared with the American people much new information about the terrorist Jeremiah, and promised to bring him to justice soon," Laura said. "In the second half of *American Chronicle*, we will seek reaction to the president's speech from a variety of expert analysts, as well as a sampling of our viewers, who can call in or contact us on-line at the numbers and E-mail address shown on your screen.

"Right now UBC will present a tribute to those who died in the bombing two days ago in Boca Raton, Florida."

The tribute, heavily skewed to Speaker Howard and the other dead politicians, began with UBC's exclusive, spectacular helicopter footage of the blast.

31

In a reversal of pattern, an airplane flying over Boca Raton the morning after the bombing dropped pamphlets containing the fifth chapter of *The Book of Second Jeremiah*.

When interviewed later that day by the FBI, the pilot said he usually didn't read the flyers he regularly dumped on the coastal area, since most contained food and beverage advertising. He only vaguely remembered the man who'd paid cash for the service.

Someone on the ground who picked up the pamphlet immediately posted it on the Internet, for "discussion purposes."

THE BOOK OF SECOND JEREMIAH

CHAPTER FIVE

¹ No Man is a greater abomination than he who abuses the public trust, sayeth the LORD. For these Evil creatures, those wielding the LORD's sword will be swift and certain in their purpose.

² Washington, capital of the united states, is

the modern-day equivalent of the Whore Babylon, sayeth the LORD, and the Evil that taketh root there is Greed, Overweening Pride, and the Lust for Power.

3 The LORD sayeth:

Invest in some Men the power to make decisions,
and power blinds them to the true needs of the people;
greed and lust overwhelm purpose and compassion,
and the only constituency they represent is Evil.

4 But should there be no government? asketh Jeremiah. The LORD sayeth, in response:

Government is a necessary function of a civilized society,
but it should be severely limited in scope, enforcing
God's law, not making Man's law; providing for the
common defense and planning economic priorities.
Government cannot do for Man what Man will not do for
himself. Observing God's law is the path to Paradise.

Political power corrupts a Man and
sows divisions among Men;
therefore, government is best that is direct and not
representative. All New Americans can
vote on issues not
decided by God, and the majority vote
shall prevail.

5 Man-made declarations, constitutions, con-
tracts, laws, and regulations should not be cast in
stone, revered, and used to guide the nation into
a future that is not the past. Only God's Word is
immutable!

6 The only contract Man need concern himself
with keeping is set forth in the Bible, including
the Social Contract of Second Jeremiah. This pre-
scribes a life of goodness, values, equality, fairness, obedience, and order, and it is the Word of
God!

7 New America, the Chosen Land, will be
formed and commanded by Jeremiah the Second,
who will be the Law and interpret the Law, so
sayeth the LORD.

8 The LORD sayeth:

In a system of bartering one's labor for
essential goods,
the lack of money, and the unnecessary
practice of

appropriating tax money, will eliminate the basis of much

Evil and the reason for most government activity.

A tax on wealth produced by labor is an absurdity, for no

Man can own another, nor the product of his labor.

9 The LORD sayeth:

Unlike its predecessor, the united states of america,

New America will emphasize the duties of its citizens,

which are to abide by God's Law, live the life of Christ,

care for the family, educate one's self to the fullest,

and yield not to the Evil that lurks in the human breast.

Do this and your rewards will be beyond expectation.

10 From duties are derived certain rights, sayeth the LORD, which include the right to work and live in a society of values and the right to espouse those values, to expect that the rule of God will prevail and that social order will be kept, to live free of fear and crime, and to avoid

exploitation by marketplace manipulators and rapacious politicians.

11 The LORD sayeth:

There is no unlimited right of free speech,
any more than a sensible person would allow
a maniac to yell fire in a crowded place, or an Evil man
to bring into question the Word of God.
12 The cult of the personal car will be restricted in New
America because it is destructive to the environment
and related to excessive pride, rampant individualism, and
the division of Men by money. Public transportation,
walking, and bicycling accomplish the same purpose whilst
promoting humility, neighborliness, and good health.

13 Those accused of crimes against their fellow Man or the state shall not enjoy a presumption of innocence, nor be entitled to a trial by a jury of fellow citizens; the determination of guilt or innocence shall be made by impartial tribunals of

legal experts, who must abide by God's law or Jeremiah's interpretation of law.

14 There is no right of immigration into New America, since citizenship can only be earned and can be taken away if one succumbs to Evil.

15 Those who violate the Social Contract can be expelled from New America, along with their families.

16 The LORD's commandment is: Thou Shalt Not Kill; therefore, no private citizen of New America has the right to carry on his person a weapon, be it a knife or a gun or anything that can be used to harm another, unless that citizen becomes a member of New America's state police or armed forces. Only God orders Men to be killed, and the LORD speaks only through Jeremiah in this generation of Men.

32

Three hundred miles east of Cape Hatteras, Jeremiah piloted the yacht *Exodus* toward a rendezvous with the Indonesian freighter *Semarang*, which sailed from Constanţa, Romania, on December 12.

Just before sunset on the seventeenth, the ship's crane hoisted a crate out of its hold and swung it over the side, lowering it onto the bow of the yacht. On the gently rolling ocean, the transfer went smoothly, which Jeremiah considered a good omen. In treacherous seas, it would have been a difficult task.

He watched the *Semarang* resume steaming north toward the Gulf of Saint Lawrence, where she would ease upriver to Quebec City. There the other half of the cargo would be unloaded and trucked overland through Quebec and Ontario provinces and eventually into New America, heretofore known as the Dakotas. Uncle Walter would supervise that operation.

"About twelve to fourteen hours, did you say?" Adam Doyle asked, standing beside Jeremiah in the enclosed wheelhouse.

"We'll enter the mouth of Chesapeake Bay about

dawn tomorrow." Jeremiah looked disdainfully at Doyle. "Do you plan to worry all night long?"

"Probably! Christ, look around you!" the former army major said, fear etched in his face.

Jeremiah knew Doyle hadn't had a moment's peace of mind since President Carpenter had threatened on national television to arrest him. Furthermore, as they sailed west toward the mainland, the weather had changed. Using a sophisticated on-board radar system, the crew tracked a storm now centered in Alabama. By nightfall this northeaster would generate rains and high winds in their path. Even now the winds grew in intensity and churned the waves.

"Relax," Jeremiah told Doyle. "Have some coffee."

"Will we have any problem getting into the bay?" Doyle asked.

"Certainly. You watched the president's address. The Coast Guard will be on high alert, although our people in Europe and the Middle East tried to divert their attention with a disinformation campaign."

"What do you mean?"

"Rumors circulated that the bombs left Odessa in the hold of the *Lysander* and were transferred to a commercial airline in Tripoli. Security in the United States is therefore concentrated on airports."

"How will we get by the Coast Guard?"

"Let me worry about that. Why don't you go below and sleep."

"I can't."

"If they stopped us short of the coast, we could always threaten to detonate the bomb at sea," Jeremiah said, toying with Doyle.

"How would we get away?"

"Personal sacrifices would have to be made, Adam."

The horrified look on Doyle's face caused Jeremiah to break out laughing. "Of course, I'm not going to do that. Don't worry, we'll get the bomb to its proper location. Do you want to know where that's at?"

"No," Doyle said, slopping coffee into a cup while trying to find his sea legs.

Jeremiah told him, anyway. "We'll transfer it to a van, drive the van into Washington, D.C., and park it on Pennsylvania Avenue, halfway between the White House and Capitol Hill. We'll retreat to a mountain hideout several hundred miles away and conduct the negotiations."

"That's good."

"It's a one-megaton bomb, about five times the size of the bomb the Americans dropped on Nagasaki. Our scientific friends have prepared a computer simulation of the damage. The initial explosion would create a crater two hundred feet deep and a thousand feet in diameter."

"I had no idea."

"The explosion will destroy all the symbols of the American republic, leveling all buildings within a radius of a mile and a half, including the White House, Capitol Building, Supreme Court, Smithsonian Museums, National Archives, Department of Justice, and Washington Monument. And the FBI building. Let's hope Steve Wallace and Peter Thompson are at work that day."

"I'd like to personally kill that bastard Wallace."

Privately Jeremiah agreed. He'd have to make certain Laura wasn't at her UBC office across the Potomac, because the winds, flying debris, and "overpressure" generated by the atomic blast would damage buildings as far as seven miles away, causing fires and secondary explosions.

"The atomic blast will kill everyone within a half-mile radius of the bomb and inflict five percent casualties up to five miles away," Jeremiah said. "Given the District's population of over six hundred thousand people, and another quarter of a million commuters and tourists, there'll be several hundred thousand dead, including the president and that pack of hyenas on Capitol Hill.

"And it gets even better, Adam. Depending on the speed and direction of the wind, I'm told that radiation fallout over a ten-day period will eventually kill everyone remaining in a downwind area ninety miles long and ten miles wide. Another fifty percent could die as far away as one hundred fifty miles if they stay in the area for three weeks. With a nice north-easterly wind like that predicted over the next few days, we could contaminate Baltimore and Philadelphia.

"Given the possibility of all this death and destruction, do you think President Carpenter will grant our demands, Adam?"

"Unless he's crazy."

"They're simple enough. We'll show them how to disarm the bomb if they allow our mercenary forces to occupy U.S. military facilities located in New America's territory. That would provide our forces with state-of-the-art weapons of war, including artillery, tanks, aircraft, and more nuclear weapons. I'm especially covetous of Ellsworth Air Force Base outside Rapid City."

"What's there?"

"Two dozen B1 stealth bombers. We'll fit them with nuclear weapons and New America will become a world military power overnight."

"You think it will work?"

Jeremiah shook his head. Doyle, obviously a doubting Thomas, stuck with the program only because he hoped to achieve money and power. What did Doyle think he'd be in New America? Mayor of a city? A high-ranking military officer? *The very nature of man will cause New America to be infected with the same diseases that crippled old America,* Jeremiah knew. He'd have a lot of housecleaning to do in the new nation.

"Of course it'll work. It's a historical imperative. Always bet on change, Adam. It's the one constant of the universe."

"How'd you get involved in this?"

"God called me," Jeremiah said, sternly, and couldn't help but smile at the look of horror on Doyle face as he realized his slip of tongue.

"I'm sorry," Doyle said.

Jeremiah sipped from his coffee and looked out at the night sea. He could turn the helm over to one of the expert sailors within the crew, but he knew he couldn't sleep. He wanted to pilot the boat until the sunrise formed a halo around his head, announcing the arrival of a new king in the Americas. Doyle was someone to talk to.

"Walter planned all this, of course. It amounts to his life's work. There are many elements in place that would astound our enemies. Alliances Walter formed over decades with dissident groups and organizations throughout the world. Europe, the Middle

East, the Far East, South America. Walter was among the first to see the power of the computer, and he had people creating information bases decades ago. The names of dissident individuals and groups. Sympathetic politicians. Mercenaries, terrorists, criminals. Greedy businessmen." Jeremiah smiled at Doyle. "People who could steal atomic bombs."

"And all these people will come to New America?"

"Let's hope we attract a better citizen base. That's what our recent campaign was about, including your public meetings, Adam."

"Oh, yeah."

"One of Walter's more interesting projects is to identify budding young scientists and influence their political beliefs. He has this idea of a giant science center that will make the new nation a leader in technology and science."

"It's a good idea."

"Walter had many good ideas and the wealth to implement them. Unfortunately, it took him a lifetime to put it all together, by which time he was too old to pull it off alone. He needed a successor."

"You, his nephew."

"Yes." He wouldn't tell Doyle everything, because he didn't want anyone, other than Walter, to know all the facts. They would detract from his mythology.

His mother had married a U.S. soldier, who had returned home to the life of a carpenter and seasonal laborer in Sioux Falls, South Dakota. Back in Germany, Walter had rebuilt the family fortune lost during war.

In South Dakota it had been a hand-to-mouth existence, with his father unemployed much of the time and his German-born mother housebound with homesickness and the handicap of never quite mastering the English language. She had threatened continuously to go home to Germany, just as soon as her only son grew up. But she'd died first, a victim of back luck and poor choices. Jeremiah never forgot that lesson.

Walter had no sons, only Katrina. And his brothers and sisters produced mainly female offspring. Therefore, Walter had invited him to Europe at the same time he erased official German records of their family relationship.

"When Walter first made his proposal to me, I thought he was crazy," Jeremiah told Doyle. "Terrorist isn't exactly the first occupational choice that comes to a young man's mind."

"No, you have to live in the world awhile," Doyle said.

That's insightful, Jeremiah thought. But when he was eighteen, he couldn't have cared less about philosophy, theology, and politics. He had listened to Walter only because his uncle had money and material possessions—houses, servants, cars, sailboats. Additionally, he'd gotten to know intimately his willing, exotic female cousins, first Katrina, and then Emma Dietze. At the time, Trent would have paid any price to fuck beautiful teenagers who got off in a foreign language. And Walter hadn't cared.

In time, however, some things began to seep through. "You're right, Adam. When you get older, you start to look more closely at the world around you, and what you see makes little sense. Man is not far removed from the animals. In fact, he is in many ways the worst of all animals."

Jeremiah wondered now if Uncle Walter hadn't subtly adjusted his recruitment message when he'd found a theme that resonated with his young protégé—the message of economic equality. As a poor boy from South Dakota, he'd been on the bottom of the economic pile. He'd known that some people, including his mother and father, could never climb that mountain, no matter how smart and hardworking they were, because the current economic system required wage slaves. It had forever been the case and always would be, until revolutionary changes came about. The rich wouldn't give up their power and privileges without a fight.

In the end, however, Jeremiah had come to his calling for simpler reasons that had nothing to do with philosophy. As Walter had insightfully noted during their recent conversation in Prague, man is not a complicated animal. Trent Dillman had had to do something in the world, and this opportunity for wealth and power lay right before him. Otherwise, he'd have had to return to Sioux Falls and become a carpenter. Or sell insurance with his high school friend, Davey Schropa. It hadn't been a hard choice.

Still, life had almost gone in another direction. "I'll tell you a secret, Adam, that no one else knows."

"You can trust me, Jeremiah."

"If Emma hadn't been killed, I wouldn't be here today."

"I remember her. She was a beautiful woman. A great athlete."

Emma Dietze, his first cousin. When he and Davey

had arrived in Germany, Walter had sent his daughter, Katrina, to meet him and bring him to the chalet in Garmisch. Katrina had romantic designs on him, which he didn't reciprocate, nor fully understand. Even Walter had encouraged this relationship. Still did. Maybe he saw it as a bonding agent.

But he had loved Emma: blonde, possessed of great physical beauty, athletic prowess, and captivating charm. He could see her clearly today in his mind's eye. He'd stayed in Germany all those years "studying and training" with Walter, but really waiting for the tennis prodigy to grow up. The day after she'd won Wimbledon and turned eighteen, they'd announced their plans to marry, which Emma's parents and Walter vociferously opposed at first.

He'd traveled the tennis tour with Emma, staying always in the background. Eventually her parents had accepted them. Even Walter had agreed it was the perfect cover for Jeremiah to move about the world, meeting with other members of "the movement."

"After Emma bought a beach house in Florida, we were going to give everything up. She was twenty-five and ready to retire from tennis. I wanted out of all this. We were just going to live and let the world and all its problems go to hell."

"Did they ever catch the guys who robbed and killed Emma?" Doyle asked.

Jeremiah shook his head. Even he hadn't been able to find them in the army of criminals that occupied America. For the opportunity of killing them, he'd have burned down the entire world, and maybe would yet.

* * *

As soon as they entered American waters in the early hours of the next morning, the U.S. Coast Guard sent a message that the *Exodus* would be boarded and searched.

The yacht had picked up passengers in Fort Lauderdale on the night the tobacco industry was lit up in Boca Raton, and thereafter had sailed the Caribbean, putting in at several ports of call. Now they were ostensibly headed to Annapolis.

The 105-foot-long motor sailer, with its two masts and twin Mercedes-Benz engines, belonged to a wealthy French-Canadian—one of Jeremiah's many supporters throughout the world. Jeremiah spoke flawless French and had impeccable Canadian citizenship and identity papers.

"They're going to board us!" Doyle repeated, frantically.

"Naturally."

"They'll have our descriptions! Photographs!"

"And you were at a forward army post in Germany, with a mission to repel an invading Soviet army," Jeremiah taunted.

"I was an engineer, for God's sake!"

"Go to your cabin, Adam. Let me take care of this."

The *Exodus* had three staterooms and crew's quarters, as well as a galley and separate dining area, plus four heads. Ten skilled, well-equipped soldiers of New America, including four expert frogmen, hid below.

As they slowed their forward movement, with the Coast Guard cutter to their starboard and astern, Jeremiah watched the frogmen slip over the port side in the dark and begin their underwater swim to the cutter. Hopefully the *Exodus* reeked of so much wealth that the element of surprise would be on their side.

The boarding craft launched by the cutter lashed onto the stern of the *Exodus*, and four armed Coast Guardsmen climbed aboard.

"Gentlemen, how can we help you this evening?" Jeremiah asked, coming out the back of the wheelhouse to greet them. A recognizable French accent overlaid his English. He wanted to stand right in front of them, daring them to recognize him.

"We need to inspect your ship, sir," a young ensign replied. "We'll need to see your ship's papers, as well as passports for all passengers and crew on board."

"Proceed at your pleasure," Jeremiah said, opening his arms. The shape of his face, especially his nose, had been altered through the use of several small appliances, expertly applied by a makeup artist. He'd grown a mustache and goatee, in the style of the French. A realistic scar on his cheek made people want to look away. *Little things make a difference.*

Two Coast Guardsmen went below deck, while the other two, accompanied by four of *Exodus*'s crew, including the captain and first mate, inspected the topside. Jeremiah aimed his binoculars at the cutter, where the captain stared back at him, unaware of the frogman behind him with a knife.

When gunfire erupted on the cutter, Jeremiah's crew killed the four Guardsmen on board, using knives and automatic weapons.

Jeremiah went below and abruptly entered Doyle's stateroom, where he found himself staring at a 9-mm automatic.

"Jesus, you scared me!" Doyle explained, lowering the gun. "What happened? I heard all that gun-fire!"

"We killed them, of course. Now we have bodies to get rid of."

"Jesus!"

Jeremiah looked at Doyle with amusement and then disdain. "You shouldn't take the Lord's name in vain so often, Adam. He doesn't like it."

"I'm sorry."

"It was a nice, long talk we had last night, Adam. I haven't been so chatty in years. I suppose it's the tensions of my job."

"Everything you told me will be held in the strictest confidence, Jeremiah."

"Maybe. Give me the gun, Adam."

Doyle looked at the automatic. "Why?"

"Are you the anointed of God?"

"No."

"I am. Give me the gun."

Jeremiah watched Adam—God—make the decision. It was another test of God's plan. The Coast Guard could have won the battle topside. Adam could kill him now and take over the movement. *What does God want?*

"Okay," Doyle agreed, handing over the gun butt first.

How convenient, Jeremiah thought, as he accepted the gun and immediately shot and killed Adam Doyle. God's will.

Topside, Jeremiah yelled at his crew, "Some of you strip the uniforms off these dead Coast Guardsmen and put them on. Weight down the bodies and dump them overboard. Then get over to the cutter and sail it into the Chesapeake Bay, right ahead of us. Answer all communications you receive from Coast Guard command.''

As the *Exodus* crossed over the Chesapeake Bay Bridge Tunnel connecting Virginia Beach to the peninsular arm of Virginia, it sailed by the Hampton Roads area, within twenty land miles of the U.S. Atlantic Fleet berthed at the Norfolk Naval Base, as well as the aircraft of the First Fighter Wing at Langley Air Force Base in Hampton. Both had enough firepower to stop an invading armada, Jeremiah knew, let alone a yacht with a Coast Guard escort.

But they sailed through unchallenged, and Jeremiah ordered his men on the cutter to sail it to the mouth of the York River, scuttle it, and wait to be picked up by car.

The *Exodus* sailed toward Point Lookout, Maryland, an hour's drive south of Washington, D.C. *Nothing can stop me now*, he thought.

33

Steve found Laura in front of the White House, standing in the middle of that portion of Pennsylvania Avenue blocked off for security purposes. She and a camera crew were filming a demonstration taking place in Lafayette Park, a favorite rallying site for protesters.

"What's going on?" he asked, startling her.

"What are you doing here?"

"Looking for you. This is where your office said I'd find you."

Laura shook her head in disgust. "Can you believe this shit? There are actually people who support that bastard."

Steve watched protesters march up and down the sidewalk, waving their signs at the White House and the television cameras. One placard lumped all of Jeremiah's victims together: CROOKS, CAPITALISTS, CONGRESSMEN, CLONES. Other messages on display read: NO MARSHAL LAW; ON TO NEW AMERICA; II JEREMIAH 5:1—NO MAN IS A GREATER ABOMINATION THAN HE WHO ABUSES THE PUBLIC TRUST, SAYETH THE LORD.

"A lot of people hate the targets he's attacked,"

Steve said. "But that doesn't mean they'll follow him. This is America. They're just exercising their lungs."

"We're about done here," Laura said. "You want to go to lunch?"

"How about going to Quebec City instead?"

"Why?"

"That's where the latest lead takes me. There's a plane leaving Andrews at eleven A.M."

"They'd let you take me along?"

"I didn't ask."

"You trying to get fired?"

"What's the difference? You said you were rich."

"Filthy."

"I figure this will end soon. The public needs to know everything about Jeremiah and his supporters. This information shouldn't be locked up in the National Archives for the next hundred years."

"Let's do it. Can I bring these guys?"

"The more the merrier."

On the plane, Steve told Laura about a commando assault on the Indonesian freighter *Semarang*, presumably taking place as they talked. "The two bombs are supposed to be in the ship's hold," he said.

"Says who?"

"According to Thompson, that's the conclusion of American, British, and Israeli intelligence. It's a complicated story. Apparently Dorfler's people planted information leading everyone to believe the bombs were on board a freighter, *Lysander*, bound for Tripoli. That was part of a disinformation campaign designed to get everyone focused on Libya.''

"Meanwhile, the bombs were really on the *Semarang*?''

"Which sailed from Romania.''

"This is great news," Laura said. "The marines get the bombs back and Jeremiah becomes nothing more than a killer on the loose.''

"Let's hope so. Here's a new tidbit compliments of the CIA. They interrogated Katrina Dorfler in Nuremberg. She had a thing for the young Trent Dillman, but he threw her over for another first cousin, Emma Dietze, who at the time was fourteen.''

"Apparently Jeremiah's New World Order has nothing against inbreeding.''

"He's just trying to keep the master race within the family.''

Laura leaned back in her seat, visibly relieved at the fortuitous turn of events. "This is really a nice plane. You always travel first class.''

"Hardly. This is a Gulfstream transport the air force uses to ferry around congressmen and other VIPs.''

"Like me. I'm the justification for you getting a ride on this thing.''

"Exactly.''

She put her head on his shoulder and lowered her voice. "Let me complete the fantasy for you. Think about us in the head, thousands of feet above the ground. Me with my hands against the wall, dress up over my head, panties down around my ankles. And you standing behind me. What do you think about that?''

"I think I'd be pawing the floor, blowing smoke through my nose.''

"Take a deep breath, then, 'cause I gotta pee.''

*   *   *

They landed at the airport in the suburb of Sainte-Foy, a twenty-minute car ride into Quebec City, set high on a hill above the Saint Lawrence River and the Plains of Abraham, where a British army defeated the French general Montcalm in 1759. As Steve knew, nothing had been the same for succeeding generations of French-speaking Canadians.

While he huddled in the airport terminal with his Canadian counterparts and CIA agents, Laura and her crew rented a van to carry them and their equipment.

"Here's the deal," Steve said, coming to stand beside Laura, who straightened his tie and tried to press his rumpled dark suit with her hands. "We're going to the Île d'Orléans. A guy named Claude Dumont lives there."

"Who's he?"

"A rich French-Canadian separatist, I'm told. More important, he owns a yacht, the *Exodus*. The Coast Guard boarded this yacht shortly after dawn. Later, the Coast Guard cutter was found abandoned in a river, with its crew missing. The yacht was seized near Annapolis, but some people were seen getting off at Point Lookout, Maryland."

"Who?"

"I'm afraid to guess. I'm also afraid to think the *Semarang* and the yacht might have rendezvoused at sea."

Dumont lived in a Normandy-style manor on the Île D'Orléans, a twenty-mile-long island in the middle of the Saint Lawrence River, downstream from the city. The manor faced south, toward the main channel of the river. A Canadian cop riding with Steve and Laura explained that the island architecture and culture were throwbacks to an earlier time, with many houses dating from the seventeenth century. The island's lush orchards provided fresh produce daily to Quebec City.

Dumont's house was set back from the road several hundred yards, behind an imposing stone and iron fence. Steve got out of the van near the front gate and watched Laura and her crew shoot B-roll footage of the house. Steve smiled at the sight of Laura, who had put on calf-high leather boots and a parka to ward off the cold.

Armed with a search warrant, the Canadian police scoured the mansion. Steve interviewed the two house servants, who told him the Dumonts had packed their bags and left two days ago, saying they planned to spend the winter in their Florida condominium.

The search of the huge mansion proved equally fruitless. If Dumont lent his yacht to Jeremiah, he'd already gone underground, like Walter Dorfler.

Outside the mansion, a groundskeeper approached Steve. "You are from the United States?" the man asked, taking off his hat in an Old World sign of respect.

"Yes," Steve answered, showing his FBI identification, which the old man examined carefully.

"My two sons run a landscape and nursery business," he explained. "I help out sometimes. They got us this job." He jerked his head in the direction of the house. "My sons are like Dumont. Separatists. I was in the army. The Canadian army."

Steve heard the proud way the groundskeeper said, "Canadian."

"I voted against separatism," the old man confided, referring to a recent referendum on Quebec independence that voters narrowly defeated. "But I don't make a big thing of it with my boys. So Dumont, he thinks I'm one of them." The old man smiled slyly. "I watch what goes on."

"And?"

"Two days ago, just before the Dumonts left, they had an unusual visitor. I noticed his accent. German, I think. He was a big man."

Steve took a photograph of Walter Dorfler from his pocket and held it out for the groundskeeper to see.

"Yes, that's him."

Dorfler. Surprise, surprise! Why is he in Quebec? Why not? It's a good place from which to infiltrate the U.S., and the Semarang's destination was Quebec City.

"Did this man leave with the Dumonts?"

The groundskeeper shook his head. "No, I don't think so. I was standing out front, shoveling ice from the driveway, when the German left in his limo. I could hear him talking with Dumont. The German had a bad cough. Dumont said he would send a doctor around to his hotel."

"Do you know the Dumonts' doctor?"

The groundskeeper smiled triumphantly. "Yes, I know the doctor's name."

Steve wrote the name in his notebook, thanked the groundskeeper, and walked to the gate and the road beyond it. He had his orders, which were to cooperate with the Canadian officials, without forgetting the paramount interests of the United States. Some of the local police might have separatist sympathies and couldn't be trusted with the information about Dorfler.

"What's up?" Laura asked.

"We're leaving," Steve said, getting into the van. He used his cell phone to call the American embassy, where another CIA team waited. He told the team leader to locate Dumont's doctor and call him back. The CIA man told him only one bomb had been found aboard the Indonesian freighter.

"Where are we going?" Laura asked.

"Back into the city, while I wait for a telephone call."

An hour later, they met the CIA team in front of the Château Frontenac, built in the seventeenth century inside the old walled city as the administrative and military headquarters of New France. Its green copper roof rose conspicuously above the city.

The leader of the five-man CIA team took Steve aside. "Dumont's doctor tried to stonewall us at first, but we got the information out of him. Yesterday he was called to this hotel to treat a German suffering from flu, dehydration, and a mild case of pneumonia."

"Let's find out if he's still here," Steve said.

The hundred-year-old hotel exuded Old World charm and advertised luxurious rooms featuring four-poster beds, antique furniture, and marble fireplaces. An appropriate place for "Baron" Walter Dorfler to stay, Steve thought.

"Why the fuck you letting this news crew tag along?" the CIA man asked. "That's Laura Delaney, isn't it?"

"My boss, Peter Thompson, deputy director of the FBI, wants videotape of anything important, like a last interview with Dorfler, in case he dies. This crew is handy," Steve lied.

"It ain't smart to involve the media."

They went to the room number the doctor gave them, and one of the spooks picked the lock. They CIA agents moved into the room with military precision, followed by Steve, Laura, and her crew.

The German greeted them with a coughing spasm as he lay in bed watching CNN. "Who are you?" Dorfler asked, an amused expression on his face.

"Steve Wallace, Federal Bureau of Investigation."

"And these other boys must be from the Central Intelligence Agency. I think all of you are out of your jurisdiction."

"Shut up," the CIA team leader barked, eliciting a withering look from Steve, who said, "Leave two of your guys here on guard and go arrange transportation. We'll be leaving in half an hour."

"You better know what you're doing," the CIA man growled. "I know how to get this guy to talk, fast."

"I'm sure of that, but I'm also certain your superiors told you to take orders from me. Am I correct?"

"I'm going to interrogate him and you film it," Steve told Laura. "At the end, I'll let you ask him a few questions, and UBC can use that footage. Okay?"

Laura saluted insincerely and conferred with her

colleagues, one of whom shouldered a camera and moved in close.

Steve sat on the edge of the German's bed. "You're alone?"

"*Ja.* Sometimes when I travel, I bring along this young fräulein, but not this trip. I hadn't planned on going back, you see."

"On to New America, huh? What were you going to be, deputy führer?"

Dorfler laughed and coughed at the same time. "That's a good one! I know about you. You're the one who almost killed Jeremiah in Kansas City, *ja*?" Dorfler smiled easily. "In history, every great man spawns a great adversary. Did you know that?"

"Like Hitler and Roosevelt."

Dorfler's smile faded. "No, like the Old Testament Jeremiah, who spoke the words of God, and Pashhur the priest, who would not listen. Do you know your Old Testament?"

Steve ignored the diversion. "Where's Jeremiah?"

"Jeremiah the Second, who speaks for God, is preparing to lead his people to their promised land."

Steve looked closely at Dorfler, trying to determine whether he truly believed or had just delivered the party line. "What's he going to do with the other bomb? I assume he has it."

Dorfler exhaled and his body seemed to sink deeper into the bed. "Judah had to be destroyed and Jerusalem sacked because they ignored the word of God."

"Cut the crap, Dorfler. You'll tell us what we want to know one way or the other. I'm the easy way. The guy who just left is the hard way. Make your choice. We don't have much time."

The German regained his smile and looked directly at Steve. "I don't know what I can tell you that you don't already know. It's hardly a secret what Jeremiah intends. He's published the details for America and the world to read. He's explained himself on Ms. Delaney's programs." Dorfler waved at Laura and said, "I watch you on television all the time in Germany. You are much more beautiful in person!" He redirected his attention to Steve. "Yes, he has an atomic bomb. I hope he isn't forced to use it on Washington, but he may. I can't tell you if he will. I can't tell you where he is. I can tell you about the movement, though."

"Oh, I know all about that. The Fourth Reich sprouts up in America. Why not Bavaria?"

Dorfler's eyes sparkled. "Not enough room! You Americans have all this empty land out west! But let's quit making these comparisons to Nazism. National Socialism had its good points. Strong rule, racial pride, high social values, dignity for the workers, economic self-sufficiency, a world purpose. Hitler wrecked all that with his insanities. You can't blame National Socialism for Hitler, any more than you can blame the failures of Christianity on Christ!"

"And Hitler was going to either rule the world or destroy it, just like Jeremiah, your nephew. You constructed his personality, didn't you? Psychological brain surgery. Made yourself a Frankenstein monster."

Dorfler shook his finger at Steve and chuckled. "You have very colorful language! No, it's more complicated than that, Agent Wallace. In the beginning I was the teacher, but Jeremiah is his own man now. He's very resourceful and he knows how to get the job done. You'll see, New America will come to pass and it will work.''

Steve looked at the cameraman standing near him and at the two CIA agents standing near the door. "Why not just take out some newspaper advertisements, recruiting people for New America? Set up a utopian community somewhere. Buy up North and South Dakota, if you like. Apparently you've got the money. Try your little experiment there. You didn't have to go to this extreme.''

Sweat rolled down Dorfler's face, yet he shivered. "A utopian community! That would attract only intellectuals. They can't do anything but talk. The people in Washington wouldn't allow New America to exist without a fight, any more than Britain would let the colonies go without a war. It's the way of the world, my friend.'' He lifted himself in his bed to get closer to Steve. "Jeremiah has tapped deeply into the frustration and anger in your country, just like your American revolutionaries did. He will raise an army that can't be stopped. You'll see.''

Steve stood. Maybe Dorfler didn't have much more to add. He needed to get him back to the U.S. and into a hospital, probably Walter Reed Army Hospital or Bethesda Naval Medical Center.

But Steve had one more question. "Do you really think some ragtag army of social misfits has a chance against the American military?''

Dorfler spit up blood into a handkerchief. "You don't know everything yet, do you, Agent Wallace?''

Steve motioned for Laura to take her shot, while he used a two-way radio to tell the CIA team leader they were about ready to go. They'd need a gurney and an ambulance.

Laura sat on the edge of the bed and smiled at Dorfler.

"Forgive me for not rising in the presence of such beauty," the German said.

"That's okay. I like to get the handsome fellows right into bed."

Dorfler laughed and coughed until his face grew bright red. "You are naughty, too! I like that."

Steve listened, interested to see how Laura would approach the old man.

"What do you want to tell me, Walter?" she asked.

He looked at her curiously, then smiled. "Jeremiah has a weakness for women."

"That doesn't make him unusual."

Dorfler grinned, then frowned. "He's too possessive."

"A stalker. Insanely jealous."

"*Ja*," Dorfler confirmed, reluctantly.

"That's his Achilles' heel?"

Dorfler nodded. "He was so obsessed with my niece Emma, I had to do something, so he would complete God's work. And it certainly worked."

Steve recognized the significance of his remarks and interrupted. "What did you do?"

"That's not important now," Dorfler said. "I only mentioned it because it just occurred to me that Laura is the only one who can—how do you say— sidetrack him again."

Steve thought he understood. Jeremiah had risked his life unnecessarily to try several times to abduct Laura. The old man seemed to be saying the terrorist wouldn't quit. Steve felt a shiver pass up his spine.

Suddenly Dorfler said, "Please hand me that bottle

of pills on the nightstand, Laura. It's time for my medicine.''

Dorfler put a pill in his mouth and reached for a glass of water on a nightstand, although he didn't drink from it. ''What will happen to me in the United States?''

Laura looked at Steve, who shrugged. ''I don't know. They might extradite you to Ukraine, or hold on to you as a material witness once Jeremiah's caught and put on trial.''

''Either way, I'll spend the rest of my life in jail.''

''You should have thought of that,'' Steve said.

''I did.'' Dorfler bit down on the pill, and white foam and slobber gushed out of his mouth. He gasped, struggled for breath, and collapsed into his pillow.

Laura jumped up from the bed and screamed. ''What happened!''

Steve rushed over and felt Dorfler's neck for a pulse.

''Is he dead?'' Laura asked.

Steve picked up the pill bottle, emptied several out into his hand, and smelled them. ''Cyanide.''

''Oh, my God!''

''Shit! A thousand secrets died with this guy.'' *And I fucked up again*, Steve thought. *I should have anticipated this suicide attempt.*

He stared at the lifeless body. Like Goering at Nuremberg, Dorfler had cheated the hangman.

34

Ten miles north of Point Lookout, Maryland, where they'd transferred the bomb from the *Exodus* to a van, Jeremiah looked out the passenger's window as they approached an intersection and saw a battered red pickup truck barrel through a red light, heading right at them. Jeremiah closed his eyes and prayed.

Jeremiah's driver jammed on his brakes, causing the pickup to plow into the right front fender of the white van, which had the name of a plumbing company painted on the side.

The force of the collision propelled both vehicles through the intersection. The van spun around completely, coming to rest in the outside lane of southbound traffic. The pickup wound up on the median strip.

Jeremiah felt dizzy and his heart pounded furiously.

"You okay, boss?" the driver asked.

"Yeah." Jeremiah undid his seat belt so he could turn and look at his three soldiers in back. "Anyone hurt?"

"Jeff's unconscious," one of the armed men said.

"Stay put," Jeremiah ordered, as he stepped out of the van. He and the driver inspected the damage. Several people gawked at them from the front of a nearby service station. In the distance he heard the wail of an approaching police car.

Two Maryland State Police cars soon arrived on the scene. A corporal got out of one and took up a position in the middle of the intersection, where he began directing traffic.

The other trooper, a sergeant, walked toward Jeremiah. "What happened here?" he asked.

"That guy in the plaid shirt standing over by his pickup ran a red light and broadsided us," Jeremiah explained, pointing out the culprit. "He looks like he's drunk."

"You two okay?"

"Yeah, I think so," Jeremiah replied.

As the sergeant walked toward the pickup, Jeremiah went to the back of the van, opened the door, and said to his two soldiers, "With any luck, we'll be on the road soon, but be ready for action in case anything goes wrong."

Jeremiah watched the sergeant talk with the truck driver, who wore cowboy boots, jeans, a waist-length winter coat, and a John Deere hat. The conversation escalated in volume and ended when the sergeant grabbed the driver's arm and steered him toward the state police cars parked on the shoulder of the highway.

The drunk driver protested loudly and jerked free of the trooper's grasp, at the same time pulling the sergeant's gun from its holster.

"This was your fuckin' fault!" the drunk yelled, as he walked unsteadily in Jeremiah's direction.

"You shudda slowed down, goddammit! Wasn't my fault!"

The sound of gunfire caused Jeremiah to cringe, expecting to feel the impact of bullets. Then he realized the shots had come from behind him. His driver had pulled out 9-mm handgun and shot the drunk dead.

"Shit!" Jeremiah shouted, running toward the fallen man to snatch the Sig-Sauer from his lifeless hand before the sergeant could retrieve it. The two able-bodied soldiers spilled out of the back of the van, wielding assault rifles. One immediately ran toward the corporal, to take him into custody.

The light of realization spread across the sergeant's face. "You're Jeremiah, the terrorist!"

"That's right," Jeremiah replied, grimly. "Now, get over to the back of the van!" He screamed at his driver, "You moron! Did you have to shoot him?"

"Should I have waited until he shot you?" the gunman protested.

"Okay, okay," Jeremiah said. He knew they had precious little time to extricate themselves from this mess. The group in front of the service station had grown in number. Several cars had pulled over to the side of the road to gawk, and one driver rolling slowly through the intersection talked on a cellular phone. More police could be expected soon.

They could hijack another van and transfer the bomb to it, he thought, except that would be time-consuming and cause them to abandon the sophisticated electronics built into this special package. Jeremiah again assessed the damage. The impact had crumpled the right front fender, blown out the tire, and bent the rim. Still, the bent fender didn't block the tire rotation. Under the hood, the battery had split open, but the radiator wasn't leaking and everything else looked okay.

Jeremiah yelled at his driver and the soldier who wasn't guarding the corporal. "Get this tire off! One of you get over to that service station and find another tire and a battery. We've got only a few minutes to get this truck back on the road. And get those goddamned rifles out of sight!"

While his men hurried about their tasks, Jeremiah used the Sig-Sauer to prod the sergeant and corporal to the back of the van. "Grab my guy lying inside and dump him on the side of the road."

The sergeant did as he was ordered, but not before closely examining the bomb.

"You know what that is?" Jeremiah asked.

"I can guess. The word is all over the radio this morning. I don't think you're going anywhere."

"Really? Well, in this game of chicken, Sergeant, let me describe my weapon. That's a one-megaton atomic bomb in the van. Do you know what cesium one thirty-seven is?"

Both policemen shook their heads.

Jeremiah pointed to canisters secured to the inside walls of the van. "It's an alkali metal that will greatly increase the radioactive fallout if this bomb explodes, depending, of course, on how the winds are blowing." Jeremiah looked up at the sky. "We got a nice breeze today. The fallout could reach all the way to Boston."

"You wouldn't do that. You'd go up with the bomb."

"No shit. What choice do you think I'll make, Sergeant? Blow myself to bits or give up so they can send me to Leavenworth? You know what kind of reception I'd get there, or in any other federal prison. No, there's only one chance for everyone to avoid a monumental disaster, and that's for you to let me go."

"How're we going to stop you?" the sergeant asked.

"In case any other policemen get the idea they can shoot me and defuse the bomb, take a look at this little device." Jeremiah showed the troopers a small rectangular black plastic box taped to the underside of his forearm. On it was a numeric keypad and a clear plastic button covering a pulsating red light. Jeremiah partially unbuttoned his shirt so they could see that wires ran from the box up his arm to an elastic band encircling his chest. A small, white circular device was attached to the band directly over his heart.

"I can detonate the bomb by pressing the plastic button on the remote," Jeremiah explained. "If I'm killed and my heart stops beating, detonation begins automatically. The only way then to stop the explosion is to punch in a nine-digit code on the keypad." Jeremiah smiled wickedly. "And it's not the identification number I've given out on national television."

"We're ready to roll, boss!" the driver said.

"We're gonna let you two go," Jeremiah said. "Sergeant, you tell the rest of your friends what will happen if anyone tries to stop us."

They drove north again on State Highway 235. Within forty miles, they encountered a roadblock manned by a detachment of U.S. Army troops.

Jeremiah got out and stood beside the van as an infantry colonel approached. He held up his arm to display the remote control. "Do you know what this is?"

"I've talked to the sergeant," said the colonel, a tall, rawboned man with cold, piercing eyes. "We won't let you drive beyond this point."

"I can detonate the bomb right here and accomplish my purpose," Jeremiah replied, bluffing.

"Then we'll be traveling to hell together, sir."

Jeremiah laughed. "You got some tough bark on you, Colonel. I could use a man like you in my new army."

"Fuck you, sir."

"So what do you plan to do?"

"My orders are not to let you drive north toward the capital. If you'll wait here, negotiators representing the president will arrive shortly."

Jeremiah climbed into the van and thought about the impending negotiations. He'd lose. Obviously he wasn't going to detonate the bomb and go up with it. They'd know that. If he had been able to drive into Washington before being spotted, he'd have parked the van on Pennsylvania Avenue and retreated to a negotiating site far away.

Despite the setback, he still had an advantage. They weren't sure what a religious fanatic would do if cornered. They'd give him plenty of room for a while.

"Where to, boss?" the driver asked.

"West on that road." Jeremiah pointed. "It'll take us across the Potomac. Then I'll give you directions.

Don't stop for anything, including roadblocks.'' He looked at the two in back. "Be prepared to shoot our way through, if necessary. But I don't think they want a confrontation now. If we move fast, we can get where we need to be.'' A place where he could make his demands to the president and the nation and then perform his greatest miracle, sure to attract thousands more to the cause.

35

The air force Gulfstream flew Laura and Steve from Quebec City to Dulles International Airport in the northern Virginia countryside about thirty miles east of Laura's farm. It was after dark before the executive jet stopped on the runway near a limo and two dark green army sedans.

As Steve and Laura disembarked, FBI Deputy Director Peter Thompson rolled down a limo window and motioned for them to get in. Military police escorted them off the airport property onto a state highway leading west.

"Why is this maniac at my farm?" Laura asked. "How'd he get there?"

Thompson briefly explained Jeremiah's odyssey through southern Maryland and Virginia to Laura's farm. "He wants to do a television interview with you, Laura, after which he'll let us know his plans. My orders from the director and the president are to go along with him. We really have no other viable choice at the moment."

They sat in a gloomy silence as the limo sped through the Virginia countryside, every intersection manned by army troops and law enforcement officials.

*   *   *

Near Laura's farm, the limo slowed on the state highway lined on both sides with police and military vehicles, and then turned west on the blacktop road leading to the entrance gate.

"Give Jeremiah his interview," Thompson urged. "I've arranged for UBC technical people to be here, Laura. However, we have two conditions for the interview, which are that Jeremiah's three soldiers surrender and that Steve accompanies you into the house."

"He's in my house!" He'd forever defiled her retreat, her dream home, her private Texas. How could they ever be comfortable there again, knowing how easily he'd infiltrated the farm on two occasions? Of course, that wouldn't matter if he exploded an atomic bomb on her property, Laura realized.

"You want me to overpower Jeremiah while Laura's interviewing him?" Steve guessed.

Thompson looked at Steve. "Only you can make that judgment once you get inside and assess the situation. If you can get him to stand up in the middle of any room with windows, a member of the hostage rescue team will take him out."

"So you don't believe his story about the timing device set to his heart rate?" Laura asked.

"With him, it's hard to tell, as you know," Thompson replied. "It could be just a ploy to prevent us from shooting him."

"And if it is true?"

Thompson looked at Steve to provide the answer. Steve explained to Laura, "A head shot wouldn't stop his heart immediately. There'd be several seconds in which to grab the sensor on his chest, even with my hand, so it would begin picking up my heartbeat.''

"Then our bomb experts will figure out the number code to deactivate the atomic trigger,'' Thompson concluded.

"When we're inside with him, why don't your guys just get into the van and defuse the bomb?'' Laura asked.

Thompson shook his head glumly. "Jeremiah's given us plenty of reason in the past to respect his electronics expertise. My guess is the bomb's booby-trapped, and the experts will need lots of time to work around that. Also, the minute we open the van doors, Jeremiah could receive a signal on that remote control device and he just might detonate the bomb. But if we can capture him or kill him quickly, before he can do anything, we'll have all the time we need.''

"He won't kill himself,'' Steve said, confidently.

"I don't want to take that chance,'' Thompson replied, "not if it could result in a nuclear explosion that would contaminate much of the East Coast, including the capital.''

"I don't know why Jeremiah'd go for any of this,'' Laura said, skeptically. "He knows what you're going to do.''

"He'll go for it,'' Steve said.

"Why?'' Laura asked.

"Because he can't miss an opportunity to speak to the nation on this the eve of his plans almost coming true. We've all seen it in his eyes before. I saw it on the old German's face. The cause is all that matters to them. Jeremiah will think up some rationale for driving around with an atomic bomb, which he'll explain to the nation. Then he'll surrender and carry on his crusade from prison.'' He paused, thoughtfully. ''Or he may believe there's some way out of here.''

Thompson said, ''I hope you're right about the possibility he'll surrender. There is no way out. In any event, someone has to go in there. Are you two willing?''

Laura stared at her house on the hill. ''I guess we have no choice,'' she replied. ''I can't say no to the interview, not if that would cause him to detonate the bomb.'' She turned to Steve and put her arms around his neck, laying her head on his chest. ''God, I don't want to die in there, not before we've had a chance to live!''

Steve held her away from him and looked into her eyes. ''The only person who's going to die today is Jeremiah! Trust me.''

Thompson used a cell phone to call Jeremiah inside the house and dictate the FBI's terms. Meanwhile he waved out the window at the UBC broadcast truck, which followed the limo through the front gate and up the driveway to the house, surrounded by FBI agents. Large portable lights lit up the house as if it were midday. Laura saw snipers positioned in several locations.

They parked near Jeremiah's van, a nondescript white Ford with a ''dirty'' nuclear bomb inside. As Laura climbed out of the limo and stood beside the van, she felt deathly cold.

''I'll be in the broadcast truck, listening,'' Thompson told them. ''In case Jeremiah shuts down the camera and the sound, this will do the trick.'' Thompson handed Steve a partial dental bridge that

snapped neatly in place in his mouth, its electronic
components hidden behind his own upper front teeth.

"It'll broadcast everything that's said, including
your softest whisper," Thompson continued. "We'll
listen to Jeremiah's demands and see if there's any
way we can negotiate an end to this impasse."

"I doubt that," Steve said.

"In that case, we'll turn to other options. The
UBC cameraman with you will actually be one of
our agents, and he's a very skilled fighter. If he gets
a chance to take Jeremiah down alive, he'll do it. So
be prepared, Steve. Also, the camera is rigged with
a special gun that doesn't look like a gun. It's a last
resort. Always keep us informed of your location in
the house. As I said before, if everything else fails,
maneuver Jeremiah near a window and the snipers
will take him out."

"You take down Jeremiah and you might hit
Laura and me, too."

Thompson looked at both of them. "Let's hope
not."

Steve and Laura waited with the cameraman near the front porch as two of Jeremiah's soldiers came out of the house and surrendered, turning
over their weapons to the FBI agents.

Steve and Laura stepped into the first-floor entryway and Laura called out, "Where are you?" The
cameraman followed, as technicians on the porch
played out a transmission cable.

A man dressed in black, carrying an automatic
weapon, appeared from a door under the staircase,
leading to a cellar that Laura had converted into a
wine room. *This is not good*, Laura thought, as she

heard Steve whisper, "Basement wine cellar" into his new teeth.

The black-clad soldier came forward and wordlessly frisked Laura, Steve, and the cameraman. Once they were at the doorway to the cellar, Jeremiah's soldier said, "He's downstairs."

Laura went down first, followed by Steve, then the cameraman. Laura looked over her shoulder to see the remaining gunman help with the cable and then squat on the landing at the top of the stairs.

"Laura, how good to see you again!" Jeremiah said, coming forward. Like his men, he wore black and held a gun in his hand. He startled Laura by drawing her close and kissing her on the cheek.

"Leave her alone! Why's your man at the top of the stairs?" Steve asked, angrily. "You agreed they'd all come out and surrender their weapons."

"I lied," Jeremiah admitted, showing them the small black box taped to his forearm. "If you jump me, he has orders to open up with that assault rifle."

It seemed to Laura the red light flashing on the box was telegraphing a warning: bomb, boom, bomb, boom!

"Thompson told you about the device monitoring my heartbeat?"

Steve sneered. "You have a heart?"

Jeremiah chuckled. "Walter Dorfler has a theory about opponents. You should hear it sometime."

Laura worried that Steve would tell Jeremiah about Dorfler's suicide, and she feared the terrorist's reaction. But Steve only smiled.

"Let's begin," Jeremiah prompted.

The FBI agent/cameraman turned on a bright light and Jeremiah positioned himself in front of a wine rack, about six feet away from the camera.

Laura reluctantly moved close to Jeremiah and looked into the camera lens. "This is Laura Delaney, broadcasting live from my farmhouse in northern Virginia, where Jeremiah the terrorist is surrounded by the FBI, federal troops, and other police."

She turned to Jeremiah and put a microphone close to him. "Jeremiah, you have an atomic bomb outside in a van that also contains radioactive material. Why would you explode this bomb with all its awful consequences?"

The cameraman focused on Jeremiah, who said, "The area from Washington to Boston is already a wasteland of evil. The Lord has said it shall be cleansed . . . unless an acceptable arrangement can be negotiated."

A gunshot exploded in the small cellar, nearly causing Laura's heart to stop. At first she thought the cameraman had shot Jeremiah. But then the cameraman staggered backward, a dark red stain spreading over the front of his white shirt. Steve supported his fellow agent and lowered him to the floor. Laura watched the agent's eyes close, as a final, long breath escaped from his body.

Keeping the gun on Steve, Jeremiah bent over and picked up the camera. Laura watched as he stripped tape off a device that looked like a fountain pen. "Very cute," he said, handing the camera to Steve. "Here, you do the honors now."

Laura looked at the camera and saw the flashing red light, meaning it was running. She wordlessly stuck the microphone back in Jeremiah's face.

"I will not detonate this nuclear weapon if the United States government withdraws all its troops, including state National Guard units, from all states north of a line from San Francisco to Saint Louis to Pittsburgh. That is New America, as decreed by God. All weapons of war contained at all military installations in that area, including nuclear weapons, will be abandoned in place. These are the armaments of the Army of New America, units of which are now forming in the Dakotas and Canada. We will not hesitate to use these weapons to defend ourselves, if necessary. When I am informed by my soldiers that they have taken possession of several specific army posts and air force bases, I will defuse the atomic weapon, provided the federal government guarantees me safe passage to New America.''

"You don't really believe the president of the United States will agree to these demands?" Laura asked, incredulously, as Steve continued taping the "interview."

"Then he'd better get out of the White House," Jeremiah said, bluntly.

"You're crazy," Laura said. "You're a murderer and terrorist. No one believes you speak for the Lord.''

Jeremiah smiled confidently. "For those of you who do believe, open your Bible to Jeremiah of the Old Testament, chapters two and four, and read: 'What wrong did your fathers find in me that they went far from me, and went after worthlessness, and became worthless?

'A lion has gone up from his thicket, a destroyer of nations has set out; he has gone forth from his place to make your land a waste; your cities will be ruins without inhabitants. For this gird you with sackcloth, lament and wail; for the fierce anger of the Lord has not turned back from us.' ''

Laura shook her head incomprehensively and asked, ''And you think you're that destroyer?''

''Yes. Through word and deed, I have identified the evil, immorality, injustice, and inequality that exist in old America. The economic system that the Lord Himself calls worthless, the cause of all greed and human division and suffering. The government that is a sham. And you have been given a new book and a new way.

''Those of you who believe, gather up your belongings and move into the new land and establish a base of power. Those of you already in New America, rise up and seize the arms of the oppressor to defend yourselves against the evil forces of the government. Read the last chapter of Second Jeremiah. I will soon be among you.''

Jeremiah stepped forward, took the camera from Steve's shoulder, and threw it on the floor.

''Now what?'' Steve asked.

''Now we wait for the president's decision,'' Jeremiah replied. ''Maybe open a bottle of good wine and have a party.'' He moved close to Laura and stroked her hair. She recoiled and Steve stepped toward Jeremiah, who pointed his gun at both of them in a threatening manner.

Suddenly automatic-weapons fire sounded on the level above them. The door to the basement splintered in a dozen places as bullets riddled the gunman on the landing. He crumpled and dropped his rifle, which clattered down the stairs.

In the midst of this diversion, Laura saw Steve's leg and foot shoot out, knocking the gun from Jeremiah's hand. He dived for the gun, rolled into a kneeling position, and pointed it at Jeremiah.

Except Jeremiah had moved behind her and held a knife to her throat, as he had in the Kansas City hotel room.

"Shoot the sonofabitch!" Laura screamed, adding to her sense of déjà vu.

"He won't shoot me!" Jeremiah said. "But you have caused me to alter my plans slightly. Back up the stairs, Steve, or I'll slit her throat!"

"Kill him!" Laura snarled, struggling in vain to escape, but Jeremiah held her tightly against him with his left arm thrown over her shoulder, grasping her right breast. He pressed the knife blade so hard against her throat that it broke the skin, and she felt blood running down her throat.

She saw it scared Steve, who began to back up the stairs, although he kept the gun aimed at Jeremiah.

When Jeremiah forced her out onto the main level, Laura saw three FBI snipers dressed in black, wearing helmets and pointing assault rifles at them.

"Don't shoot!" Steve pleaded.

"That's right!" Jeremiah echoed, keeping the knife to her throat, although he now held the remote control in his left hand, the one that had been groping her. "Shoot me and I'll push this button! You guys won't even have time to think of the wife and kiddies before you're vaporized!"

As if he knew the house layout well, Jeremiah moved toward the kitchen and the adjacent mudroom, which led outside. Laura watched as Steve and the other FBI agents followed cautiously.

"Laura Delaney and I are coming out of the house, Mr. Thompson," Jeremiah said, as if he knew about the transmitter behind Steve's teeth. "If you shoot me, I'll press the button. I'd give this a few more minutes if I were you."

Outside the house, Jeremiah forced her

into a Chevy Blazer and ordered her to drive toward the north pasture. When she hesitated at the gate, he jammed his foot on the accelerator, causing them to crash through it. In the rearview mirror she saw other vehicles speeding after them.

"Drive right up to the edge of the pond dam," Jeremiah ordered. "Park the truck sideways, so it's between us and them."

He forced her out the driver's side, and again got behind her with the knife, using her body as a shield. He stepped backward, pulling her farther onto the dam. FBI agents targeted them with car spotlights. Thompson appeared with a bullhorn.

Jeremiah whispered into her ear. "It's almost like that moonlit night, isn't it, Laura? Too bad it wasn't you and me. We'd make a great team. You'll never guess how long I've been watching you."

"Give up!" Laura said. "You don't have a chance!"

Jeremiah smiled. "Dear Laura, I'm sorry I had to bring you this far. But don't fear, you won't be killed. You can't be. Our son someday will lead New America! It's prophesied. Read the Lord's word. In this war between good and evil, Laura, don't mistake the first battle for the last."

Without warning, he shoved her away and she turned to see him dive headfirst into the pond's dark, cold water. Everyone seemed momentarily stunned.

Then FBI agents hustled her off the dam and delivered her into Steve's arms.

Thompson asked her, "Did he press the remote button?"

"I guess not." There had been no explosion, she thought, stupidly, as if they'd still be here if there had been.

"It wouldn't operate underwater, anyway," Thompson said, talking to himself. Then he started running back to his car, although shouting over his shoulder. "Get his body out of that pond!"

Steve grabbed her hand and dragged her toward a car. "Where are we going?" she asked.

"Anywhere but here!"

They drove west toward the mountains, getting through several checkpoints with Steve's FBI credentials. They had no destination in mind, other than to put maximum distance between them and the bomb.

36

During the dramatic events unfolding at Laura's farm, the last chapter of *The Book of Second Jeremiah* appeared on the Internet.

THE BOOK OF SECOND JEREMIAH

CHAPTER SIX

1 God sent Moses to lead His People out of Egypt, and God has sent Jeremiah the Second to lead the Chosen People to New America.

2 Thus spake the LORD of Hosts, the God of Israel and New America, saying:

3 Ye who oppose My people should read the Old Testament,

for I will send afflictions on you as I did on Pharaoh,

except yours will be greater by far, causing much

death and destruction and a pox on future generations.

So it is said, so it is written in The Book
of Second Jeremiah,
My guide for the future of Mankind.

4 The Chosen People will abolish Chaos and
Evil, restore God's values, eliminate the excesses
of government, establish the Wealth Exchange,
ensure the equality of Men, set Mankind on the
path of Knowledge, and establish the leadership
of Jeremiah, the Anointed of the LORD.

5 New America will be a white, Christian society composed of those
descended from the Caucasian race. All
races of men
and all species of insects and animals
were created by Me
for different purposes and therefore are
of value;
but segregation is the natural order of the
Universe.
Like attracts like and opposing forces repel.

6 Diversity is not a desirable goal of New
America, not only as it applieth to race and custom, but to fractious politics, law, government,
social and economic policy, philosophy, and religion. There is but one path for New America and
that has been ordained from the beginning of
time. Follow that path unerringly or seek thy own
way elsewhere!

7 In times of confusion about principles and values, look thee to My Word, or the leadership of Jeremiah.

8 New America will be independent and aloof among nations;
it does not have a mandate from God to tell others what
to do or how to live, since that is My work. When
threatened by others, the Chosen People can use any
weapons available to defend themselves against Evil.

9 The LORD sayeth:

These things will come to pass. Jeremiah will be thought of as
dead, but He will be in God's hands, while others carry
on the Exodus. Jeremiah will be reborn through Me and
return. A great battle will occur in the New Year
Three, and New America will prevail by Divine
intervention and greatly expand its borders.
10 Scientists of New America will make several momentous

discoveries, including a genetic key that will

conquer disease and increase longevity. A quantum leap in

computer processing speed and capacity will set the

stage for evolutionary advancement. So sayeth the LORD.

11 In the New Year Twenty-seven, a number of great significance, a New Leader of New America will emerge, the Inheritor, Anointed by God, Announced by Jeremiah the Second.

12 The LORD Creator of the Universe sayeth:

When New America achieves its goals on Earth, I will reveal

the origin and fate of the Universe and Mankind.

Those who believeth and obey will reach the Omega Point,

understand all, and be resurrected to Eternal Life.

37

They started coming in the spring of the next year: people who climbed the fence around Steve and Laura's farm and walked across the pasture toward the pond. These people who admired the "prophet" and his teachings would stand there respectfully, pray, throw flowers on the water, stab white crosses into the ground, or leave mementos lying about—letters, verse, or bound copies of *The Book of Second Jeremiah*, in which they'd inscribed their thoughts.

One day Steve and Laura stopped working in a flower bed north of the house to watch a family of four, including a boy and girl both under the age of ten, walk slowly and orderly toward the pond.

"It never seems to occur to them that this is private property," Laura said, as much in amazement as disgust. "Or that they might need permission."

"Would you give it to them if they asked?"

"Hell, no."

"I wonder what most of them really believe."

"The public opinion polls are evenly divided between those who think he drowned and those who think he got away." Laura clearly put herself in the latter group.

"The official FBI position still is that they don't know what happened," Steve said.

Laura liked his reference to the FBI as "they." Steve had retired at the first of the year. "It suits their purpose to muddy the waters," she said.

"I understand their tactics. If a certain percentage of people think Jeremiah's dead, it might decrease the numbers of his followers migrating into the Dakotas to establish New America."

Laura completed Steve's thoughts. "And if they keep alive the idea that he's alive, the public and Congress will support their efforts to find him."

"It only makes sense in Washington."

"It's all bizarre," Laura said, returning to her gardening. "Especially the rumor that he drowned in his escape attempt and his followers who were waiting spirited away his body."

"That rumor obviously is intended to parallel Christ's Resurrection. He may have more appeal as a martyr than as a prophet."

"That *is* sacrilege." They dropped the subject then, as they usually did, but it never left their minds, she knew.

Last December, FBI demolition experts had successfully disarmed the nuclear bomb in the van, which included a detonation device set to go off ninety minutes after they'd concluded the television interview in the wine cellar. *The remote control taped to Jeremiah's arm might or might not have been real,* Laura thought, *but he clearly intended to explode the bomb if his demands weren't met.*

Divers searching for Jeremiah's body that day had

found nothing, prompting the FBI to drain the pond the next day. What they'd found still astounded Laura and everyone else. Partly buried in the lake bottom was a thirty-six-inch-diameter pipe that extended through the base of the dam into a stand of pine trees fifty yards away—the same wooded sanctuary Jeremiah probably had escaped into that night he'd spied on her and Steve. The pipe emptied into a culvert that emptied into a creek on the other side of the fire road.

After the FBI had interviewed the contractor who built the pond, the mystery had evaporated. Ponds in the area that weren't spring-fed built up with algae and occasionally needed to be drained and cleaned. Inside a ground-level box on the dam, a wheel could be turned to open a valve on the underwater pipe and slowly drain the pond.

Jeremiah apparently had added an air lock to the three-foot-diameter pipe, creating a safety valve for himself. Obviously he'd envisioned using her farm as a base of operations. Some might call it prescience, but Laura only conceded the terrorist was good at contingency planning. It had worked. The FBI had spent hours that day last December searching the pond for the terrorist's body, while he had already crawled out the drainage pipe and run to freedom in the dark.

"You want to get married?" Steve asked, jarring Laura from her ruminations.

"What? You serious?"

"Sure. You're rich and I'm single and unemployed."

Laura put her arms and dirty hands around his neck. "I'd need a prenuptial to make certain you don't take advantage of me.''

"I've already done that.''

"Many different ways. Remember the flight to Quebec? Okay, I'll forget the prenuptial.''

"Forget all that legal crap. Let's just declare ourselves man and wife right here in the midst of the pansies.''

"I do and always will.''

"Me, too.''

Laura hugged him tight and images of the future flashed through her mind, including the children they'd have. Try as hard as she might, though, Laura couldn't prevent Jeremiah's last words about *their son* from intruding upon her happy thoughts.

Davey Schropa attended the groundbreaking ceremonies for the Science Center of New America, located northeast of Pierre, the capital of South Dakota. He wanted to meet "New Americans" relocating to the state, and sell them insurance.

The state needed new blood, anyway, he conceded. South Dakota only had a population of three-quarters of a million people on seventy-six thousand square miles of land. Only Alaska, Montana, and Wyoming had fewer people per square mile. The newcomers bought large chunks of cheap land and created mobile-home cities on the prairie overnight. Like Anathoth, another thirty miles north of the Science Center site.

"What do you think about this?" someone asked, and Schropa turned toward the sound of the voice. An old man with a shawl draped over his shoulders sat in a wheelchair beside him.

"You mean the Science Center?" Schropa asked.

"Yeah."

"It's gonna be huge, they say. Five thousand acres. Ten million square feet of building space. A hospital, university, research labs. It's either gonna be the economic miracle a lot of us hoped for, or the biggest construction boondoggle in history."

Schropa saw the old man nod his head in agreement. "Yep. It's a gamble, for sure."

Schropa doubted the old man knew anything, but you could never tell about people. "Have you heard about this New America Economic Development Corporation that helped finance this place? They have to have hundreds of millions to do this project."

The old man with the wispy white hair and large hearing aid over one ear squinted up at him. "Yep, I know a lot of people who've invested in the corporation. Got quite a bit of my own money tied up in it."

"Really. I'm Davey Schropa. I sell insurance in Sioux Falls. Thought I'd come out here and see what's going on. You from around here?"

"Born and raised."

Schropa squatted down, so as not to be lording it over the old man. "What do you think about these newcomers? I hear there's religious extremists, utopians, isolationists, secessionists, white supremacists, militia members, foreigners. Even socialists. The God-awfulest collection of nuts you can imagine."

The old man hee-hawed. "Welcome home, I say. South Dakota's always had the highest incidence of mental illness and incest of any state in the union. It's comes from being cooped up inside all winter long."

Schropa laughed at that joke, variations of which

he'd heard as far back as high school. "On the other hand, there's obviously some money here."

"More than you can imagine, Davey. More than you can imagine. All these people moving into the state will rev up the economy. They'll attract businesses looking for cheap labor. There'll be a big demand for new retail stores. The folks who work at this Science Center will demand services. Money will flow into South Dakota and surrounding states. You could sell a lot of insurance to these folks, Davey, if you had the inside track."

"What did you say your name was, sir?"

"Just call me sir, Davey. Say, if you want to get in on the ground floor of this new movement and make yourself some real money, you stop by my hotel room in Pierre. I'm at the Best Western. Room one-oh-seven."

A broad-shouldered young man dressed in black materialized and pushed the wheelchair and the old man away.

Intrigued, Schropa showed up later at the hotel room. The old man's attendant let him into the room and then left.

"A relative?" Schropa asked.

"Bodyguard."

"You rich, or wanted by the law?" Schropa quipped.

"What did you think about Jeremiah?" the old man asked. "Have a seat, Davey. First help yourself to a beer from the refrigerator."

"Don't mind if I do," Schropa said. "How 'bout you?"

"Not me. Alcohol use is banned by *The Book of Second Jeremiah.*"

By the time he heard that, Schropa already had the beer in his hand, and considered putting it back. *To hell with it,* he thought, twisting off the cap and sitting in a chair. "I never paid much attention to Jeremiah. It all happened back east. You know how that is, living out here. Those folks always got some controversy going. I'll tell you this, sir, he killed a helluva lot of people."

"Seems to me most of 'em deserved it."

"Can't argue with you on that," Schropa said, thinking he wasn't going to argue with the old man about anything. He just wanted some business leads.

"Here's the thing, Davey. All those nuts you referred to are migrating into what they call New America, whether the folks in Washington, D.C., like it or not. I can tell you on good authority that there won't be any problem attracting several million people to New America. Then they'll be in the majority here and easily take over the political machinery."

Schropa nodded. "Yeah, I can see that, although I don't really understand what motivates them, you know."

The old man screwed up his face in contemplation. "Theology, philosophy, adventure, greed. Like you said, some of 'em are just nuts. Some of 'em are actually being paid to come here."

"Paid?"

"By the people running this show."

"Who're they? I wouldn't mind meeting them."

"You should, Davey. Before New America is officially recognized, there'll be a transition stage. The newcomers will elect themselves a governor, a couple of senators, and several congressman. They'll control the state legislature and every locally elected office. In fact, I can see you in one of those jobs, Davey.''

"Really?"

"How'd you like to be governor of South Dakota?"

Schropa began to snicker and almost choked on a mouthful of beer. "Now, that'd be something."

"All things are possible, Davey. Just watch."

Schropa watched the old man get out of the wheelchair and stretch to a height he wouldn't have imagined possible. He pulled off a skullcap to reveal curly, blond hair. He peeled latex off his face and removed rubber appliances from around his eyes, nose, and mouth. The old man got younger by the minute, it seemed to Schropa.

"I don't understand."

"Sure you do, Davey. Just think about it a minute."

The man standing in front of him braced his shoulders, jutted out his chin, and smiled broadly.

"It can't be," Schropa said, feeling sick to his stomach.

"Died twice, resurrected twice."

"I don't believe it."

"Davey, do you ever think about Mona from Nuremberg?"

"Oh, my God!"

Look for

New America

Available now in hardcover

1

As Laura brought the coffee mug to her lips, an indistinct shape ran into her peripheral vision. Looking out the kitchen windows, she saw a burly man dressed in black rushing up the hill toward the house. As his legs pumped and his arms churned, a gun grasped tightly in his right hand jerked about wildly.

Laura jumped up, dropping the heavy earthenware mug. It bounced on the table and spewed hot coffee toward her husband, Steve, who threw aside the morning newspaper as he scooted back in his chair.

"What's wrong!" he yelled.

Speechless, Laura could only point.

Steve looked in the direction of her finger. "Goddammit!"

As the man leaped onto the front porch, Steve jerked open a kitchen cabinet drawer, and took out a black 9-mm Sig-Sauer.

Through the east window, Laura watched the trespasser kick the front door, the sole of his heavy boot landing with such force the wall vibrated. But the door held.

"Where are the guards?" Laura screamed. "Where's Maria?"

"Stay here," Steve commanded, as he rushed out of the kitchen toward the front hallway.

Laura felt rooted to the floor of the kitchen nook as the nightmare unfolded in slow motion. One of their bodyguards, Shawntel, ran into view. Through the open window, she heard him shout at the gunman, "Stop, or I'll shoot!"

The armed invader whirled around and shot first, causing Shawntel to collapse on the front lawn. The gunman resumed his assault on the door, which suddenly gave way with the sound of wood cracking. The man charged into the house.

Gunfire erupted. One shot, loud and deadly, followed by two shots so rapid their sounds nearly blended. An awful silence then prevailed, causing Laura to almost quit breathing. Her heart pounded furiously and her temples throbbed. Someone walked heavily toward the kitchen.

Suddenly, he came into view and Laura let out her breath. She ran into Steve's arms.

"It's all right," he said, his voice husky with emotion.

Clinging fiercely to her husband, Laura looked over his shoulder at the intruder lying in the entryway, half in the house, half on the porch. The smell of exploded gunpowder hung heavy in the air.

"Is he dead?" Laura asked.

"I think so."

At that point, Maria burst into the house, both hands wrapped around a handgun pointed at the man Steve had shot. Her eyes darted wildly from the fallen intruder to Steve and Laura. "I'm sorry," she said.

Is that all you have to say? Laura wondered, as

Steve broke away from their embrace, picked up a phone and dialed 911.

An hour later, Laura stood near the living room fireplace as Steve and Maria Inglesias, head of their private security detail, pieced together the story for the county sheriff, Bo Hendricks. His deputies swarmed over the house and grounds of Steve and Laura's northern Virginia farm.

Steve sat on the edge of a sofa, the Sig-Sauer lying ominously on the coffee table in front of him. Maria stood beside Hendricks, who sat on a chair across from Steve.

Laura's hands shook as she hugged herself against a pervasive chill, even though she wore a yellow sweater over a white blouse and jeans. She glanced anxiously at Steve, who occasionally looked toward the entryway where the dead intruder lay, covered by a blanket. The sickeningly sweet smell of spilled blood caused Laura to choke back vomit rising in her throat.

"Three men got out of a car parked alongside the highway and climbed the fence," Maria explained. She wore a dark blue windbreaker with yellow FBI lettering on the back. Shortly after he retired three years ago, Steve had given it to her as a present. "They ran toward the pond, and two of my guys went to head 'em off."

"This one must have come from the southwest edge of the property," Steve said, nodding toward the body. "Shawntel saw him first and took out after him."

"How is he?" Laura asked, referring to the gunshot bodyguard who had been taken away by ambulance to the hospital east of Leesburg.

"It's a serious wound, but he'll survive," Steve answered.

Laura cast an accusatory look at Maria, who responded defensively, "I was down by the front gate. Someone buzzed the house and said there was a delivery."

"It was an elaborate ruse, Laura," Steve suggested, "so he could get close to us."

Laura looked helplessly about the room, then shrugged her apology to Maria, who'd become a close friend over the past four years.

Hendricks said, "Don't worry, we'll find out who this guy is." The sheriff was bald and so thin his uniform appeared to be draped over a clotheshorse.

"He's one of *them*," Laura said, sounding indignant and fearful at the same time. *Isn't that obvious to everyone?* The dead man was one of the disciples of Jeremiah, the Terrorist Prophet. One of thousands of his acolytes who'd made the pilgrimage over the past three-and-a-half years to their farm located in the foothills of the Appalachians; specifically, to the small pond in the northwest pasture where Jeremiah had mysteriously escaped the FBI in 1995, after threatening to detonate an atomic bomb located in the back of a van parked in front of their house.

"Laura's probably right," Hendricks said, pursing his lips. "This business certainly has taken a new turn."

"Yeah," Steve agreed. "Usually they just throw some flowers in the pond, pray, or stand around and gawk."

"They've thrown eggs and rotten fruit at the house

before," Laura objected sarcastically, "and shouted threats at us." Laura fixed the sheriff with a withering stare. "It wouldn't have happened if we'd been able to electrify the fence."

"Laura, you know I supported you on that," Hendricks said, wearily. "And so did the local district judge. It was the appellate court that said no."

Laura mimicked the essence of the ruling: "Our property rights don't include *endangering the lives of innocent people expressing religious convictions.*' What crap! I hope those judges are ashamed of themselves now."

Laura swiped the hair off her face, took a cigarette out of a pack lying on the mantel, and lit up. She remembered the quaint fence of hand-stacked stones that had once outlined the front of the property and had been joined to a traditional white post-and-board fence around the horse pasture. Then came the chainlink fence topped with razor wire, but *they'd* cut through that, or found ways to climb over the top.

Hendricks coughed and stood, hitching up the pants of his dark green uniform. "When my report's typed up, I'll ask you all to review the findings and sign it, if you agree." He tried to console them. "It seems an open-and-shut case to me. An armed intruder intent on mayhem. You were perfectly justified in using deadly force, Steve."

Laura disdainfully blew a plume of smoke into the air.

Later, when everyone was gone from the house except her and Steve, Laura once again stood in the kitchen. She looked through the windows down the driveway toward the road; the direction from which the gunman had come. April showers indeed had brought May flowers. Delicate white blossoms decorated the perfectly shaped pear trees flanking the driveway. The forsythia bushes near the front gate sported bright yellow buttons. In the woods across the road, the angular dogwood trees blazed with pink and white flowers. It was the season of renewal. Even the mare in their barn was about to foal.

Laura caught a glimpse of her own reflection in the window, causing instant self-analysis. Even at thirty-eight, she had much of the beauty pageant loveliness that had carried her to the top of the television news business. Her shoulder-length hair was naturally blonde and she hadn't gained a pound in retirement, despite her teasing threats to Steve to grow fat as a result of repeated pregnancies. But there was no baby. *The big disappointment.* Even worse than the invasion of their home and privacy.

Steve walked up behind her. "What are you thinking about?"

"Nothing," she lied, pouring him a cup of coffee from an urn sitting on a hot plate. *Maybe this time we'll get to finish it,* she thought, sitting at the table.

Steve joined her. "Be truthful."

As she looked up at him, Laura became aware for the first time today that Steve was dressed as if going to work—a white shirt, dark wool-blend trousers, dress shoes. She doubted anyone could tell he had recently been in a life-and-death struggle.

"I was thinking of the night you first moved in here," she admitted.

"I remember that red teddy you wore."

"It wasn't really edible." *Our usual banter is nice,* Laura thought, *even if awkward given the situation.* "You remember what I said."

"You said you couldn't ever imagine leaving here, or anything coming between us," Steve replied.

"Yeah," Laura said, her chagrin obvious. At the time, nearly four years ago, Steve had been an FBI agent—head of the bureau's counterterrorism unit, in fact. He'd been assigned to protect her after Jeremiah decided to use Laura as his mouthpiece; rather, to use *American Chronicle,* the twice-weekly newsmagazine show she'd hosted then, as the channel for broadcasting to the nation his twisted philosophy. "Now I can imagine leaving."

Steve nodded. "I understand, but I'm not sure that's necessary. We just have to find a new strategy."

"We had a strategy? Beyond just reacting to whatever his followers decided to do to us?"

"Yeah. The fence was a strategy. An imperfect strategy, but the best we could do when it appeared they only wanted to harass us."

"Now he wants to kill us."

Steve smiled. "Not us, Laura. Me. He'd never kill you; you know that. He has an obsession with you. Always has had."

Laura shivered, remembering Jeremiah's words whispered in her ear during the standoff down by the lake: *"Dear Laura, I'm sorry I had to bring you this far. But don't fear, you won't be killed. You can't be. Our son someday will lead New America! It's prophesied. Read the Lord's word. In this war between good and evil, Laura, don't mistake the first battle for the last."*

"Who shot first?" Laura asked, nodding toward the front hallway.

"He did."

"Were you afraid?"

"Sure. Afraid he'd kill me and I'd never see you again."

"Oh, baby," Laura said, climbing onto Steve's lap, peppering his face with kisses; tasting the salt from her renewed tears. She didn't doubt he'd been afraid, just that his idea of fear was different from hers. She'd have been paralyzed; Steve meant his senses and reactions had been sharpened.

"What's changed all of a sudden?" she asked.

Steve sighed. "I don't know, Laura. We've always known Jeremiah was out there. Hiding. Waiting. Watching his followers flood into the Dakotas. Now he's ready to start the next phase of his campaign, whatever that is."

Laura felt like a coward for asking. "Steve, would it seem like I was running away if I went home to Texas for a few days? I really want to see my mom and dad."

Steve gently stroked her cheek. "Sounds like a good idea, sweetie."

"Will you come with me?"

"Let me do a few things around here, and I'll join you in a couple of days. Take Maria with you. You'll be fine."

2

Evening commuters filed off the bus, including Robert Dean, who lingered at the side of the road, waiting for several friends who'd sat in back. At this time of day, commuter buses clogged state highway 83, which connected Pierre and Bismarck, the capitals of the Dakotas, although everyone Robert knew now referred to the entire area as "New America." Nearly six million people had heeded the prophet's call so far and migrated into the four-state area.

Robert stood near the bus shelter, his hands shoved into his pants pockets, as he rocked idly from heel to toe and looked out over the countryside—rolling hills covered with long, green prairie grasses sprinkled with tiny yellow, purple, and pink flowers.

"So, Robert, what was the condom count down at the shit factory today?" interrupted Winston Margolis, one of Robert's fellow commuters and a physical therapist at the nearby sprawling Science Center.

Robert laughed politely at the tired old joke about his job at the local sewage treatment plant. Truth was, most people had no idea what their neighbors flushed down the toilet. Still, Margolis's comments rankled a bit, since Robert considered his work to be socially necessary and important, as defined by *Second Jeremiah*.

Robert changed the subject by gesturing toward laborers working on the highway even during rush hour. "I hear it will be six lanes wide by next summer."

"Think about what a mess it would be if we all had our own cars up here," Margolis responded.

Personal cars were seldom seen in New America because they had been described by the Prophet in *Second Jeremiah* as being related to excessive pride and rampant individualism, both sins.

"Automobiles pollute the environment," Robert said. "They deplete the oil reserves of Third World countries, ensuring that native populations will be eventually impoverished and that America could always be sucked into a war over oil."

Margolis playfully put up both hands to stop Robert's recitation. "I know, I know. Cars are a symbol of racism and imperialism. I read the book. Still, you've got to admit, Robert, it would be nice to hop in your own buggy now and then and take off by yourself."

That's how social disorder started, Robert thought, *when everyone began thinking only of their selfish needs.* Robert vividly remembered his commute on the highways surrounding Saint Louis. Hundreds of frustrated, enraged road warriors manipulating two-ton killing machines across multiple lanes of traffic in some insane game of competition and intimidation.

Robert didn't mind riding the bus to and from his job at the new sewage treatment plant, where he was chief engineer. The atmosphere inside the bus promoted a sense of community. The ride allowed him time to read, relax, and think positive thoughts.

Robert walked with the other commuters down the main street of Anathoth, named after a village in ancient Judah that was the birthplace of the Old Testament Jeremiah. The early Jeremiah had envisioned a purged and rejuvenated Davidic kingdom. *It's been a long-time coming,* Robert thought, *and on the other side of the earth. New America, inspired by Jeremiah the Second.*

Those in the outside world might see Anathoth as a large trailer court, with all the unfortunate connotations of that phrase, but Robert understood that a community experiencing such rapid growth—nearly forty thousand newcomers in the last two years alone—had to rely temporarily on "manufactured housing." They'd build permanent homes when time allowed. Now they were busy building a nation.

Most of the roads in Anathoth remained unpaved. With residents walking wherever they went, and kids constantly running about, a dust cloud hung permanently above the settlement. *It must have been this way when these rolling prairies were covered with migrating herds of buffalo,* Robert thought. He fervently hoped New America wouldn't go the way of the buffalo.

Robert smiled as he saw a towhead running toward him. Douglas, his eight-year-old son, who the neighborhood kids affectionately called Douggie.

"Douglas!" Robert said, as the boy ran right into his arms. Robert hoisted him into the air, and then Douglas sat in the crook of his father's strong, right arm. Annie his wife, and Patty, their eleven-year-old daughter, stood up the road a ways, at the entrance to their cul-de-sac.

"What did you learn today?" Robert asked Douglas.

"More math. I can do all my multiplication tables up to ten."

"Great. Remember, math and science are keys to knowledge. And mankind's purpose in the world is accumulation of knowledge."

"So sayeth the Prophet!" Douglas recited, flashing a broad smile marred by several missing teeth.

As Robert and Douglas came abreast of the two women in the family, Annie said, "Hi, honey, how was your day?"

"Great. Patty, Douglas was telling me about his math exercises. What did you learn today."

"I learned there's a lot of smut on the Internet," Patty said, breathlessly, as she sneaked a sideways look at her mother.

"Some things you can't get away from, even up here," Annie explained, arching her eyebrows critically. "On the other hand, I believe someone was supposed to be searching cyberspace for information on photography, not pornography."

When the Dean family reached their single-wide, Robert reached out and opened the door for his family. He beamed at his wife, son, and daughter. "I just can't get over it. No locks on the door! And we don't have to worry about anyone breaking in." Anathoth truly was the "dream" Jeremiah had spoken about so often. They lived without fear.

After dinner, Robert helped Annie with the dishes, while the kids went outside to play before it got dark. Robert feared Annie would once again bring up the subject of money. It was all they talked about lately when they were alone.

She didn't disappoint him. "Are they still talking about implementing wage equality at the plant?"

"Eventually, it'll happen," Robert replied. It was in the book. *Second Jeremiah,* chapter 4. Wealth could only be created by physical and intellectual labor, usually collective labor. No man should own the product of another man's labor, which he willingly donated to the state in return for being part of a community and enjoying the benefits of a shared philosophy. All labor in socially necessary work was therefore equal. Wage equality would be achieved through a sophisticated computer-run barter system still in the conception stage. The Wealth Exchange.

"I just worry about how we'll make out if you don't get your wage differential," Annie repeated. Concern, even fright, was written on her face.

Robert shrugged. He currently received a higher salary than unskilled labor at the treatment plant because he had a college degree in engineering. Despite rumors about a new currency, New American wages were paid in old American dollars.

"It's one of the reasons we were able to move here," Annie noted, pointedly.

"Yes, but we also knew there'd eventually be a transition to a fairer reward system," Robert gently reminded her. He considered himself lucky to have such a worthwhile job, even though it might be a joke to some of his neighbors. Some people, he knew, were *assigned* necessary jobs. Everyone worked. It's what had to be done to allow New America to survive and prosper. In Robert's mind, state economic planning made more sense than workers having to chose among jobs made available in a marketplace manipulated by shadowy Wall Street figures for the sole purpose of *profit*. Planning allowed implementation of social goals. For example, several clothing and shoe factories had been established in New America so they wouldn't be dependent on foreign workers to clothe them.

Annie rose and began clearing the table. "It's just that I don't understand how it will work. Right now, we need money to live. If we're going to have another baby, we'll need a bigger place. You know how long the waiting list is for a double-wide? Will we ever be able to afford to build a real home here?"

Robert took his wife in his arms. "It'll work out, Annie. Look at all the wonderful things that are happening in New America. Take the kids. We get to school them at home, and in the neighborhood teaching coop. Isn't that working out?"

"I agree, it's wonderful, Robert."

"You and the other wives can teach the basics and the Bible. We don't have to worry about what will happen to our kids in public schools. We don't have to worry about them being assaulted, or pressured into sex and drug use, or having to listen to all kinds of evil ideas."

"You're right," Annie agreed, although still shaking her head.

Robert rubbed her back. "You just have to have faith, Annie. With faith, everything will work out."

"I know, I know," she said, but he felt hot tears running down the side of her face. He pressed her slender frame close to him, so he could feel her stomach. Was a seed already planted there?

* * *

Later, Robert walked alone in the neighborhood, wanting to enjoy a few minutes of solitude and the wonderful spring weather. They'd moved here a year ago last February, when the wind chill yielded temperatures the equivalent of twenty below. Still, he loved life in Anathoth. The "big sky" above the prairie seemed to indicate there was room here for everything under the heavens.

Anathoth was largely contained within an outer ring road. Inside the circle, two intersecting straight roads formed a cross. Within each quadrant were figure-eight roads providing access to many tear-shaped cul-de-sacs, like the one Robert and his family lived in. Someone had told him that from the air the design resembled a giant pendant, combining elements of the Christian cross and the ROSE flag carried by the New America National Guard.

Robert didn't like to think of the military. He hadn't even approved of Jeremiah's use of terrorism to attract followers, although Robert would never tell that to anyone else. He had come here just to lead a different lifestyle, based on God's revelations to Jeremiah. Fairness, equality, justice, a high moral purpose; that's what Robert wanted, whether the Prophet was alive or not.

As he walked on a makeshift dirt path linking two cul-de-sacs, Robert heard a commotion behind some bushes. He peered through an opening and saw three men wrestling another to the ground.

"What's going on!" Robert demanded.

"We caught this degenerate exposing himself to some kids!" replied Sgt. Vincent Dale, who wore the

distinctive uniform of the New America State Police:
campaign hat, taupe-colored shirt, jodhpurs, and knee-
high, black leather boots. Every community in New
America had a resident policeman who enforced the
Social Contract set forth in *Second Jeremiah*.

"It's all a lie," the accused flasher protested.

The man had a day or two's growth of dark beard
and his hair was uncombed and matted. He wore
baggy, light-gray pants that were clearly stained. *Has
he been masturbating?* Robert wondered. *My God,
were the social diseases of Saint Louis and old America infecting Anathoth?*

"Two people saw you!" Sergeant Dale said, shoving the handcuffed man forward. "The rest of you
come with me. Everyone needs to witness this."

The policeman pushed the man down several
streets toward the community stocks. As news of the
crime spread, the procession increased in number.
Robert watched as some began to kick and hit the accused. One woman repeatedly lashed him with a large
switch that appeared to be a branch from a sapling, although precious few trees grew on the prairie.

Near a community hall still under construction, Sergeant Dale uncuffed the man and forced him into one
of the stocks, which closed like a vice around his
hands and neck, causing the prisoner to bend at nearly
a ninety-degree angle from his waist. Five other members of the community were similarly incarcerated.

The alleged exhibitionist continued to loudly pro-
test his innocence. "I didn't do nothin'!"

"That's not what the kids say!"

"They're lying! Those goddammed kids lie all the
time."

"A woman saw you," Sergeant Dale snarled.

"She's a bitch! She hates me 'cause she says I stole a lawnmower from her yard."

"So you're a thief, too!"

"No, she's lying 'bout everything."

"You're not fooling anyone," another voice boomed from the crowd. "There's no presumption of innocence here. *Second Jeremiah* 5:13."

The man in the stocks replied angrily, "Ain't suppose to be any taxes in New America. Same chapter, verse 8. No representative government, either, but the so-called leaders of this community have been 'round to my place telling me who to vote for. Asking for donations so we can put up this so-called community center. What's the difference between taxes and somebody forcing you to make a donation?"

Robert looked around, surprised at how large the crowd had grown. Many people shouted out responses:

"Rome wasn't built in a day!"

"You should be happy to help this Christian city grow!"

"Go back to wherever you came from!"

Robert agreed with most of what was said. The accused man's remarks bothered him, though. *Second Jeremiah* decried representative government and advocated a direct democracy, presumably to be conducted over the Internet. Yet New Americans were still asked to go to the polls and elect city and county officials, members of the state legislature, and members of Congress. The official justification put out over the state news network was that New Americans had to have their own kind in elective office to protect everyone's rights. Direct democracy would come later.

Sergeant Dale disappeared into the crowd and ree-merged moments later with a man Robert recognized as the community tattooist. Those put in the public stocks for a serious infraction had a numbered code tattooed on their body. In the case of this pervert, it would be across his forehead.

The tattoist efficiently went about his work with needles and ink and a satisfied murmur rippled through the crowd.

"I don't have any problem with you locking up a pervert," a woman shouted to the crowd, "but what about my boy!" The woman pointed to a teenager in the stocks. He had a distinctive appearance Robert seldom saw in Anathoth, or anywhere else in New America, for that matter. The boy's hair was close-cropped two inches above his ears, then long and braided. He had a barbed-wire tattoo around his up-per arm. He wore a T-shirt on which several obscen-ities were imprinted. The boy's jeans rode so low on his hips that the top half of his boxer shorts could be seen. However, the effect of this in-your-face out-fit was offset by the prisoner's near state of collapse. His body sagged so much that Robert feared he might strangle in the stocks.

"What's Rex here for? his mother asked again. She had close-cropped blonde hair and black semi-circles under her eyes. Robert saw she smoked a cig-arette in clear violation of a prohibition set forth in *Second Jeremiah*.

"I'll tell you why. It's because you people don't like him. Don't like his haircut, don't like the way he dresses, don't like his music." She released pent-up energy by jabbing at the heavens with the two fingers holding the cigarette. "This place is like Nazi Germany!"

A woman stepped out of the crowd, her face equally twisted in anger, "That's right, Mary Ann, we don't like Rex! Everyone knows all about him. He's a wannabe street thug who smokes, curses, and bullies other kids."

"People have caught him with alcohol."

"He steals!" someone else shouted out.

"Fuck all of you!" Mary Ann retorted, and an ugly buzz swept through the crowd.

"Go back to LA!"

"Believe me, we're outta here," Mary Ann shouted, defiantly. "Just as soon as you let Rex go."

"Good riddance," said a man standing beside Robert. "I know your husband, Mary Ann. You two came up here just for the construction work. To make big money, quick. You never shared our values, but you thought you'd flaunt yours in our faces. We came here to get away from trash like you and your boy."

As Mary Ann again cursed her adversaries, Robert watched another woman open her personal copy of *Second Jeremiah*, and read in a loud, singsong voice, " 'The life of cleanliness, orderliness, self-sacrifice, dignity, prayer, and reflection is much beloved by the LORD; the loud, boisterous, disorderly, and obnoxious are a grievous vexation to the LORD.' "

Mary Ann gave the crowd the finger, prompting Sergeant Dale to walk over and slap her face. "I think you can join your son for a day or two." He began to wrestle her toward an empty stock.

"Wait a minute!" a man called out, and Robert looked in his direction, as did all others in the assemblage. The man stood on a small hill located behind the stocks. He was dressed in black, as was the custom among many community leaders, most of whom had emerged by the force of their personality. This man looked vaguely familiar, although Robert couldn't place him. Certainly, he projected a commanding presence.

Equally intriguing to Robert were the three individuals standing beside the man in black. They looked to be a television news crew: two men and a beautiful young woman. Robert looked more closely at a camera held by one of the men and made out the words: "MIDWEST NEWS SERVICE."

"Outside media agitators" weren't allowed in New America, but Robert noticed that Sergeant Dale hadn't made an effort to run off this crew.

The man dressed in black walked to a spot in front of the stocks, where he faced the crowd. "I've been listening to all this and it makes my heart ache," he said. "I hoped I'd left all this behind. People breaking the law without any fear of consequences. Inadequate punishments that don't really deter criminals. Greed. Endless bickering, with a thousand points of view represented, but no consensus ever achieved. No firm philosophical ground, just moral quicksand. You know when it was I committed myself to Jeremiah and the concept of New America?" He paused, although not really waiting for an answer to his rhetorical question. "It was when Jeremiah said people had a choice between good and evil. They weren't compelled to do evil by Satan, or society, or their genes, or anyone else. It was a *choice* they made.

"Jeremiah said good people should separate themselves into a new land. That's what we did. That's why we're here in New America. We're building the good life. We've chosen it freely. As for the many who won't make that commitment and choice, remember what the Prophet said, 'Obey or die!' ''

Robert saw many in the crowd nod vigorously.

The man looked over his shoulder at those in the stocks, then back at the crowd. "I say let this woman and her boy get on the road to Los Angeles right now. He can get back into his old gang, selling dope and shooting innocent people. His mom and dad can sit isolated in their small apartment, smoking and boozing it up, and worrying about money."

Robert shoved his hands in his pockets and looked at the ground in shame for his wife's worries.

"As for the scum who exposed himself to children, we know what he's likely to do next. Cast him out also. If you see him again anywhere in New America, with the mark of a Sodomite on his forehead, kill him." The man paused, smiled, and then melted into the crowd.

Robert watched Sergeant Dale unlock the stocks and free Rex, as well as the man accused of exposing himself. The policeman talked briefly to all three violators, who then hustled away. All the while, the camera crew continued filming.

Some in the crowd began returning to their homes, but Robert edged closer to the news crew. He couldn't help but stare at the young woman with the microphone. She was more beautiful than anyone he'd seen in a long time. Blonde, busty, wearing a short, tight skirt that barely covered her beautiful, long legs.

As the camera continued to roll, Robert listened to part of her stand-up report, "This is Julie Burton reporting from Anathoth, in New America, giving many of our viewers their first look at justice, New America style, which seems like a throwback to colonial times. There was an extraordinary scene here today . . .''

As Robert walked home at sunset, he thought about the last man's speech to the crowd: obey or die. Robert had come to fervently believe in that philosophy. He knew it seemed harsh back in Saint Louis, where many people, including some of his relatives, thought everyone in New America was a nut or racist. They just didn't understand the beauty of social order and shared values.

But Robert knew that real evil involved breaking the expanded commandments the Lord gave to Jeremiah the Second, which were referred to in New America as the Social Contract, 2 Jeremiah 2: 6–26.

Why is it so hard for people to do good? he wondered. You just did it. But for the last two thousand years, most people did just exactly as they pleased, motivated by selfishness or their obsession with power and greed. *They won't even obey God's word, let alone man's law.* Unless the punishment was so severe that fear compelled them *not* to do evil. It was harsh, but it was true. Robert would have preferred that people do the right thing because it was the right thing to do. But they wouldn't, and the Prophet had come up with a better way: obey or die.

All it will take to make New America a utopia is committed, hard-working, righteous people who choose to do good, Robert thought. He was committed to being one of the chosen few. The last thing he wanted was to return to Saint Louis.